] *A Bouquet of Rue*

Mysteries by Wendy Hornsby

A Bouquet of Rue

A MAGGIE MACGOWEN MYSTERY

Wendy Hornsby

2019 Perseverance Press / John Daniel & Co.
Palo Alto / McKinleyville, California

A Perseverance Press Book
Published by John Daniel & Company
A division of Daniel & Daniel, Publishers, Inc.
Post Office Box 2790
McKinleyville, California 95519
www.danielpublishing.com/perseverance

Distributed by SCB Distributors (800) 729-6423

Book design by Eric Larson, Studio E Books, Santa Barbara, www.studio-e-books.com

cover photo by Keith Ferris / iStock

10 9 8 7 6 5 4 3 2 1

LIBRARY OF CONGRESS CATALOGING-IN-PUBLICATION DATA
Names: Hornsby, Wendy, author.
Title: A bouquet of rue : a Maggie Macgowen mystery / by Wendy Hornsby.
Description: McKinleyville, California : John Daniel and Company, 2019. |
   Series: Maggie MacGowen mystery series
Identifiers: LCCN 2018059489 | ISBN 9781564746078 (softcover : acid-free paper)
Subjects: LCSH: MacGowen, Maggie (Fictitious character)–Fiction. | Women motion picture producers
   and directors–Fiction. | GSAFD: Mystery fiction.
Classification: LCC PS3558.O689 B68 2019 | DDC 813/.54–dc23
LC record available at https://lccn.loc.gov/2018059489

For Paul, always

There's fennel for you, and columbines. There's rue for you, and here's some for me. We may call it herb of grace o' Sundays. O, you must wear your rue with a difference!

SHAKESPEARE, *Hamlet*, act 4, scene 5

] *A Bouquet of Rue*

] *One*

FROM THE BUTCHER TO THE BAKER to the *café tabac*, word spread through the village of Vaucresson that Monsieur Jean-Paul Bernard had moved a woman into the house he had ever so recently shared with his wife, Marian. Such a lovely woman, the deceased Marian, the butcher offered with a sad shake of his head, gone so young and so suddenly. The customer he was waiting on, a prosperous-looking matron wearing sensible yet somehow stylish shoes, shook her head in sad agreement. Poor Monsieur Bernard, *oui*? Left to raise their boy alone.

The next person in line, a similarly carefully yet casually groomed young woman with a toddler by the hand, paused for a respectful moment as an expression of sorrow over either the unexpected loss of Madame Bernard or the swiftness with which Monsieur Bernard had replaced her; I couldn't tell which. When she finished her reverie, she said, "If something happened to me, I hate to think how quickly my Hubert would be looking about for someone to replace me."

"More to the point, Madame," offered the butcher's assistant as she slapped my fat roasting hen onto the scale, "if something happened to your Hubert, how soon before you would find an excuse to call on Monsieur Bernard yourself?"

"*Oh-là-là.*" The woman smiled as she offered a coquettish little shrug. "Monsieur Bernard, now there's a catch, *oui*?"

Next door, at the boulangerie, while the baker cut a wedge for me from a massive multi-grain *poulaine* loaf, I overheard another customer tell the baker's wife that a friend had seen a large delivery truck in Monsieur Bernard's driveway just the day before yesterday. Box after box the driver and his assistant had carried in. This new woman, whoever she was, was certainly wasting no time asserting herself as *châtelaine* of the Bernard household, was she? She'd probably already cleared away anything left to remind poor Monsieur Bernard of his wonderful wife.

An outsider, I seemed to be invisible among the shoppers as they discussed Monsieur Bernard's apparent change in status. That morning, after the commuters exited toward Paris, the people out loose in the village were, for the most part, older men and women and young mothers or nannies with little ones in tow. They all seemed to be familiar with each other and the shop keepers, and they all seemed to have fond memories of the late Madame Marian Bernard. In shop after shop, I heard echoes of the same refrain: Such a shame, such a shame, such a shame.

The tone of the discussion concerning Monsieur Bernard's new companion was a bit cheerier in the *café tabac*. At least it was cheerier among the cadre of white-haired men leaning elbows on the zinc-topped bar while they tossed back a morning shot or two. How long had it been, the proprietor asked as he wiped the counter in front of them. Three years? At least that, maybe four, the men agreed after exchanging a series of Gallic shrugs and head wags. A long time for a young and healthy man like Jean-Paul Bernard to be alone, *non*? Only natural he would want the company of a woman to warm his bed at night, the proprietor offered, leaning forward as he placed his index finger alongside his nose in case his customers hadn't understood his meaning. Clearly, they had. Indeed, yes, I thought, smiling to myself as I carried my coffee to a table near the front windows where the women seemed to congregate. Relative to Monsieur Bernard's team of supporters at the bar, at fifty he probably seemed quite young. The man in question, I knew for a fact, was indeed a healthy and handsome specimen. Perfectly natural he would seek out female company.

With my spirits somewhat lifted by that conversation, I drank my coffee and shamelessly eavesdropped on the conversations around me. I could tell myself that I was merely working on my less-than-perfect conversational French, but the truth was that I was simply nosy. I have made a career of being nosy. Besides, I wanted to know what was on the minds of the people who were my new neighbors in this Paris suburb. Surely there were other things to talk about than Monsieur Bernard.

There were, I was relieved to learn. Fifteen-year-old Ophelia Fouchet had run off with her boyfriend after a school event Friday night, and no one had seen them since, according to the women at the table next to mine. No surprise, they seemed to agree; Ophelia had always been such a quiet child and then all of a sudden at fifteen the rebellion began, *oui? Mon dieu*, that hair, those black clothes! The parents could only blame themselves, you know, the mother rocking a sleeping baby on her lap opined in such a low voice that I caught myself leaning back to hear her. A child needs rules of course, but *oh-là*, there are limits, yes? Yvan Fouchet was simply too strict with his daughter, Ophelia. How could she develop the judgment necessary to manage independence under such a heavy thumb? They agreed that the parents did not approve of the boyfriend, an Arab boy she knew from the school orchestra. Who knows who his parents were? Not that Yvan would approve of any boy his daughter spent time with; she was only fifteen.

I left them to work through the dynamics of family Fouchet, and walked three doors down to the fishmonger, hoping he had haddock and no interest in either runaway teens or Monsieur Bernard's living arrangements. But no. The proprietor, a grizzled old gnome named Gomes, according to the gold lettering on the front window, was telling his only other customer that Monsieur Bernard picked up this new woman when he was on a diplomatic post in Los Angeles. A Hollywood film actress, he said. The only response from the customer, a comfortably round woman wrapped in a heavy hand-knit cardigan though the late spring morning was very warm, was to point at the tank of murky green water near the window and tell him, One, please. Probably has fake tits, Monsieur

Gomes posited as he slid his left hand into a long rubber glove before plunging the hand into the water. They all do, you know, film stars, he added with a wag of his bald head as if, indeed, he was an authority on the topic of Hollywood actresses and their tits. I glanced down at my chest. Nothing to brag about, maybe, but everything there was absolutely the original equipment. Indeed, the only bit of surgical enhancement I had succumbed to was a nose job I was talked into, many years ago, by the executive producer of the Dallas television network affiliate that hired me to read the evening news. I now blame youth and unfocused ambition for agreeing to the surgery, and I regret that I had it done. But done is done where nose jobs are concerned.

As the fishmonger pulled a live, slithering eel out of the tank, the sweater-clad customer glanced my way and gave me a little noncommittal shrug that I took to connote neither agreement with him nor its opposite. She said nothing. Maybe the woman had merely turned toward me because she didn't want to watch as Monsieur Gomes picked up a giant cleaver and hacked off the eel's head with a single whack before he dropped the still writhing carcass into a plastic bag, and not because she wanted to engage me in the conversation. I answered with my best impression of a French noncommittal shrug, which she acknowledged with a subtle head wag.

The fishmonger's wife came in from the back lugging a bucket of crushed ice to shovel over the fish in the display case. Monsieur Gomes watched her dispassionately as he wrapped the bagged eel in pink butcher paper. As he handed it to the customer, and to no one in particular, he offered that poor Bernard seemed to have lost his compass since his wife died. First, he brings that damn Arab into his house, and now an actress; they're all whores, you know, actresses.

The actress remark didn't bother me because it was nothing more than ignorant gossip. But the "damn Arab" remark raised my hackles, suggestive of something dark in the heart of Monsieur Gomes. His wife must have seen something in my expression that I had not intended to reveal because while eyeing me she shot an elbow into her husband's ribs. When he looked up in surprise, she said, "You talk too much nonsense, Gus."

"What nonsense?" he countered, rubbing his side. "You'll see. Monsieur Bernard will come to his senses soon enough and throw them both out."

It was Monday. On Sunday, during lunch at a local brasserie and later waiting in line at the movie theater, the discussions I overheard largely had to do with summer vacation plans and the high school principal's sudden leave of absence. Was he sick? Would he be back in the fall? I wondered what the community topic du jour would be on Tuesday, by which time, surely, the principal's situation would no longer be a mystery, young Ophelia would be home again, and speculation about the private living arrangements of Monsieur Bernard would have run its course. And they would all be discussing something else.

I bought the haddock I came for, said, "*Merci, Madame*," to the fishmonger's wife who served me, and left.

A light spring rain began to fall as I drove into the garage of the home in that Paris suburb that I now shared with poor, apparently compass-less Monsieur Jean-Paul Bernard, whom I intended to marry as soon as I had established French residency. While I was out shopping, Ari—Doctor Ari Massarani, the damn Arab the fishmonger referred to—had kindly broken down the moving boxes that I had unpacked earlier that morning, bundled them with twine, and stowed them next to the recycling bin outside the back door. He was running a vacuum over the living room rug when I entered the kitchen. I set the shopping bags on the counter and looked around the doorway into the next room, giving Ari a wave when I caught his eye. A refugee from the ruins of Aleppo, he suffered from PTSD and I didn't want to startle him. He waved back and continued with his task of sucking up the bits of packing material my moving-in inevitably trailed. As I set about putting away groceries, I went through a mental inventory of what was left to unpack.

Three weeks earlier, still at home in Los Angeles when I filled the boxes that were now stacked in various parts of Jean-Paul's house in this Paris suburb, it had seemed to me that I was only taking a few essentials. Into the boxes went clothes, some family photos, books I intended to read one day, various film project notes, a few mementoes from my now-twenty-year-old daughter's life so far, legal documents and other records, a few domestic things like a favorite chopping knife and a set of non-metric measuring cups and spoons, my pillows, a disassembled and much-scarred work stool crafted by my late father, and not a whole lot more. It wasn't very much considering that I was starting over–new job, new spouse, new home–on a far continent. At least, it didn't seem like much when it all went into boxes and was carted away for shipment overseas. But on Saturday, apparently under the watchful eye of the neighbors, when the boxes came off the truck parked in Jean-Paul's driveway it seemed that their number had multiplied in transit. And now the issue was where to stow everything.

For the record, it was not I who cleared away the intimate possessions of the late Marian Bernard. The widower, Jean-Paul, and his eighteen-year-old son, Dominic, had taken care of that task before they welcomed me, Maggie MacGowen, into their home. Though I had never met Marian, I had great respect for her, just as Jean-Paul had for my late husband, Mike Flint. But if Jean-Paul and I were going to establish a life together, I fully intended to be the *châtelaine*, the woman of the house, wherever that house might be and no matter whose ghosts lurked in the shadows, so long as Jean-Paul was with me.

I had just finished putting away the groceries when Ari came through on his way to the laundry room to stow the vacuum cleaner in its cupboard. He was tall, dark, and lean, about my age–mid-forties. He had an easy manner with people, as befits a pediatrician, and a quiet outward cheerfulness that did not quite cover the deep sadness he bore.

"Your fish," I said, patting the long pink bundle on the counter as he passed behind me.

"*Merci*, Maggie. Old Gomes had haddock today?"

"He did."

"Excellent."

On his way back through, Ari stopped and picked up his fish. "So, you're finding your way around all right?"

"I'm beginning to," I said. "I still feel invisible. Everyone seems to know each other."

"They'll know you soon enough," he said, chuckling. "Trust me on that. And they'll know all your business."

"Apparently they already do. This morning I learned that Jean-Paul has taken up with a surgically enhanced young Hollywood film star with loose morals. I hope they aren't disappointed to learn that I'm just a drab middle-aged documentary filmmaker."

"Hardly drab," he said with a gallant little bow. "You heard this, perhaps, from Monsieur Gomes?"

"The same. He seems to be a man of strong opinions."

"And one who certainly has no hesitation about sharing them. If he is not more careful, one day someone may thrust that big cleaver he wields straight into his skull."

I wasn't sure whether this was offered in jest. I looked into Ari's face, but I found him difficult to read. I often did. As preparation for my move-in, Jean-Paul had explained to me why this very cultured and accomplished man was living in the small guest house in a corner of the backyard behind the lap pool and was taking care of mundane household chores like vacuuming and dusting and mowing the patch of lawn. Ari, too, was a widower, and more. Tragically, two years ago he had lost his wife and both children during the shelling of Aleppo, just hours before the family was to be evacuated. Because of Jean-Paul's advocacy, Ari was now in a safe and quiet place, but he was a long way from recovering from his loss.

After some hesitation, I asked, "Has Monsieur Gomes ever said anything to offend you?"

"That he intends as offense?" He shrugged, an acquired Gallic gesture that, along with a particular frown, connoted he knew that the world was a very strange place, indeed. "Yes, of course. Generally, he tries his best to; that is his way. Chances are that he knew perfectly well who you were when he said whatever he said this morning."

I had to laugh at myself because of course the old bastard probably had said what he said for my benefit. "So," I asked, "why do we shop there?"

"Because Gomes has the best fish in town. I can go to the supermarket or wait for the Thursday farmers' market, but tonight I want something very special for my guests. So, what can I do but turn to Monsieur Gomes? I thank you, Maggie, for saving me the errand and braving the fishmonger for me."

"Any time," I said. "I mean that, Ari. Any time you want something from Gomes, I'll be happy to fetch it."

"Thank you, but no. I don't want a buffer. Instead of avoiding the beast, I think I might invite him to dinner next time he says something particularly rude. You and Jean-Paul will join us, of course."

I laughed. "You're a peacemaker, Doctor Massarani."

"Maybe I was once, but no longer." Though we usually spoke with each other in French because we both needed the practice, he switched to impeccable English to say, "What I am is a work in progress. Every day, I struggle against the demons of my anger."

Then he took a breath, tossed the fish into the air, caught it, and said, with a smile, "Inviting Gomes to dinner is something Jean-Paul would do. He says that when people sit down to eat together, civilization and the needs of the belly replace anger with peace. At least for the duration of the meal. And that is progress, yes?"

"Sounds like something Jean-Paul would say." I said.

"Good advice, I think. Now if you'll excuse me, I have soup to start," he said. "Dinner then, *chez moi*, at seven, yes?"

"Oh dear," I said, feigning horror. "Have I done something to rouse the demons of your anger?"

He laughed. "Decidedly not. We will dine as friends. Seven o'clock then?"

"Yes," I said. "I'm looking forward to it."

On his way out, he said, "If the sky clears, we'll eat on the terrace. The apple tree is in bloom."

With that, it was back to the chore of settling myself in. I shuffled some boxes into the ground-floor room, Marian's former office, that was to be my work room. To spare me, Jean-Paul had so thoroughly purged the space of evidence of Marian's occupancy that there wasn't even a bent paper clip wedged into a corner of a desk drawer for me to discover. Purged of detritus or not, it was still Marian's desk, and that bothered me more than I thought it should. The room itself was a bit of challenge to work with. To begin, it was pie-shaped, a corner cut off the even more irregularly-shaped salon, as the living room is called in France.

The house, very modern and quite interesting, was in the form of a giant scalene triangle; it had no equal sides, no equal angles. Two sides of this wedge, the sides visible from the street, were stark, bunkerlike, made of concrete and stone with narrow slits for windows. But the third side, the longest side, the one that faced the walled backyard, was wood-framed glass from floor to soaring ceiling. The design created a very private enclave, secretive even. I thought the house was a strange choice for the very laid back and open Jean-Paul as I had come to know him. On my first visit, with a bit of self-effacing chagrin, he explained to me that the house was not chosen for its avant-garde architecture, but for its location adjoining the *Haras de Jardy*, a vast public recreation area. Historically a premier breeding farm for thoroughbred horses, the *haras* still had an equestrian center where Jean-Paul and his son, Dominic, boarded their horses. Horses were an interest we shared, though mine, left behind in Los Angeles, were rescued nags and his were rather more genteel in both behavior and origin.

At noon I made myself a sandwich out of a length of baguette spread with Camembert, fresh basil, and tomato, carried it into my new office, sat down on the floor and tried to decide how to arrange this oddly shaped space to suit my needs.

Though the house might seem stark and a bit formidable from the outside, the furniture inside was clearly chosen for comfort. Easy, casual comfort. Except for this room which with its heavy silk drapes and dark, oversized office furniture was an odd contrast of ponderous pomposity to the other living spaces. Marian was an accountant who worked for a big international corporation. I thought it unlikely she would have brought clients she wanted to impress into her home. What, then, did this weighty room, Marian's private lair, furnished for her I assumed, say about the woman?

In the end, I decided that it didn't much matter, because Marian was no longer there, and I was. First thing, I took down the heavy drapes to bring in light from the big windows facing the backyard. Did I, or maybe could I, fit in here? *Here* being not only this house, but this country.

My immersion in France began about a year and a half ago when I discovered that the woman who raised me, Mom, was not my biological mother. I was, instead, the by-product of an affair between my father, a physics professor, and a French graduate student named Isabelle. I was raised in California by my father and his sainted wife and knew nothing of Isabelle's existence until recently. Her death in Los Angeles was the catalyst for all that has followed, including meeting Jean-Paul. Sometimes good things do come from bad.

Since the discovery of my origins, I have been trying to sort out my odd new situation and the people who came with the discovery—my ninety-three-year-old grandmother, a half brother named Freddy, a brace of nephews, an uncle, and a confusing collection of cousins, cousins by marriage, cousins by proximity, godmothers, and so on, and so on—and the way I feel about it all, in the best way I know how. That is, through the lens of a camera.

To that end, a year earlier under contract with an American television network, my film partner, Guido Patrini, and I spent several months filming on my newly discovered family's farm estate in Normandy. Last fall, at home again in California, as we edited the unstructured mass of footage we had shot, I could finally bring some order to my thoughts about the very strange circumstance that brought me back into their midst, and where I fit and did not among them.

But before the edit was finished, on the whim of a new network executive the Normandy project was dropped, and Guido and I were sent off to work on something altogether different. That second film was now set for broadcast, but Guido and I would not be in the States when it aired. Our contract with the network had expired, and we were not invited to negotiate a new one, nor did we pursue one. After a few calls to people with the right connections, and some bargaining, a French television network agreed to pick up the unfinished Normandy film, with us attached.

Somehow, what started as a one-off, the film about my family and their farm—I now know more about carrot cultivation and cheese making than I ever thought necessary—and my discovery of my French origins, ended up as a contract for a series about the status of small-scale family farming generally. The first episode scheduled for broadcast in France, of course, was to be the very personal Normandy piece, and we would explore outward from there.

Three weeks ago, Guido and I went back to Normandy to shoot some fill-in footage. Then on Friday, immediately after kissing my ancient grandmother, my half brother, some nephews, and many, many cousins good-bye, we decamped for Paris, our new home base, to edit the piece for broadcast. At the moment, Guido was happily turning the Left Bank apartment I inherited from my bio-mother, Isabelle, into bachelor quarters and transforming a vast empty space in the building's basement into a work room. And here I was in the suburbs stewing over how to accommodate myself to a room as it existed, when I knew even before I took the first bite of my delicious sandwich that it was impossible for me to work there as it was.

I pushed everything I could into the middle of the room, found a tape measure in the kitchen junk drawer, and measured the space. After getting a good look, and with numbers to work from, I sat back down on the floor with my laptop in front of me, and went shopping for basic, functional furnishings and supplies that would accommodate my needs: a long work table, chairs, open shelving, and several good lamps. Because French outlets deliver 220 volts, and my American appliances were made for 110 volts, I'd left behind everything that needed plugging in. So, while I was at it, I ordered a new desktop computer capable of handling film editing. I found an odd sort of comfort browsing the offerings of the French branches of the same stores I would have gone to in the U.S., collecting things I knew I would find in each one. I also picked up some new vocabulary: while a lamp is a *lampe* and table is a *table*, a paperclip is a *trombone* and a computer is an *ordinateur*. Whatever it was called, I was promised that all of it would show up on my doorstep by Thursday afternoon.

After inflicting severe damage on a credit card, I rolled up off the floor and shook out some kinks. The rain had stopped and the sun was promising to emerge from behind the clouds. With nothing pressing until it was time to pick up Jean-Paul at the train station, I decided that it was time to go out and explore the new neighborhood on foot. I went upstairs and changed into running clothes, did some stretches on the back terrace, then went out through the side gate in the garden wall, directly onto a foot path that led into the *haras*.

The sun was more-or-less out again, and the park was full of people enjoying the remains of the daylight. I stayed to the left side of the cinder path, out of the bike lane, and started running. Truthfully, my gait for the first half mile could hardly be called running, but I found my stride as I passed the tennis courts and set a course that would give me an overview of the huge park.

A group of women emerged together from a parking lot adjoining the courts, spread out and began taping flyers to light poles, walls, and fence posts. As I passed one of the women, I saw the words ENFANTS DISPARUS–missing children–in bold atop a flyer about the teenagers who hadn't returned home Friday night that she was taping to a light pole. I barely glanced at the flyer because my eye was drawn upward to the top of the pole where a CCTV camera watched over the park, and I resumed my run. Once you've been stalked by video, as Jean-Paul and I too recently had, you become aware of the damn things. As I ran, I paced off the distance between the cameras and looked for open spaces that were out of their range. If the missing kids had been in the park, Big Brother surely would have captured their images, at least as they came and went.

Instead of circling back the way I came, I left the park, turned down a side road, and turned again into the end of Jean-Paul's street. I confess that as I passed each house and yard I gawked, trying to decide who might live around us. Generally, the houses were newish, big, and well groomed. Most, like Jean-Paul's, were set well back from the street, each of them with landscaping that provided a heavy layer of privacy, a cultural convention, I supposed, and something I would ask him about.

The first living soul I spotted was a woman who was on her knees in a flower bed in front of the house next door to ours, working mulch around carefully trimmed roses. When she saw me, she stabbed her trowel into the earth, stood, and with a wave made a beeline toward me. After pulling off her garden gloves, she extended a hand.

"Hi, neighbor," she said in pure American English. She looked to be in her thirties, trim, pretty, Asian DNA somewhere in her history. "I'm Holly Porter."

"Maggie," I said, taking the offered hand. "Let me guess, you're west coast, not east."

"Long Beach, California," she said, grinning. "You?"

"Originally, Berkeley. Lately, L.A."

"I am so happy to meet you. When I heard an American woman had moved in next door, I almost did a little dance. I've been looking for an excuse to knock on your door."

I laughed. "Do you need an excuse?"

After checking to see if anyone was near us, she leaned in closer, and said, "Showing up uninvited is just not the done thing around here."

"Then, Holly, you are hereby invited to come in for a cup of tea." I was a post-run mess, but with her grass-stained knees she was hardly dressed for the prom, either. "Or a glass of water?"

"Well, thank you, I would love a cup of tea." She tucked her gloves into a pocket of her shorts and walked me home. Because she was a guest, I showed her in through the front door, the first time I had ever used it; we always went in through the garage. On the way from the entry hall to the kitchen, she paused just long enough to give the salon a good looking over. As she took a seat at the kitchen table unbidden, she said, "Forgive me for being so nosy, but I have been dying to see inside this house ever since we moved in next door. It's not at all what I expected. Suits of armor wouldn't have surprised me, but this is just homey-looking."

"Surprised me, too," I said, taking a package of cookies and a plate out of a cupboard. During the time it took for me to boil water and put tea bags into two mugs, I learned that Holly had a seven-year-old daughter and that her husband, Kevin, was a sales exec for Toyota. France, she told me with a sigh, was their third posting in six years.

"Kevin might as well be in the military, for all the moving around we do. At every new assignment, there's so much to get used to. I'm still working things out here, hoping not to humiliate myself or Kevin or our American mothership in the process. You know, where we grew up, we didn't kiss much of anyone outside of family. But in France, instead of shaking hands with people they hardly know, they kiss them; *les bises* they call it. Except when they don't. So, when does one kiss the air beside cheeks and when offer just a handshake? And then, who gets three smooches instead of a mere two?"

"I wait for the other person to lean in or offer a hand as my cue before I do anything," I said.

"Good strategy," she said, taking a cookie from the plate I set on the table. "I don't mind all the moving around, except I never have time to really learn the language in one place before we go on to the next. I do get hungry for someone to talk to. I mean, really talk to. Besides Kevin, of course. Maybe that's the hardest part of being the foreigner all the time, just having someone to talk to. Are you finding that?"

"At first, yes," I said, sitting down opposite her. "Things get easier over time. I still speak French like someone's maiden aunt, you know, in complete sentences, no slang, the way I learned it in school. But I can hold up my end in a conversation now, with some mistakes."

She laughed. "They'll jump right up to correct you, too, won't they?"

"They will. I practiced the French R roll until my throat hurt, but I still get corrected. It's a good way to start a conversation, though. Make a flub, meet someone new."

"With that attitude, you'll be okay here," she said, using her cookie like a pointer. "Now, Maggie, the minute I become a pest, you must say, Holly go home. Promise me."

"I promise," I said, laughing. "I'm happy to know someone else who speaks fluent California."

She studied me as she finally bit into her cookie. It was when she had her mouth full that her face lit up. After swallowing, she said. "I know you. I mean, I know who you are."

"Oh?" I had a pretty good idea what was about to follow. It happened to me sometimes in the U.S., though fortunately not in France. But here it was.

"You're Maggie MacGowen."

"Guilty."

"Don't say guilty. I think that's pretty amazing. I like your programs on TV. We stream them on international access wherever we are. I make Kevin sit with me and pay attention so he'll have something other than cars to talk about." She took another bite. "So, are you just visiting Mister Bernard? I've never met him, but I see him and his son and that other man who lives here come and go. I heard that you moved in–I saw the truck–but maybe I heard wrong; I don't even speak French like your maiden aunt yet. You just visiting?"

"I'm here for the duration," I said. "I work for a French television network now."

"Making more documentary films?"

"That's what I do."

"Well, that's big news." Cradling her tea mug, she said, "You know what would be a good subject for you? These kids that went missing. The teenagers. A real Romeo and Juliet story."

"Is it?"

"I think it is. The girl's parents don't approve of the boyfriend, I hear," she said, leaning forward. "Think of it, right when you move into little Vaucresson, *boom*, that happens."

"I don't know what happened," I said.

"No one does."The phone tucked into her shorts pocket buzzed. She tapped a button to silence it, and with a sigh, she rose. "Duty calls. Time to go get my munchkin from school."

"It's a pleasure to meet you, Holly," I said, because it was.

"The pleasure is all mine, believe me."

I walked her to the door. As she left, she turned and pointed a finger at me. "You think about what I said. Those missing kids could be your next subject."

"We'll see," I said. "We'll see."

It was nearly four when she left, or sixteen hours–*seize-heures*– according to the French twenty-four-hour clock. I made myself a second cup of tea with the intention of sitting outside for a bit with a book. But when I approached the tall glass doors that led from the salon to the terrace, I saw that Ari was already there, and he had a visitor, a dark-haired young man. They were deep in discussion, their heads close together in front of a laptop screen. I knew Ari did some tutoring, so the youth was probably one of his students.

Not wanting to interrupt, I took my tea upstairs, set the alarm for five o'clock, and stretched out on the bed to read for an hour. The fuss and bother of moving, culture lag, three weeks of filming in Normandy with my ninety-three-year-old grandmother under-foot, the smell of apple blossoms through the open windows: I fell right asleep and didn't move until jangled awake by the alarm. I showered, pulled on clean jeans and a pullover, put a bottle of white wine from Languedoc into the fridge, and drove out to meet the five-fifty-two train from Paris.

When I left, Ari was wiping down the chairs on the terrace, and the boy was nowhere to be seen.

Jean-Paul, looking perfectly fresh somehow after a long day of meetings about issues involving French exports and the European Union, came off the train searching for me among the crowd near the exit to the parking lot. I waved to catch his eye and started toward him along the platform. A man, similarly suited but clearly in need of pressing and a shave, rushed up behind him and caught him by the arm. After their exchange of perfunctory greetings, Jean-Paul glanced my way and held up a hand to stay me. I went to the railing on the far side of the platform to get out of the way of the exiting commuter stream and waited. Jean-Paul's contribution to the conversation with his friend, if indeed he were a friend, amounted to nothing more than a calm nod, a shrug, upraised palms from time to time while the other man spilled an apparently angst-filled plight. Jean-Paul listened for a bit before he put his hands on the man's shoulders and, looking him in the eye, said a few words that seemed to bring a measure of relief to the other. Then they shook hands and walked off in separate directions. I stayed where I was, alternately counting CCTV cameras—there were six—and watching the man until he exited the platform.

Jean-Paul kissed both my cheeks, and then kissed them again. With his face next to mine, he said, "I came off the train and saw my Maggie waiting. Tell me it's not a dream."

"If it is, I hope you don't wake up."

Arm in arm, we headed for the car park. "Good day?" he asked.

"A full day," I said. "I learned in the village that some American movie actress has moved in on you."

"*Vraiment?* Is she beautiful?"

I tugged at the front of my sweater. "She is surgically enhanced."

He laughed. "Is it possible you were buying fish when you learned this?"

"Ari asked me to pick up some haddock."

"I hope that means he's making us his wonderful soup tonight. What time does he want us?"

"Seven." I passed him the keys to his car. He handed me in on the passenger side, and when he was behind the wheel, buckling up, I asked, "Who was that man you were talking to? He seemed agitated."

"He is at least that. Distraught, I think. Yvan Fouchet. His daughter is missing."

"Ophelia? The missing girl everyone is talking about?"

He nodded, watching traffic behind us as he backed out of the space.

"What did he want from you?" I asked.

"A miracle."

"Do you have one?"

"Sadly, no." He put the car into drive and we joined the queue heading toward the street exit. "Fouchet thinks I have connections that I don't. A missing child is a matter for the local police. But he says the police aren't doing enough because they believe she's a runaway. Her boyfriend is missing, too. They're fifteen, Maggie. Kids that age, sometimes they get ideas, *oui?* Chances are that Ophelia and the boyfriend will turn up when they run out of money and get hungry."

"I hope so. What a nightmare for the parents in the meantime. Can you do anything at all to help Fouchet?"

With a little shrug, he said, "I told him that I'll call a contact at Interpol who helped set up the European Union's missing children hotline. Their focus is sex trafficking, which isn't likely in this case. I know my contact will tell me this is a matter for the local police, but maybe they'll put out an international alert, just to appease the father. Other than that, what can I do?"

My turn to shrug; I was still learning the rich vocabulary of French body language. "Do you know either of the kids?"

"The boy, no. But Ophelia, yes. Or, I did until she was about twelve. She rode in the youth riding club I coached. A nice enough youngster, I thought, eager to please. She had a natural saddle seat, worked quite hard, looked after her horse, took direction well, got along with the other kids. A bit quiet, but a pleasant girl. That's all I can really tell you. She's a few years younger than Dominic so she wasn't in and out of the house with his pack of friends."

"Did Dominic ride with the club?"

"Oh yes. Dom was the only reason I was involved. But he gave up riding when we left for the consular post in Los Angeles. Since our return, school has kept him too busy to prepare for hunter-jumper competition. So, I have seen nothing of Ophelia or the rest of family Fouchet for more than three years. I don't know what sort of young woman she is becoming."

"And the boy?"

He shook his head. "I don't recognize his name."

We talked about everything else the rest of the way home. But

we were both parents, and the specter of a pair of missing young-
sters hung in the air around us.

Jean-Paul and I were standing in my pie-shaped office, sip-
ping that very nice wine from Languedoc and talking about what
to do with Marian's furniture when we heard Dominic's scooter
come up the gravel drive out front. Jean-Paul, with a little smile,
cocked his head and listened: first the garage door, then the kitch-
en door, footsteps, a cupboard door, the clink of glass, the beloved
eighteen-year-old's heavy book bag hitting the floor somewhere
near the stairway. And then the youth himself appeared, glass of
wine in hand, looking a bit worn out after a long day of classes and
tutorials, but still cheerful. Dominic was nearing the end of the first
year of his grueling two-year preparatory course before entering
one of the nation's elite *Grandes Écoles*. The promise of summer
holidays made the daily grind bearable for him.

"*Ça va,* Maggie?" Dominic kissed my cheeks.

"I'm fine, thank you," I said. "And you?"

"*Assez bien.*" He turned to his father to deliver the same set of
smooches. "*Et tu, Papa?*"

"Amazing. Fantastic. Perfect. The way I always feel when
you walk through the door intact." Jean-Paul ruffled his son's
helmet-flattened hair. Dominic wasn't as tall as his father, his features a bit sharper, his hair lighter. But he was unmistakably a twig
from the same tree. That is, heartbreakingly, quietly handsome.
"Tell us about your day, Dom."

"Same old torture chamber." Dom glanced at the piles of boxes
and the disarranged furniture. "So, I love your décor, Maggie. *Très
chic.*"

I clinked glasses with him. "Glad you approve."

Jean-Paul reached over and grabbed his son in a one-armed
bear hug. "So, *mon petit malin,* I'll need your help to haul this stuff
out of here."

"Tonight?" Dom asked with some dismay, releasing himself
from his father's grip.

When Jean-Paul turned to me for the answer, I said, "No hurry.
I'm solidly booked with meetings at the network and editing

sessions with Guido until Wednesday. There's new furniture coming sometime during the week, so everything can wait until the
weekend."

Still also working on my vocabulary of French slang, I asked,
"What does *petit malin* mean?"

There was a father-son exchange of Gallic shrugs, raised palms,
and moues before Dom said, in English, "Smart ass."

"*Exactement*," Jean-Paul said with a nod.

After taking another look at the jumble, Dom asked his father,
"What do you plan to do with Grand-père's things?"

"Do you want any of it?" Jean-Paul asked.

"I could use one of the file cabinets, if that's okay."

"*Bien sûr*," Jean-Paul assured him. "Only one?"

"Sorry, yes, only one." He shrugged. "Actually, I don't want any
of it, but I thought, well, to keep the peace I would take one."

"That isn't necessary, Dom. Not for your mother's sake, and not
for your own."

"Grand-père's things?" I asked, curious.

"*Zut*," Dom said with a shake of his head, clearly not happy
with the topic.

"There's a little history, yes," Jean-Paul said. "When Marian's
father retired, he made a gift to her of his precious office furniture.
At least, all that he could squeeze in here. He even had his drapes
cut down to fit these windows. Where are the drapes, by the way?"

I pointed to the pile on the floor behind the desk.

"Good place for them," Dom said. "*Maman* hated them. She
hated all of Grand-père's old furniture."

"But she kept it?" I said.

"Where her father was concerned," Jean-Paul said, "Marian
chose her battles carefully. A roomful of ugly furniture, she decided, wasn't worth a war."

"Oh dear," I said, thinking that through. How often did Marian's father visit? And what would he have to say when he got a
look at what I fully intended to do to the room? And did I care?

At that moment, Ari opened the terrace door and announced,
"*À table, mes amis.*"

As we trooped out toward the backyard, Jean-Paul asked Dom, "When was the last time you saw Ophelia Fouchet?"

"Around Easter, I think." He reached into a back pocket and pulled out an untidy wad of paper that he handed to his father. "But she didn't look like this at all. She's gone totally Goth now. Dyed her hair black, black clothes. If they want to find her, they need to use a different photo."

The paper, we saw when Jean-Paul had smoothed out the folds, was the flyer for the missing girl and boy that the women had been posting all over the *baras*. In her picture, the girl was fair and sweetly pretty. The boy was dark-haired with olive skin. Her I did not recognize. The boy I did. He was in our backyard that afternoon, deep in discussion with Ari.

] Two

"*AHMAD NABI?*" Ari studied the color photos on the missing persons flyer. "Who says he's missing? He was here for his tutoring session just this afternoon."

"So, then, he's back," Jean-Paul said as he took his seat at the table on the terrace. "I hope that means the girl has returned as well."

"Do you know the girl, Ari?" I asked as he handed me a basket of warm flatbread.

"Ophelia Fouchet?" He shook his head as he began ladling rich fish soup into bowls and handing them around. "No. I can't think of a reason our paths would cross."

I accepted a bowl from him, and after an appreciative sniff of the fragrant steam rising above it–tomatoes, grilled fish, onions, garlic, peppers, and fresh oregano–asked, "How do you know Ahmad Nabi?"

"From the Islamic Community Center in La Celle Saint-Cloud," he said, picking up his spoon. "I can't practice medicine in this country until the results of my licensure exams come in. But I can offer lay counseling and do some preliminary pediatric medical screening. Most of the kids who come to the center are quite recent immigrants. Refugees, to be exact. They have all sorts of issues: academic, physical, emotional. If I spot something, the center staff can direct kids to the help they need. Sometimes they can, anyway."

"What sort of help does Ahmad Nabi need?" Jean-Paul asked.

"Among other things, academic," he said. "The secondary school Nabi attended in Afghanistan offered no science courses. He needs tutoring to catch up with his peers in anatomy, chemistry, biology. He's a serious boy. He works hard and he wants to succeed. More than that, he wants desperately to fit in."

"Good to know he is no longer among the missing," Jean-Paul said. "I'll call Ophelia's father after dinner and congratulate him now that the ordeal is over. And I'll notify Interpol to cancel the alert."

"Not yet, Papa." Dom had been quiet, listening intently, so far. "Doctor Massarani, what time was Nabi here?"

"Four o'clock, give or take, until five. He comes straight from school on Mondays."

"It was after six o'clock tonight when I dropped my friend Nathalie at her parents' bistro. All the mothers were in the village handing out flyers." He tipped his head toward the flyer now folded on the table beside his father. "Madame Aubert, Cécile's mother, gave me that one."

"Maybe word isn't out yet that the kids are found," Jean-Paul said.

"But Ophelia's mother was there, too, in front of the *patisserie*. Wouldn't she know if her daughter was back?"

Jean-Paul turned toward Ari to say something, but when he saw that Ari had his phone in his hand and was tapping in a text, he sat back and waited until he was finished and had set the phone down on the table.

"Texting Nabi?" he asked. When Ari nodded, Jean-Paul took out his own phone and began punching in numbers. Ari reached over and put a hand on his arm.

"Before you call anyone, as a favor to me, my friend, I ask you to wait just a bit. Give Nabi a chance to respond to my text."

Jean-Paul rubbed his chin, thinking, deciding. In the end, he acceded to Ari's request and put his phone away.

"How terrible for the boy's parents," I said, remembering the state of Ophelia's father at the train station.

Ari shook his head. "Nabi has no parents. No family now except his grandmother. As far as he knows, only he and the grandmother survived when the boat smuggling them to Italy capsized in the Mediterranean; thousands of refugees don't survive that crossing. Nabi is certain his parents and siblings drowned because he has heard nothing from them. And sorry, I don't have a phone number for his grandmother."

"Do you know where they live?" Jean-Paul asked.

"No. But the center might. I'll call there if I don't hear from Nabi soon."

Though everyone's gaze strayed from time to time toward the screen on Ari's phone, waiting for it to light up, the conversation moved on. There was an edge, a hesitation, to everything that was said, with that dark telephone screen serving as the centerpiece.

After the soup, Ari brought out a tray of cheese and fruit. As he placed a small plate and knife in front of me, he said, "Maggie, I had hoped that tonight with my humble offerings I could wish you, one immigrant to another, good success in your new country. The circumstances for you and I finding ourselves so far away from everything that was once familiar to us are certainly very different. But no matter why we are here, the adjustment can be difficult at times. As you said this morning, in the village you felt invisible. These French people—" With a smile, he looked from Jean-Paul to Dom. "As charming as they are, they can be mysteries to us. I caution you to be patient with them, and sooner or later you will cease to be an invisible stranger."

"Thank you," I said. "Though I think there may be some advantages to invisibility."

From there, a general conversation followed about adding a fourth cog, me, into the workings of the household machinery. My first concern, the native Californian and freeway veteran, was, how would four people with four very different schedules manage with one car in the household? When I suggested that I might look into acquiring a second car, the others asked, almost in unison, "Why?" So far, there had been no need. Dom, who was not yet eligible for a driver's license, assured me that he took his Vespa almost everywhere he needed to go. When Ari needed a car, which was rare, he would ferry Jean-Paul back and forth to the train, as I had done that very day. Because Ari observed Islamic dietary rules, he kept his food, kitchen, and food preparation utensils entirely separate from ours, and generally did his own shopping. Everything he needed, he told me, except meat from a halal butcher, he could walk or ride a bike into the village to acquire. Most days, Jean-Paul said, the car sat all day in the train station parking lot gathering dust. I wasn't persuaded, but until I knew my work schedule and where my work might take me, and considering the other issue hanging like a pall over the evening, I let the subject drop. For now.

The cheese course was finished, coffee came and went, dishes were carted back into Ari's little kitchen in the guest house. And still no word from Nabi.

Dom and I gave our thanks to Ari, said good night, and headed toward the house, but Jean-Paul hung back. He put a hand on Ari's shoulder, looked into his eyes, and said, "We have to call the Commissariat of Police."

Ari nodded. "Do what you must."

Within fifteen minutes of Jean-Paul's call, two police detectives, a somewhat rumpled older man and a starchy younger woman, were at the front door. They could have been American senior police, a bit world-weary, know-it-all, skeptical, except that their suits were better, and when Jean-Paul offered them wine they accepted. The man drank his in a single long quaff and did not turn down a second pour. She took a sip and set her glass on a table.

While her partner, Detective Lajoie—an ironic name for such a dour-looking man—took care of asking who we were and the reason they had been summoned, the woman detective, Fleur Delisle, surveyed the room as if it might hold some answers to yet unasked questions. With her head back as she studied the soaring ceiling, she finally spoke.

"Monsieur Bernard, a large black spider is spinning a web up in that corner."

Jean-Paul followed her gaze. "*Oui.* Lots of spiders this time of year. They trap all sorts of pests, so I leave them alone to do their work. And they leave me alone."

She brought her focus down to study him for a moment, her expression as contained as the tight bun at the back of her neck. "We'll need to see your identification. All of you."

Jean-Paul, Dom, and Ari reached for their pockets while I went in search of my bag. Quickly, Delisle scanned the national I.D.s of the two *Messieurs* Bernard into her phone and handed them back. Delisle lingered over Ari's papers, looking from them back at Ari several times.

"Syria?" she said. "Refugee?"

"Yes, to both."

"How long?"

"Just over two years."

"And that is how you are acquainted with Ahmad Nabi?"

Ari puzzled over the question for a moment. "Are you asking if I know him because we are both refugees, or are you assuming that all refugees are somehow connected?"

Her only answer was the smallest shift of her left shoulder; she never took her eyes from his face.

He said, "A couple of days a week I do some counseling and some tutoring at the Islamic Community Center. I met Nabi there. He was having difficulty catching up in school, so he started coming to me here once a week for help. Today he came by after school as usual, and we worked on his chemistry lessons. Just as a point of information, Ahmad Nabi is from Afghanistan, and he has been in France for barely a year."

She made a quick note in a small pad. "What did he say about Ophelia Fouchet?"

"Nothing. I never heard her name until young Monsieur Bernard showed us the flyer he picked up in the village this evening."

With an open palm, she drew a line from Ari to Jean-Paul. "You two know each other how?"

Jean-Paul answered first. "I met Doctor Massarani at a refugee camp in Turkey shortly after he was evacuated from Syria. It took a while, but with help from our friends at Doctors Without Borders we were able to arrange a French visa for him."

"*Doctor* Massarani?" She made a note. "You were in the camp as a physician or as a refugee?"

"Both," he said again.

"Monsieur Bernard, why were you at a refugee camp?"

"From time to time, on behalf of the European Union's consortium on refugee resettlement, I conduct inspections of the camps."

Lajoie uttered his first sound for a while, a short "Hmm," as he thought over, perhaps, some implications of Jean-Paul's mention of an affiliation with the EU. Delisle pivoted her focus to me, holding out her hand for the passport in mine.

"Margot Eugénie Louise-Marie Duchamps Flint," she recited as she studied my passport. "You are born in France?"

"French mother, American father."

"Father is Flint?"

"Father was Duchamps."

"So, his background is French?"

"No," I said. "American Immigration misspelled my grandfather's name when he got off the boat from wherever he came from. I don't know what the Eastern European original was."

"And Flint?"

"My late husband."

"What did he do, your Monsieur Flint?"

"He was a homicide detective with the Los Angeles Police Department."

"Late husband? He died in Los Angeles? Gunshot?"

"He had cancer." Which was true. But I sure as hell was not going to tell her that Mike Flint used his service weapon to decide the timing of the inevitable before cancer could take him. I also did not mention that my *nom de guerre*, my TV name, Maggie Mac-Gowen, wasn't on my passport. The MacGowen part was a leftover from husband number one, another folly of youth but one that had an excellent legacy, my daughter Casey.

"You have a *passeport talent* work visa," she said, a statement, not a question, as she looked up from my passport.

"I do. I'm a filmmaker. I have a contract to work with a French television company."

"A filmmaker," she repeated, glancing at Lajoie with a sarcastic little sneer as she handed the passport back to me. "I had no idea that French television is in such a sorry state that we must import talent."

"Detective Lajoie," I said, catching the partner's eye. "Does she ever let you speak?"

He chuckled. "I let her play bad cop until she gets her foot so far up someone's ass that I need to step in."

In English I said, "She is certainly a pain in the ass."

She only shrugged, but he laughed again, letting me know that he understood some English; no clue about her. She wasn't finished with me: "You saw Ahmad Nabi this afternoon?"

"I did. He was in the backyard with Doctor Massarani at around four o'clock, just as Doctor Massarani said. He was gone when I left before six."

"Do you know Ophelia Fouchet or her family?"

"I do not. I'm new here. I don't know much of anyone."

The palm came up again, drawing in Jean-Paul and Dom. "But you do know the Fouchet family, yes?"

"Yes." Jean-Paul spoke for them both. "More precisely, we did once. My son and I were away for several years and lost contact with them."

"You were away?"

"I was appointed to a consular post in Los Angeles. My son and I were there until this past fall."

"Ah, Los Angeles," she said, glancing at me. "I see."

"I saw Ophelia in the village recently," Dom volunteered. "But she didn't look anything like the photo on the flyer. She has black hair now. Blacker than Nabi's."

Again the detectives exchanged knowing looks as Delisle snapped her notebook shut.

"Thank you for calling." Lajoie handed out his card. "If you hear anything–"

"Of course," Jean-Paul said. Ari said nothing.

When they were gone, we all stood silent, frozen for a moment, lost to our own thoughts. Dom was the first to speak.

"I have some reading." He said his good nights, grabbed his book bag from the bottom step where he dropped it when he arrived home, and went upstairs to his room. Ari, quiet, took his leave as well. I went to the kitchen and rinsed the wineglasses.

Jean-Paul reached past me to get a towel to dry the glasses. "Welcome to Vaucresson, *ma chère* Maggie. A quiet little suburb where nothing ever happens."

"Fleur Delisle," I said. "With a name like that she probably has to be tough. But, sheesh, such a hard ass."

"Cops," he said, smooching the back of my neck. "The same all over, yes?"

"That's not a study I plan to make." I dried my hands and hung the towel on its hook and nothing more was uttered all evening about cops or missing kids. We turned out the downstairs lights and arm in arm went up to get ready for bed.

While I brushed my teeth, I watched Jean-Paul in the mirror as he stripped off the starched dress shirt he had put on that morning. He wadded the shirt and raised his arm to lob it into the laundry bag, a movement that puckered the red scar over his collarbone, a souvenir from a very bad day in February. I had seen the wound when it was still fresh and watched the skin mend over time. For some reason seeing the scar at that moment, all shiny and angry under the bathroom light, triggered a wave of memories that filled me with sudden dread.

He came over and patted my back. "Something go down the wrong pipe?"

I took a deep breath and nodded as I laid my hand over the scar. "Looks better."

"All better." He took my hand and kissed the palm and very soon we were happily tucked up in our bed together between new sheets. I fell asleep knowing that at that moment, in that place, wrapped in each others' embrace, I was home.

] Three

SOMETIME BEFORE DAWN, I woke to the racket of a trash truck rumbling down the street below. The clock on the bedside table said it was ten past six. There was no way I could get back to sleep, so I slid out of bed as quietly as I could, trying not to waken Jean-Paul. I pulled on a sweater over my T-shirt and pajama bottoms because the house was chilly and went downstairs to make coffee. After wrestling with the cafetière—grind the beans, pour in hot water, wait, press the plunger—I made a mental note to shop for an automatic coffeemaker like the one I left in California.

Mug in hand, I went to the big windows in the salon to watch for the sun to come up over the garden wall. The morning was overcast, threatening rain again. I used that quiet moment to call my daughter, Casey, in Los Angeles, where it was still the night before. The nine-hour time difference made finding a good time to actually speak with her instead of texting difficult. Casey said everything was fine, she was in her dorm room studying. Now that the women's volleyball season was over, she was able to make up for the light academic load she took in fall to accommodate practice and team travel. She was on track to graduate on time next year, good news for my aching bank account, but the heavy schedule didn't leave her time for a social life. And by the way, could I send money? She'd bought new jeans for the summer when she would be working again at the *fromagerie* on Grand-mère's farm in Normandy. As soon as we hung up I made a transfer from my account to hers.

Slowly, as I watched through the window, the gray sky brightened then turned vivid rose. All seemed serene and orderly. Except, someone had left a coat or a blanket on one of the chaises longues on the far side of the pool. As the sky grew lighter, I could see that the dark lump was the protective cover that should have been stretched over the chaise. Had wind in the night blown it loose? Barefoot, I went out to put it back in place before the promised storm arrived.

One tug and the cover heaved upward. Eyes like black holes, wiry hair gone wild, a specter rising through the long morning shadows.

"Ahmad Nabi?" I said, dropping the cover.

He looked around as if searching for an escape path.

"You must be hungry," I said, trying to sound calm though my heart jackhammered in my ears and I struggled to breathe. "Come inside. Let's get you something to eat."

I turned and started for the house. Behind me there was silence at first, and then the gentle thump of the heavy chaise cover landing on the pool deck. Footsteps followed. I was pouring milk into a mug of coffee when Nabi made it as far as the kitchen door. Extending the mug toward him, I said, "Have a seat. I'll make some eggs. Toast? There's brioche from yesterday."

Reticent, clearly frightened, he sat on the edge of a kitchen chair. There was no reticence, however, about gulping down the hot coffee. I poured him a second cup, pushed the basket of fruit that sat in the middle of the table toward him, and set about scrambling eggs and making toast. Jean-Paul appeared at the door, surveyed the scene, and without comment, poured himself the last cup from the cafetière and refilled the kettle. He carried his mug over to the table, took two bananas out of the fruit basket, handed one to Nabi, and peeled one for himself.

"Looks like you've had a rough night, young man," he said, taking the chair opposite the youth. "I've roused Ari and asked him to come over. You have any objection to that?"

Tears rose in the kid's eyes. He struggled for composure but somehow managed to hang on. Until Ari appeared. He was out of his chair, sobbing into Ari's neck, clinging to the man with the sort of desperation that he must have felt when he clung to whatever it was he had used to stay afloat after the boat under him and his family collapsed into the Mediterranean.

Still standing in the doorway, Ari patted Nabi's back, rocking him back and forth as all of us who have been parents once rocked children to calm them. Jean-Paul slid a box of tissues within arm's reach for Ari, and in a few minutes Nabi was blowing his nose and wiping his face. When he was breathing more-or-less regularly again, I set a plate of eggs on the table and Ari guided Nabi to sit in front of it. One last sniffle, and the boy had a fork in his hand and eggs disappeared, followed by toast with great slatherings of my grandmother's homemade raspberry jam.

Ari, cradling a cup of coffee with both hands, leaned against the counter, one ankle crossed over the other as if at ease, and spoke in a calm voice. "People have been looking for you since Friday night, Nabi. Where have you been?"

After looking at each of us in turn, the boy said, "I don't want to say."

"Where is Ophelia Fouchet?"

"I can't say."

"Can't or won't say?" Ari asked.

Nabi dropped his head. And said nothing more.

Jean-Paul leaned back in his chair and studied the boy. "Nabi, you don't have to talk to us. But we do have to call the police, and eventually you will absolutely have to tell them what you know. Before they get here, young man, we want to know what sort of trouble you might be in so that we'll know how best to help you. Trust me, you don't want the police version to be the only story that gets out. So, now will you answer Doctor Massarani's questions? Where have you been, and what do you know about Ophelia?"

Nabi checked with Ari. After he got the nod, he said, "I was working. That's all. Just working. I don't understand why people think I'm missing."

"It's because no one has seen either you or Ophelia Fouchet since Friday when you left a school event together," Jean-Paul said. "Have you seen her since Friday?"

The boy shook his head. "No."

"Where have you been?"

"At my job. I work for a guy over in Garches who makes halal sausage. Every weekend, we go around to farmers' markets and sell them. He picks me up right after school on Friday and takes me home on Sunday night."

"But Friday you were at a school event, not at work," Jean-Paul said.

"Sure. But it wasn't exactly an event. The school orchestra had a nighttime rehearsal for the big end of term concert. My boss, Marco, had to drive all the way to Arras and he wouldn't wait for me because the market sets up early on Saturday. If he waited he wouldn't get to bed until after midnight and he'd be too tired the next day; Marco is an old guy."

"How far away is Arras?" I asked.

"Over a hundred miles," Jean-Paul said, doing the conversion from kilometers to miles for me.

"If you weren't with this Marco on Friday—" Ari began.

"But I was," Nabi insisted. "Sort of. It was about two in the morning when I finally got to Arras."

Ari asked, "Was Ophelia with you?"

After some thought, Nabi shook his head. "I promised not to say anything."

"Promised who?"

"Ophelia."

"Young man," Jean-Paul said. "Some promises are not worth keeping, even promises to people we love. We need to hear this: where is your girlfriend?"

"I don't know. And Ophelia is not my girlfriend. She tells everyone she is because she knows it will really piss off her parents if they think she's with some refugee kid. A Muslim. But I'm not anybody's boyfriend."

"You go along with her lie?" I asked.

"She keeps me from getting beaten up all the time, so yeah."

"You haven't told us how you got to Arras," Ari said.

"I went over by the expressway and caught a ride."

Ari didn't like the answer. "With whom?"

Blushing furiously, the boy said, "A truck driver. I don't know his name. He said he was going to Amiens. He drove me as far as his turnoff and dropped me at a truck stop café. I had to wait with my thumb out for more than an hour before a Belgian trucker picked me up and took me the rest of the way."

"Have you any idea how dangerous that was?" Ari demanded.

"Sure." Nabi pulled a five-inch folding knife out of his pocket. "I was prepared. But I never had to show this."

Jean-Paul turned and looked up at me, dismay on his face.

"Jesus, Mary, and Joseph," I said. "Better call a lawyer."

"I did nothing," Nabi protested, some heat behind his words.

"Where did you get that, son?" Jean-Paul asked.

"Ophelia gave it to me," he said. "She said that if I just show it, no one will bother me. She carries one, too."

Ari held out his hand for the knife, but Jean-Paul stopped him, opened a kitchen drawer, and instructed Nabi to drop the weapon in, himself.

"Was Ophelia with you?" I asked while this was going on.

"No. Well, yes, some of the time. She asked me to walk her as far as the car park at the train station. We said good-bye, and that was it."

"Did she say where she was going?"

He shrugged. "She said it was none of my business."

Jean-Paul folded his hands on the table and leaned forward. "I'm sure the police questioned your grandmother, Nabi. Wouldn't she have told them that you were at work and not missing?"

"Probably not. If she said anything at all, she would say she didn't know where I was."

"She doesn't trust the police?" Jean-Paul asked.

"No, she doesn't. But that's not why," he said. "I'm only fifteen, I can't legally work. If anyone finds out, I'll lose my job. If that happens, then you might as well just throw me into the sea and let me drown with the others."

Ari let out a soft chuckle. "Such drama, Nabi. Don't tempt me or I might throw you into the pool to wake you up to the seriousness of your situation. You don't go hungry, you have a roof over your head. So, what is so pressing that you have to work?"

"To pay my violin teacher," he said, looking at the floor.

Ari seemed to think that made some sense. To me and Jean-Paul he said, "Nabi's father was perhaps the finest violinist in Afghanistan, a teacher. He trained in Europe, and that's what made him a target of the Taliban, and that's why the family had to flee. Am I right?"

Nabi nodded. "I promised my father that I would keep up my music study, no matter what. But it's expensive."

"Okay," I said. "How did no one see you between the time Marco took you home on Sunday and the time you showed up here Monday for your regular session with Doctor Massarani?"

"Marco didn't take me home Sunday. His old truck broke down on the way out of Arras and we had to wait for the garage to open on Monday to fix it. They didn't have the right part, and–" He sat back, shaking his head as if reliving the frustration of the day. "I missed school yesterday. I barely made it back in time for my appointment with Doctor Massarani. Marco dropped me off in the *haras* by the bike path and I ran all the way."

"That explains the state you were in," Ari said.

A bit embarrassed, the boy agreed. "After I left here, that's when everything really went to hell. That's when I saw the posters about us being missing; they were pinned up all over the park. I thought it was a joke with that stupid picture of Ophelia on it. I mean, if they're really trying to find her, why don't they use a new picture so people will recognize her? Maybe, I thought, her parents want to find the girl she used to be, and not the girl she is now."

"Interesting thought," I said, turning to Jean-Paul. He hadn't said much for a while, just listened. His response to me was a barely perceptible lift of a single eyebrow, but I had a feeling the wheels were turning inside that handsome head.

"I didn't know what to do," Nabi said. "All I could think was to hide, so I locked myself in a park restroom until I thought everyone was gone for the night."

"And then you came here and went to sleep on the terrace," Ari said.

"I didn't know where else to go."

"Where is Ophelia?" Jean-Paul asked Nabi yet again.

"I'm telling you the truth; I don't know. All she said was, she had something to do."

"That's all she said?" he asked, skeptical.

"Except, she wanted me to say I was with her if anyone asked. She told her parents the school orchestra was going out for pizza after the rehearsal, so they were letting her stay out until twelve."

"Was there a pizza party?" I asked.

"No. She lied to her parents so they would let her stay out late. They are very strict about curfew. I had to get to Arras, so I walked her to the station and said good-bye."

"Was she meeting a boy?" Jean-Paul asked.

"Maybe. I don't know. She never talked about a boy."

After exchanging a glance with Ari, Jean-Paul again turned toward Nabi. "We have to call the police. I want you to say nothing to them except your name until we get a lawyer in to counsel you. Do you understand?"

"But I didn't do anything," the boy protested.

"You don't know what sort of trouble you might be in," Jean-Paul said. "I know Ophelia's parents. It won't matter to them that whatever is going on was Ophelia's doing, they will blame you. And they will do their best to make your life miserable, Nabi. Trust me."

"Listen to Monsieur Bernard, Nabi," Ari said. "We are strangers here, you and me. Let him be our guide through this mess. Yes?"

After a profound sigh, Nabi held up his grubby hands. "May I wash?"

Jean-Paul stood and looked under the table around Nabi's feet. "Do you have a bag?"

"I left it on the terrace."

"Sure, go wash. But leave the bag where it is."

While Ari chaperoned the washing up, Jean-Paul made two phone calls. The first was to a lawyer, and the second to the town Commisariat of Police.

"The charming Detective Fleur Delisle is on her way," he told me as he set his phone on the table. "I asked Éric Aubert to drop over. He's a good man, a neighbor, a very experienced *avocat*. His kids are Nabi's age, and I think that gives him some advantage in helping Nabi."

"An *avocat*?" I said. "A criminal lawyer?"

"In Éric's case, yes. After he talks with Nabi and the police, if he isn't the right person, he'll know who to call. Besides, he lives down the street. He'll be here as soon as he gets his pants on."

"Speaking of pants." During all the commotion, I had forgotten that I was still wearing the T-shirt I slept in. Jean-Paul had the presence of mind to pull on jeans before he came downstairs. "If you don't need me at the moment, I think I'll go and get dressed."

He looked up at me with his upside-down smile, and said, "I think you look charming, but perhaps dressing is a good idea."

I went up to our room and made some calls before getting into the shower. Guido and I were to meet at Isabelle's—my bio-mother's—apartment to go over the rough cut of the Normandy film we were to show the senior producer at the network and her staff that afternoon after joining them for lunch. Guido was nervous about it, worried that we hadn't read the French media market well. I thought the film was very good, for a rough cut, and tried to reassure him, but my mind was elsewhere. After he told me I sounded distracted, I gave him a short summary of the drama unfolding downstairs and we agreed that we would forgo getting together that morning because it was pointless to do anything more with the film until we had feedback from the producer. We knew what we wanted to do, and we knew from experience that the network people would likely have other plans for us. Why not let them go first and fight out the differences from there?

Scrubbed, brushed, and dressed in a black skirt, boots, gray silk shirt, and my favorite red cardigan, I followed Dom down the stairs and back to the kitchen.

"Who's here?" he asked, looking back at me over his shoulder.

"Ahmad Nabi, and maybe the police."

He seemed to find that interesting and hurried his pace.

Detective Delisle leaned against a kitchen counter, arms crossed, her tight bun in perfect order though she looked exhausted. She barely glanced up when Dom and I walked in, all of her attention focused on the quiet conversation between Nabi and the other newcomer, a man of about fifty seated at the table with an arm draped protectively over the back of Nabi's chair. The man had dressed hurriedly in slacks and a fresh dress shirt but hadn't taken time to shave.

"*Comment ça va, Monsieur Aubert?*" Dom said, giving the man a little wave as he headed toward the refrigerator. He received a smile and little wave in return. The question, How's it going? I was learning, didn't necessarily expect an answer beyond a wave, a nod, or *les bises*, or a repeat of *Ça va.*

Delisle stifled a yawn. Without asking, I poured a cup of coffee and handed it to her.

"*Merci,*" she said, sounding grateful.

"Rough night?" I asked.

Her only response was a glance over the rim of her mug.

Ahmad Nabi was a minor. He was entitled to have legal counsel and a parent with him during questioning by police. Which brought the boy's grandmother into the conversation. He told us that his telephone had been dead since Saturday afternoon because he forget the charger. That's why he didn't respond to Ari's text. It also meant that he hadn't spoken with his grandmother so she had no idea where he was both Sunday and Monday nights.

"Maggie?" Ari said. "May I ask a favor? Nabi wants me to go to his grandmother and explain the situation. She comes from a traditional background so I think she would feel more comfortable if a woman were with me. Will you come?"

"Happy to," I said, glancing at my watch. I admit I was curious about the situation, as Ari labeled it, that had dropped on our doorstep. But I had a lunch meeting at noon that I could not miss. Not if I expected to stay employed, and by that particular situation keep my current visa so that I could remain in the country without going through further immigration folderol. No matter what, I had to be on the train to Paris by eleven-fifteen.

We all decamped at once: Nabi and his entourage headed for the Vaucresson police station, his backpack and violin case in the custody of Delisle; Dom drove down our street on his Vespa in one direction while Jean-Paul, Ari, and I went in the car in the other. Ari and I dropped Jean-Paul at the train station before continuing toward the address on the far side of the *haras* that Nabi had given us.

When the GPS on the dash announced that we had reached our destination, I thought that we must have made a mistake when we wrote down the address. Nabi and his grandmother, I was told, lived on a public stipend. Welfare. But the drive Ari turned down led to an impressive mansard-roofed château set among vast, green grounds. Not at all what I expected.

As we got out of the car, I asked Ari, "Do I call her Madame Diba, or Madame Azadah?"

"Neither," he said. "Or both. Afghans don't have surnames unless they decide to adopt one. Her name is Azadah Diba. Period."

I was curious about her. We all go into new situations with a package of preconceptions based on, what? Experience, prejudice, hope? All that I knew about Ahmad Nabi's grandmother was that she was an Afghan refugee who had lost almost all her family in a desperate attempt to find a safe place for them to live. And that her late son—or was it son-in-law?—was a classically trained musician. I had learned that the current wave of refugees pouring out of mid-eastern war zones were, like Ari, more likely to represent their nation's educated urban elite than any other group. Though I did not expect Nabi's grandmother to be shrouded in a burka, when I thought of refugee grandmothers I conjured an image of white-haired rosiness. Azadah Diba was neither white-haired nor rosy-cheeked.

The woman who answered the door at this film-set version of a château was dark-haired, slender, stylishly coifed, dressed in tailored jeans with a starched shirt under an apron smock. She also had a half-year-old blond baby on her hip.

Ari, palms together at chest level, gave her a little bow. "Azadah Diba?"

Before she responded, she gave us a hard looking-over. "You are?"

"I am Ari Massarani, and this is Maggie MacGowen."

"Doctor Massarani?" she said, shifting the baby to her other hip. "You are here about my Nabi?"

"Yes. Don't worry, he's fine."

"Tell me." Stepping aside, she gestured for us to come in. We followed her through a large marbled foyer and out into the backyard where a toddler of about three was digging in a sandbox. Azadah Diba put the baby down on a pad spread on the brick patio, and said, "Sit. Please tell me, where is Nabi? I am worried."

Ari started to explain where the boy was now and where he had been since Friday but wasn't far into the story before she raised a hand to stop him. "Please, more slow. My French not so good. You have English?"

"Of course," Ari said, and started over. She had little to say until he had finished filling her in on Nabi's situation, and when she spoke her English had hints of a British accent, not surprising when I thought about it.

"I am so relieved to have news," she said, her voice quivering, though she somehow held herself together. "Nabi always calls to tell me where he is. But all weekend he didn't answer his phone and my messages went straight to voice mail. That was not like him. Then when the police came on Sunday morning looking for him, I was afraid something terrible had happened to my boy. You know Nabi, Doctor Massarani. You know he's a good boy. But adjusting here has been very difficult for him. Sometimes he gets so angry, and I was afraid that he had been–" She looked out across the lawn, checked on both children, took a deep breath. "Some of the boys become seduced by crazy imams and disappear into a hole for a while. They come back ready for war."

"Do you think Nabi is vulnerable to be recruited by a radical imam?" I asked.

"I hadn't," she said. "Until he didn't come home."

"As long as he has his music," Ari said, "Nabi will be okay."

I asked, "Are you aware that a girl, a friend of Nabi is missing?"

"The police told me that." Her attention suddenly shifted to the toddler across the lawn. "Lydia, you must not throw sand."

"Yes, Miss Diba." The little girl went back to digging.

"The girl speaks English," I said.

"Yes. My employers are Australian. They wanted an English-speaking nanny, so that's why they hired me."

"You're the nanny?" I said.

"Nanny, housekeeper, sometimes cook." She laughed softly. "There was a time when I hired nannies for my children. And now, here I am. Please don't think I'm complaining. My employers are quite generous, though they have some reservations about us. Nabi and I have the servants' quarters to ourselves–I am the only live-in staff–and we are sufficiently comfortable. I feel fortunate."

She turned to Ari. "You said that a lawyer is with Nabi now. Is he very expensive?"

"Don't worry about that yet. If Nabi is honest with the police, I believe he has nothing to worry about. We should be able to get him back to you very soon."

"Diba," I said, still feeling uncomfortable about which name to use, "do you know Ophelia Fouchet, the girl who is missing?"

"I know who she is," she said. "She and Nabi play in a string quartet at school. She's a cellist, a fairly good one I think. They played a wonderful Mozart Divertimento at the Christmas program."

"But other than that?"

She shook her head. "It is difficult for Nabi to bring friends here–my employers are quite strict about visitors–and it is difficult for me to get away until the children are ready for bed at night. So

I haven't met many of his school friends. I want to go to him now, but as you see, it is impossible. Nabi understands."

"Miss Diba!" Little Lydia came running across the lawn, grinding sandy fists into her eyes. "I have something in my eye!"

"Don't rub them, dear. We'll take care of it." Diba rose, swept up the baby and grabbed Lydia by the sandy hand. To us she said, "Please excuse me. I must tend to her. Will you see yourselves out?"

And we did. When Ari and I were back in the car, I asked, "Thoughts?"

"The resiliency of the human spirit never ceases to amaze me."

"I was right, you are an optimist."

"As I said, I am a work in progress. Now, where to?"

"Train station, please. I have a meeting."

] Four

GUIDO WAS WAITING FOR ME outside the train station across the Seine from our new studio. He had a paper coffee cup in one hand, a croissant in the other, and earbuds in his ears. He was studying French, mouthing the words in his lesson.

"Croissants, really?" I said, coming up beside him. "We're going straight to lunch, and you're snacking?"

"Yeah, but croissants, you know, right?" He pulled the buds out of his ears. "Want a bite?"

Of course I did. Somehow in the middle of all the activity in our kitchen that morning, I forgot to eat, and I was hungry. He broke off about half of what he had left and shared it as we walked toward the bridge over the river, headed for the lunch meeting with our new executive producer and her staff.

Guido was in his mid-forties, like me, beginning to gray at the temples, silver flecks in the curly black mass of his hair. His family came from Sicily, descendants of Aeneas and his Trojans, he insisted. He did look as if he could be carved in Greek marble. We had worked well together, on and off, for nearly twenty years, me taking charge of film topics and content, he with most things tech and camera related. We argued a lot, but it never meant anything in the end because our focus was always on what was best for the film; we were like family. The work we would be doing for our new employer was exactly what we had been doing for years, making investigative films. But that morning, Guido was more nervous than I had ever seen him. The hand holding his coffee cup shook.

"What's up, my friend?" I asked, putting my hand around his elbow. "Second thoughts?"

"About working over here?" he said. "No way. No. I can't remember ever wanting a job more than this one. Except maybe my first gig. I think that's the problem, Mags. I'm afraid we'll screw up. Or I'll screw up; you'll be okay."

"Guido," I said, nudging his shoulder. "Just do what you know how to do, keep your hands off French women, and you'll be fine."

He chuckled. "That second part's a bitch, huh? Some of these girls, jeez, they're so beautiful I want to go up and lick them."

I nailed him with a glare. "Promise me you won't."

He squeezed my hand. "I promise, I promise, I promise. Maggie, I've learned my lesson. Hands to myself."

"Hands and all other body parts."

"Absolutely. Yes. Don't worry."

"Uh-huh." This topic was the source of several of our worst arguments over the years. In the past, there was an obnoxious, exploitative culture of slap and tickle—and worse—in the film and television industry. But not as much recently. Not without impunity, anyway. People didn't get away with as much shit in America as they once did. Same was true in France. The French corollary of the American #MeToo movement was #BalanceTonPorc, which roughly translates as Out Your Pig. Guido needed to behave like a grown-up with our new employer or he could be outed right out of the country.

That conversation, plus however much coffee he had swilled that morning, did nothing to settle Guido's nerves. But ever the trouper, when it was time to go meet with our new bosses, he took a deep breath, smoothed his perfect hair, and put on his game face. He opened the restaurant door, bowed to me, and said, *"Après vous."* He didn't roll the R at the back of his throat and I did not correct him as I preceded him inside.

The agenda set by our new executive producer, Diane Duval, and her production staff, called for lunch first. Business was not discussed during the meal, at least overtly. Instead, there was a swapping of stories, getting to know each other. Excellent food, interesting people, casual conversation; Guido and I both relaxed and enjoyed it. The staff seemed comfortable with each other and with their boss, an easy camaraderie that, if it were genuine, would make for a good working environment. Because Guido spoke little French, yet, much of the conversation was held in English with liberal smatterings of French at times that he needed to have translated. Most of the jokes and all the puns simply weren't funny in translation, but we tried.

It was afterward, over cheese and yet more coffee, that we finally got down to serious discussion about work. The first topic was the Normandy film.

"We are very happy with what you and Guido have produced for us, Maggie," Diane said. "I am confident it will attract an impressive audience share. When will you have the broadcast version ready?"

"That depends on how much tweaking you want us to do," I said.

Nodding, thinking, she picked up a spoon and began rhythmically bouncing it on the starched white tablecloth. Studying me closely enough that I began to feel uncomfortable, she said, "So far, most of your success in America has been making hard-hitting investigative pieces. Homelessness, abandoned elders, sex trafficking, and most recently unexploded bombs left behind after war, yes?"

"Yes, among others."

"This film you have brought us about your family's Normandy farm is quite a departure for you. Very different in tone. What engages me—" With that spoon as a pointer, she swept her hand in a broad arc to encompass the other six people at the table. "—engages us, with this project is the expectation that the film will be both a powerful introduction of your work to the European audience and will establish your French roots. Or, to be more exact, your discovery of your French roots. I know that we talked about this piece as the first in a series examining family and niche agriculture within the eurozone. However–"

Under the table, Guido gripped my knee. I could feel his hand shake, telling me that he, also, was waiting for the first shoe to drop. Or the axe.

"However, after long consideration and much discussion, the production staff have decided that we prefer for you to make for us the same sort of films that your career and reputation in America are built on. Don't be afraid to tackle controversy."

"Oh." I peeled Guido's death grip from my knee. "*Quelle surprise.*"

"Does that prospect make you uncomfortable, Maggie?"

"Not at all." I felt my shoulders come down away from my ears and I began to breathe normally again; we weren't being given the sack before we began, after all. People who work in television don't know the meaning of job security. Only a year earlier, two days before Christmas, Guido and I had been terminated just weeks after we signed a new contract. And then six weeks later we were rehired by the same unit. It happens. I turned to my old partner. "Your thoughts?"

"Great." He was smiling, at last. "Yes. If it works for Maggie, I'm fine with it. Dragging cameras through back alleys and homeless camps is more familiar to me than dodging cow pies at farms."

There was a puzzled exchange of looks around the table. As explanation I said, "Cow dung. Poop."

"Poop" echoed around the table, along with some laughter.

On that note, we left the restaurant for a tour of the studio's production facilities led by Diane and her personal assistant, Bruno, an excruciatingly young, painfully hip-looking man. The network building's vast interior reminded me of an M.C. Escher drawing, a maze of hallways that connected, or didn't, in a seemingly indecipherable and possibly impossible pattern. Because of Paris height restrictions, the structure extended as many floors below ground as it did above, with offices generally up where the sun shines, and production areas down where it doesn't. After a brief stop at Diane's office suite, and a peek into the partitioned space that would be mine and Guido's, we coursed downward through layers deep below the left bank of the Seine until we reached the technical command center of live studio operations.

Guido may not have understood very much French, but he certainly understood television technology. As soon as we walked through the door of a room lined with television monitors, four or five dozen of them, all live-streaming images from external video feeds, any remnant of a nervous, hesitant Guido disappeared; this was his professional milieu. Three technical engineers sat at the long video switcher console in the center of the room, pulling up and manipulating images on the monitors. As one of the engineers toggled between a highway collision in Portugal and a weather report from Kazakhstan, Diane was saying, with some pride, "The network is part of an international news sharing consortium. We bring in live feeds from all over the globe," but my eye was drawn to a monitor near the top right labelled CCTV.

The CCTV monitor was split into four screens, each screen streaming a few seconds of live footage from a different closed-circuit camera somewhere in France before cutting to another.

I took a seat next to one of the engineers, with Guido hovering over my shoulder. "Tell me about your access to CCTV."

He shrugged, puzzled, I thought by the question. "We can pull up most municipal systems." He punched some buttons and the current scene on the street outside the studio appeared on a large central monitor. "The French haven't embraced CCTV the massive way the Brits have, but most cities have general coverage. Paris does, for sure."

"Does Vaucresson?" I asked.

"*Bien sûr*. A lot of bigwigs live there, so of course."

"Can you show me the Vaucresson train station Friday night from about nine o'clock on?"

"I can try." The central monitor screen flashed with a new image–the familiar station platform–and then split as he pulled up footage from one camera after another until each of the six cameras around the train station was displayed. More flashes as the images shifted from current live stream to the archived Friday footage. "Here you go."

"Checking up on Jean-Paul?" Guido asked, slipping into my chair as I rose from it.

"No." I went around to the front of the console for a closer look. "This morning I told you about the girl from the village who went missing Friday night. Her friend, the kid who showed up on our terrace, said he walked her as far as the station parking lot. She hasn't been seen since."

"How interested are you?" he asked

"I don't know yet." I watched people, trains, and cars come and go, hoping to spot a girl dressed all in black. "Can we single out the parking lot?"

"Hold on." The engineer, whose named we learned was Zed, sent two of the frames to an adjoining monitor. The first camera was trained on the walkway between the parking lot and the platform, the other looked toward the lot's street exit. He said, "Those cameras shoot six or eight frames per second. Decent enough resolution, but the angle isn't great for face recognition."

"Can you fast forward?" I asked. He did as Diane came to stand beside me. At time stamp 21:21:52–fifty-two seconds past 9:21 P.M.–I saw what I thought was three people walk into the parking lot off the street: a tall boy, a slender girl, and someone who was shorter and curvier than the others and who seemed to lean heavily on the boy. "Go back to 21:21:49, please, and run in slo-mo from there if you can."

"Is that the missing girl?" Diane asked.

"Maybe." I turned to Zed. "Can you freeze screen two at 21:21:18 and zoom in?" The image of the trio was clear enough to identify Ahmad Nabi. The curvy shadow leaning against Nabi wasn't a person, but a red, hard-shell cello case that he carried. The slender girl walking beside him looked like a typical teenage Goth. Black hair, baggy black jersey, black mini skirt, torn black tights, six-hole Doc Martens boots. Was she Ophelia Fouchet? All I had to compare this image with was the photo her parents posted on the missing children flyer, and the fact that she played the cello. If indeed the girl with Nabi was Ophelia, she had put a lot of effort into not looking like the sweet-faced blonde in that photo. "Can you print the frame?"

"Not from here," Zed said. "But I can send it to your company mailbox."

"I don't have a company mailbox," I said. "Can you send it to my cloud account?"

Zed said, "Not if it's out of our system, unless Diane—"

Diane turned to her assistant, "Bruno, you did set up mailboxes for Maggie and Guido, right?"

"Of course, yes."

"And did you tell Maggie and Guido that they have mailboxes, and give them access information?"

"Oh." All color was gone from his narrow face as he looked from me to Guido. "Merde. I sent the info to their mailboxes."

"Yes, Zed," Diane said with a heavy sigh. "You may send the image to Maggie's cloud account until Bruno gets off his skinny ass and gets her set up in-house."

"Thanks," I said. "Can we continue?"

There wasn't very much more footage to see. On the screen, Nabi and his companion said good-bye, exchanged bises, and he handed her the cello case. He walked back the way he came and out of frame. She continued toward the platform for a few yards, lugging the case that was nearly as tall as she. Before she reached the opening to the platform, she turned and watched Nabi until there was no more of him to see. When he was gone, she walked back into the parking lot and out of camera range stage left, as it were.

Zed put the other four cameras back up on the monitor, each of them covering a different zone of the train platform. The Goth girl wasn't captured on any of them. Indeed, by ten o'clock, the station was all but deserted. Unless the girl had instantly disguised herself as a middle-aged man carrying an umbrella or one of a pair of young men who snogged a bit on the platform as they waited, she did not catch the ten-fifteen train to Paris on

Friday night. Nor was she there to catch the ten-twenty-two toward Le Celle Saint-Cloud. So, where did she go after Nabi left her?

"See what you needed?" Guido asked.

"I saw what there is," I said. "It supports what the boy said but only adds questions about the girl."

Zed said, "Let me guess, you want the parking lot footage sent to you, too."

"Yes, please. And a few minutes of the platform. Enough to show the girl wasn't there."

A young man with spiky hair leaned in from the hall. "Diane?"

"Yes, Moby?" Diane said, turning toward the door.

"I'm told Madame MacGowen is with you," he said.

I said, "I'm here."

"You're needed in makeup."

"Makeup?" I said. "Why?"

"The interview," Diane said, checking the clock on the far wall. "Jimmy starts taping at *quinze-heures*."

That is, three o'clock. It was already past two. But I was still puzzled. "Who is Jimmy? And what interview?"

Her eyebrows rose. "You got the memo, yes?"

"Memo? No."

She spun around and nailed her assistant with a glare. "Bruno?"

"*Merde*," he said again, face paling as he looked at me. "I sent it to your office mailbox."

"Madame MacGowen?" Moby, still leaning around the door-frame, repeated, more impatiently the second time.

Diane sighed. "Sorry this was sprung on you, Maggie. But please go with Moby and get your face powdered, or whatever. You're scheduled to tape a segment on *Ce Soir* with Jimmy Jardine, one of our more popular talk show hosts. The network wants your audience to know you're here. My only advice is, don't let him bait you."

"Come, Guido," I said, rising from my chair. "Time to sparkle."

Diane wagged a finger. "Maggie alone this time; the language issue, yes? Guido, Zed will finish your tour of production facilities. And Bruno will get you set up on your office mailbox. Right, Bruno?"

Guido did not like being on camera, so he seemed relieved. I patted him on the back as I passed by on my way out and said, "Wait for me."

With a promise that he would, I went with Moby down a few floors where the broadcast studios and their appendages were.

"Annette," Moby announced, showing me into a makeup room that was like a small, fully equipped beauty salon. "Madame MacGowen is here."

"Almost finished with Jimmy. Have a seat," Annette said, flicking her chin toward the second of the two chairs in the room. Her hands were busy artfully tousling the hair of the man in the other chair. He was fortyish, tan, fit, and clearly happy with his image in the big mirror on the wall in front of us. The stylist paused what she was doing to give my face a long, hard study. "Who usually does your makeup?"

"I do."

Her answer was a grunt that connoted to me that, from the look of me, she wasn't surprised. Except when I'm in front of a camera, I rarely bother to put on anything more than some blusher and mascara, if that. I think that walking around with a bare face is my reaction against the heavy camera-ready makeup I am required to wear onscreen. A bare face can also be a disguise; fewer people recognize me.

"Madame MacGowen is it? You must be the American invader," Jimmy said, eyes shifting to take in my reflection in the mirror. "It's Maggie, right?

"Right. Let me guess," I said; remembering Diane's warning not to let Jimmy bait me, I swallowed the invader remark without commenting on it. "You're Jimmy Jardine, host of *Ce Soir*."

"Guilty as charged," he said, preening.

"So, what should I know before we go on the air?"

"Just relax and be yourself."

Moby leaned in from the hallway only long enough to say,

"First call, Jimmy. Chop, chop." And then he disappeared again. The man never seemed to come all the way into a room.

Annette brushed some shadow under Jimmy's chin, unsnapped his protective cape and snatched it aside with a flourish. "*Fini*, Jimmy."

"Thanks, *poupée*." He pushed himself up from the chair. Under the cape he wore blue jeans and an untucked pink dress shirt. He flipped up his collar and gave himself a last careful study in the mirror. After a resigned shrug and a moue, he took a denim jacket off a hook and draped it over his arm. His parting words were, "Annette, don't pretty her up too much. I don't need the competition."

It was my turn for Annette's brushes and paint pots. She was good at her job, and fast. Face, hair, a last dusting of powder, and she unsnapped my cape and took it away. I had no idea where I was to go next. As I got out of the chair, I asked her, "Where is the green room?"

"Moby will come for you." She brushed something on my lips and warned me not to lick them or drink anything. Then she stood back and took a long view of me. I had not dressed to be on TV: everyday skirt, knee-high boots, gray silk blouse, red cardigan. She tugged my skirt down, undid the top button of the blouse and pulled it open, flattening the collar to expose my sternum. Then she grasped the bottom corners of my cardigan, gave them a twist and tied them into an interesting knot at my waist, something that would never have occurred to me to do. With a little more fuss and tuck, she said, "Red's your color; you look fine. Just remember that Jimmy is a bastard, and women scare the shit out of him. And don't cross your legs on camera."

"Good to know."

As promised, Moby came to fetch me. There were three men already waiting in the green room when I entered: a writer, an art historian, and a professor of political theory, I learned as we introduced ourselves. We made small talk and watched the pre-show activity on the *Ce Soir* set via a flat-screen monitor attached to the wall.

The set was typical talk-show design–host's desk and a row of chairs for guests–except that the small audience sat behind the host where they would be seen on camera during the broadcast, and not out front. A jazz combo, stage right, warmed up the audience. While that was going on, a soundman came in and wired the four of us with remote microphones; my power pack was slipped down between my shoulder blades.

Moby appeared at the door and summoned everyone except me to follow him. Was I, the American invader, to be ignored? Or was I being overly sensitive?

"Courage," the political theorist said to me as he trooped out behind the others.

"Do I need courage?" I asked.

"If Jimmy is playing polemicist today, yes. We all will."

On the wall-mounted monitor, I watched the new activity on the set from the green room. There were last checks for light and sound, then a moment of stillness before the director, standing behind a podium between the primary cameras, gave a signal. The music rose, the audience applauded, Jimmy walked on set, flirted with the camera, took his seat behind the desk, and the show began. A short monologue, and then the writer, the art historian, and the professor of political theory came on, waving to the audience. They shook hands all around as Jimmy introduced them, sorted themselves into seats, and the discussion began.

Jimmy set the tone, challenging the writer to defend the topic of his new book, something about the relationship between patterns of human migration and global climate change. The political theorist thrust himself into the conversation. He said, "Isn't the current anti-immigration push nothing but cover for long-rooted racism? All across the eurozone, along with open Islamophobia, we've seen a surge in anti-Semitism unmatched since Hitler. In Paris, where the great majority of French Jews live, you would be hard pressed to find a Jewish child in a public school because of harassment and bullying. It seems that with every passing year our collective memory of the Holocaust fades, and that is both tragic and dangerous. How do you equate that with global climate change?"

The art historian sent the discussion caroming from there to white nationalism represented in the arts. Once the conversation reached a certain momentum, Jimmy backed off and let his guests fight things out among themselves without his input except for the occasional provocative prod. The give-and-take was noisy, sometimes angry, sometimes truly cogent, other times downright silly, no more than argument for the sake of argument. It was much more free-form than American talk shows, with the host more participant when he chose to be than referee. I watched it all with a growing sense of dread.

As a distraction, I texted Jean-Paul and told him I was waiting for my curtain call. He said he would ask Ari to go into the house and set the television to record *Ce Soir* so we could watch it later. He was supportive and funny, as expected, and that's why I reached out to him. I asked if he had learned anything more about Nabi's situation. He answered that the police verified his alibi with the sausage maker and released him. Ari took him home to clean up, then dropped him at school before lunch. There were still questions about Friday night, but Jean-Paul thought Nabi didn't have much to worry about. I was feeling calmer by the time he signed off.

Finally, Moby came for me. Annette was waiting in the passageway to touch up my face and straighten my clothes. All the time she was tucking and fussing and daubing with her brushes, Moby was giving me instructions about what to do when I got the cue. On the set there was a brief musical interlude as a break from the earlier discussion to the next segment. While I waited, Jimmy read an introduction: American filmmaker Maggie MacGowen, some blah, blah, blah about me and my history. Then, to my surprise, instead of summoning me he ran the five-minute trailer for the Normandy film that Guido and I had given to Diane Duval as part of the original pitch we made to beguile her enough that she would hire us. At the end, a new banner rolled announcing our upcoming series–I had never seen it before–the monitors faded to black, lights came up and the studio cameras were back on Jimmy and company. Moby gave my shoulder a forward nudge. I strolled onto the set as the audience applauded and Jimmy and the debate bunch rose. I waved to the audience and shook hands with the quartet on set. Jimmy took my extended hand and leaned in for the exchange of *les bises* as if we were old friends.

Jimmy's first question as I took the chair closest to his desk was, "How many German soldiers did your grandmother murder?"

"Face to face? Only one that I am aware of," I said. "Slit his throat and shot him through the heart. But what she and the women of her village did on the night she mentioned in that film clip was an act of war, not murder. They did what they had to do to survive," I said. "What fascinates me, though, is that out of a five-minute discussion about fundamental existential issues relating to traditional family farming in France, what caught your attention was a twelve-second nugget where my grandmother mentions that she and the women of her village dispatched a company of German Occupation soldiers in order to save not only their lives but their livelihood. The point of her story is, she despairs that her grandchildren don't share her commitment to the family land and its produce. The question is, will the family farm survive past this generation?"

Jimmy leaned closer to me and rested his chin on the heel of his hand. With a smarmy grin he may have thought was charming, he asked, "When provoked, are you as fierce as your grandmother?"

I remembered to smile: "You don't want to find that out, I promise you."

The political theorist dove in: "You say those murders were morally justified in order to save a patch of dirt? Morally, murder is murder, Maggie, even during war. How can you suggest otherwise?"

"Sure, sure, Étienne," the writer interjected. "But leave that for now." Turning to me, he said, "In that clip you seem to elevate the cultural importance of the small farmer—what is it your people produce, cheese and brandy?—to some iconic status, as if the artisanal producers are the veritable foundations of what defines France. I want to ask, Maggie, how you, an American, have the nerve, the arrogance, to think you can interpret life, commerce, and culture in France for a French audience. Don't you think, that as an outsider, that is impossible to accomplish?"

"Not at all," I said. I had expected some form of that question to come up.

The art historian wanted to jump into the fray but only got as far as, "Beware barbarians at the gate—" before Jimmy, upright again, shut him down by saying, "Why not, Maggie?"

"I believe it was Anaïs Nin who said, 'What we are familiar with we cease to see.' Sometimes we need an outsider to hold up a mirror so we can realize what we have become blind to. Certainly, the keenest contemporary observations about life in early America were made by Alexis de Tocqueville, a Frenchman."

"So, you believe you are the American Tocqueville come to France?" the writer said, patronizing in his tone.

"Through a different medium and in a different time, we'll see." I turned to Jimmy. "Maybe next I'll make a film about French talk shows. They look like talk shows around the globe, but oh-là, the content and tone are yours alone. Such passion for debate."

"I look forward to being stripped bare before your camera." Jimmy looked into my eyes. "You have a charming accent."

I laughed. "Every time I hear that, I wonder if it's code for, chérie, you're not one of us, are you?"

Behind me I heard a guffaw and a snort. Jimmy reached for my hand, kissed it, and still holding it turned to the cameras and said good night. The band played, the monitors faded, I reclaimed my hand, and we were finished. The audience began to file out, the soundman retrieved our mics, there were handshakes and les bises all around, and the writer suggested we all go out for drinks. I declined and said my good-byes. Diane was waiting for me when I walked off; she had been watching from the sidelines.

"Okay?" I asked her.

"Oui. Bon." She leaned in for les bises. "You'll survive here, I am confident. Guido told me to tell you that you will find him exactly where you left him. Bruno will show you the way back."

Along the way, Bruno was stiff with me, more formal than anyone had been all day. Was this his manner, or was he still embarrassed about the mailbox gaffe? Maybe he thought I would be angry and simply had his guard up. I made a mental note to bring him a cookie sometime.

"I watched you," Guido said when he noticed I had taken the seat beside him at the video switcher console.

"How do you think it went?" I asked.

"You looked like you were holding your own, but I have no idea what anyone was saying. Were they picking on you?"

"No. No more than they picked on each other. It's like a sport."

"The host—Jimmy?—was he coming on to you?"

"In a token way. Some habits are hard to break."

"Tell me about it," he said.

"You having fun with the toys?" I asked, watching him play with the video feed controls.

"The system is interesting. Some of the tech here is way ahead of ours, but some of it we dumped during the Dark Ages of analog. The interface might be tricky to navigate, but I think I have things under control. Now, you want to tell me why you're so interested in that missing girl?"

"Just being nosy, that's all," I said. "Two things bother me, though. First, what the girl told her friend sounded like she intended to get home by midnight, her curfew. But she never got home. Next, I met the friend, Ahmad Nabi, who was the last person known to have seen Ophelia. Nabi seems like a good kid. He's only fifteen, a refugee, went through hell getting here, now he's being put through hell at school. I think the footage will help him."

"Only two things?" Guido turned away from the console to watch me closely.

"Okay, three," I said. "According to Nabi, the kids had come from a rehearsal at the high school. You can see that Nabi has his violin case on his back and he carried her cello. When he hands Ophelia the cello, she almost disappears behind it."

"Cellos are big," he said. "She isn't."

"Exactly. She couldn't carry that instrument very far, so I'm wondering if she planned to meet someone somewhere very near-by. Or someone was picking her up. The question is, who?"

"That third one is a poser." After a pause, he said, "You know where to find me when the fourth thing occurs to you. The one that gets us up to our necks in something."

"You already know what it is, my friend. What did she need to talk over with this mystery third person?"

"She's fifteen?"

"She's fifteen." I looked up at the row of clocks on the wall, time zones around the globe, found Paris, and said, "I'm going home now. What are your plans?"

He told me he was going out with his downstairs neighbor, Barry Griffith, an affable Francophone Canadian who had enrolled Guido with a French language tutor and was himself tutoring Guido on local restaurants and nightlife. When I said good night, he was humming "Back in the Saddle Again." I made my way up through the caracole of the studio's underground hallways and back out into the daylight. It occurred to me as I rushed to catch the next train to Vaucresson that I hadn't stopped to wash off the television face.

Already, the late May days were long. At five-thirty, when I got off the train, the sky was still bright. The air was clear and crisp after a day of rain and it felt wonderful to be out after an afternoon largely spent underground. I texted Jean-Paul and told him that I would walk home. He asked if I minded picking up some balsamic vinegar when I passed the shops. He was home already and had put the chicken in the oven for dinner, but he was out of the bal-samic he needed for the sauce.

As we texted, I studied the camera placements along the plat-form. When I reached the parking lot, I located the two cameras there, and stopped to figure out the path that Nabi and the girl had followed when they turned in off the street. They said good-bye near the low iron fence that separated the car park from the plat-form, and went separate ways, Nabi back the way he came, and the girl, who I assumed was Ophelia, off to the left and out of camera range. There was a break in the hedge along the parking lot at

about the place where Ophelia became a ghost. I texted good-bye
to Jean-Paul and walked through the hedge and out into a narrow
alley that passed between a large old house and an optician's shop.
I continued down the alley until it ended at a main thoroughfare,
a chocolatier on the left and a bakery on the right. Had Ophelia
simply stopped in for a treat after concert practice? I checked at
both shops and was told that they closed at seven on Friday, so no.
At least, she hadn't stopped there.

My phone buzzed with a text. It was Jean-Paul: AND SOME
ASPARAGUS. I sent a heart emoji as response and went on to do
my shopping.

At the greengrocer, where I gathered the asparagus, carrots,
shallots, and some arugula because it looked good, I overheard
that the Fouchet girl's boyfriend had been picked up by the police
that morning. At the bakery, waiting in line to get a fresh baguette
for dinner and brioche for breakfast, the woman in front of me
told the woman behind me that the little Arab boy who had gone
away with Ophelia was in school today. He was late, but he was
there. The woman in front wondered if they should get parents
together to speak with *la directeur*, the new high school principal–the previous *directeur* had suddenly gone on leave just last
Friday–about the wisdom of letting the boy attend until someone
got to the bottom of things. At that remark, I couldn't help myself. I
butted in.

"If you'll excuse me," I said, "I happen to know that the boy,
Ahmad Nabi, did not go away with Ophelia on Friday. And he
wasn't missing. He was in Arras all weekend selling sausages at the
farmers' market. It's natural that everyone in town is upset about
Ophelia, but I caution that you would make a terrible mistake if
you used that boy as a scapegoat. The child has been traumatized
enough already. And another thing: While he is a Muslim, he is
not an Arab."

By then I was shaking. The woman in front seemed to cower
away from me, but the woman behind glared.

"I don't know who you are," she said.

"Let me introduce myself. I am Margot Eugénie Louise-Marie

Duchamps Flint." I reached out a hand to her. As a reflex, she took it, but I think I scared her. I said, "I don't know who you are."

"Fabienne Simon. Charmed to meet you, Madame–" She shrugged; too many names in that string.

"Maggie," I said after taking a deep breath. I managed to smile. "Just call me Maggie. Sorry if I sounded fierce, but I've met the boy, Ahmad Nabi. He's been through so much tragedy in his short life that I feel protective. I'm a parent, I understand your concern. But Nabi is no threat."

The woman in front spoke over her shoulder. "He plays the violin, you know."

"So I hear."

"Ophelia plays the cello," Fabienne said behind me. "She gave up riding, over her father's objections, because it ruined her hands. She's an interesting girl." A euphemism for wild thing?

And so the conversation went until it was my turn at the counter. I ran into Fabienne Simon again at the grocery, where we had a conversation about balsamic vinegars. She pointed out the one she used for cooking, and I, knowing nothing about balsamic vinegars, or much at all about cooking, put that one into my basket. During the conversation I learned that she and her husband lived down the street from us and had two children, a boy in middle school–the *collège*–and a girl in high school–the *lycée*. Monsieur Simon worked in a bank and Fabienne was a *notaire*, a family attorney, with a local practice so she could be on call for her children. I told her my daughter was in her third year at UCLA and gave her the short version of what I do–I work in television. She knew Jean-Paul, and of course had been on several parent committees with Marian.

"Such a shame," she said. She lived two doors beyond Holly and Kevin Porter, so we walked home together. "To die so suddenly–a brain aneurysm–and so young. A shock for everyone." Then she turned to me and smiled. "How lovely it is that Jean-Paul has found you. A man like Jean-Paul should not go through life alone. Good luck to you."

I thanked her, and then I brought up Ophelia. "Does your daughter know Ophelia well?"

"Of course, at least in the sense that they've been in school together all the way through. They were never best friends, but they are friendly. As kids get older they form into cliques." She chuckled. "Like their parents, yes? My daughter is an athlete–tennis–and there she finds her closest friends. Ophelia was with the music crowd, though I have the sense that she has always been a bit of a loner. A quiet girl, very bright. Yet fierce in her way."

"Fierce?"

She gave me the side eye with a wry smile. "You called us out for gossiping earlier."

"I was simply correcting the story," I said.

"And now you're curious."

"I confess," I said. "Very curious. Everyone is talking about Ophelia, but I know nothing about her. The police think she's run away. I'm curious about what she might run away from."

"Have you met Yvan and Claire?"

"The parents?"

She nodded.

"I haven't."

"Next time you hear thunder and lightning, look down the street before you look to the sky."

We had reached the end of my driveway. Because it was true, I said, "Thunder and lightning terrify me."

"So, you understand."

We parted at the end of my driveway. Both of us had our hands full, so we leaned in to touch cheeks and kiss the air, a casual exchange of *les bises*.

"À *bientôt*," I said.

"*Ciao*," she answered, raising a shopping bag in a sort of wave. "Regards to Jean-Paul. And welcome to you."

When I opened the front door I heard people talking. I walked into the salon and found Jean-Paul and an older woman, a beautiful older woman, deep in conversation as they looked into my office. Not wanting to interrupt, I continued toward the kitchen to put the shopping away. But Jean-Paul spotted me.

"Maggie," he said, holding out an arm to me. "Here you are. Good. I want you to meet someone."

The woman eyed me critically as I crossed the salon.

"Caroline, this is Maggie," he said, slipping his arm around my waist. "Maggie, Caroline is Marian's mother."

I set the shopping bags on the floor and offered her my hand. "Lovely to meet you."

"And you," she said with a very polite little smile, giving my hand the gentlest of squeezes. Even for a French woman she was perfectly turned out, but without appearing to have fussed at all. A silk skirt, a knit top that draped just so, an artfully knotted scarf at her neck, shiny light brown hair that fell loosely two inches below her ears. On my very best day, and this was not one of them, I could never pull off that effortless chic. Suddenly, I was aware that I still wore full television war paint.

"Maggie, I called Caroline to ask if she wanted any of this furniture."

She looked again at the chaotic state of the office with an expression that was equal parts distaste and sadness. "I was just saying to Jean-Paul that these things meant so much to Marian and her father." She dipped her chin to look up at me. "Everything is the finest quality and perfectly functional. If you're to work at home, Maggie, I don't see the issue over keeping the room as it was."

I turned to Jean-Paul. "If you'll excuse me, I think this is a family matter. I'll put away the groceries."

"Please stay," he said, looking into my eyes and smiling gently. "You're right that this is a family matter. But, Maggie, you are family." Then, still holding me close, he turned to address his former mother-in-law. "Caroline—Maman—I loved Marian very much. She will always have a place in my heart. I understand that you wish to preserve her memory in any way possible. However, this is a house, just a house, and not a mausoleum. There is no logical reason to preserve this room as a shrine when, as you said, Maggie will be doing some of her work at home and will need the room arranged in a way that is practical for her."

Caroline squared her shoulders. "But what will Roland say?"

"I'm sure my father-in-law will have a great deal to say. He always does. That's why I am offering to return his things. He can do anything he wants with them."

A sly smile crept across her face as she took another look at the jumble of furniture in the middle of the room. "Perhaps a bonfire."

Jean-Paul laughed, and so did she.

"Roland has terrible taste," she said.

"Do you want me to speak with him?" Jean-Paul asked.

"No, *chéri*, but thank you for offering. A bully shouldn't always get his way."

She declined our offer of dinner, saying she and Roland had plans with friends. "On Tuesdays we always meet at his golf club. The food is ordinary, but it has become a tradition, so Roland insists we go. And now, I'm off. Maggie, I am happy to meet you at last. I confess I have been curious. Dom has assured me that he approves, and if you make our Jean-Paul happy, then I say welcome, *ma chérie*."

"Thank you very much," I said, touched by her words because the situation, a new woman taking her daughter's place, had to be difficult for her. She leaned in to give me *les bises*, offered her cheeks to Jean-Paul, and led us to the door.

"I'll arrange for Roland's things to be picked up tomorrow," she said, turning as she stepped over the threshold. "Shall I call Ari about the time?"

"That would be best," Jean-Paul said. "What will you do with it?"

"Put it into storage with the other junk Roland can't part with. I doubt he even remembers what's there." With a last wave, she turned and walked to her car.

After Jean-Paul shut the door behind her, I said, "Hi, honey, I'm home." And received a proper greeting before he retrieved the shopping and carried it to the kitchen.

"The chicken smells wonderful," I said, following him. "How long until we eat?"

"Are you starving?" he said, giving the balsamic vinegar an appreciative nod.

"I didn't know I was until I walked in and smelled that chicken. But no hurry, really. Right now I'm going to go up and wash this TV goo off my face and then I have something I would like you to take a look at."

"Sounds mysterious."

"It is, actually." I left him to him to work on his balsamic reduction—he is a far better cook than I—and went upstairs to wash and change. When I came back down with my laptop under my arm, the chicken was out of the oven, resting atop the stove while Jean-Paul blanched the fresh asparagus I bought on the way home that afternoon. He wisely declined my offer to help, handed me a glass of wine and suggested that I relax at the table and tell him about my day. I filled him in on the bits we hadn't already spoken about and asked about his day. Meetings, he said. Nothing interesting, just more squabbling about trade policy. Though with Jean-Paul, it was entirely possible that the policy they squabbled about had something to do with swapping spies or nuclear submarines rather than cheese or cars. He, of course, would never say.

While we talked, I booted my laptop and found the file Zed had put into cloud storage for me. When I had the close-up still of Nabi and the girl, I turned the computer screen to face Jean-Paul.

"Is this Ophelia?" I asked.

Wiping his hands on a kitchen towel, he came over for a look. With a shrug, he said, "Could be. There is a general resemblance, but the last time I saw Ophelia she was just twelve, still a girl. A blonde. This is a dark-haired young woman. Dom should be home anytime now. He'll know."

I downloaded the video clip and ran it in real time.

"CCTV?" he said. "How did you get this?"

"Goofing around with the studio's live feeds. I asked one of the engineers to pull up Friday night's CCTV at the train station. Why? Is that a problem?"

"No. It isn't classified. People in England watch live CCTV feeds at home all the time; neighborhood vigilance is the idea. But over here, there is no general access. Little interest in it, for that matter." He shrugged again, just one shoulder, and went back to his asparagus. "Ari would probably like to see that clip. It does appear to support what Nabi told us. After dinner, I'll give him a call."

To be useful, I set the table. Dom came in through the garage, a force of energy something like a sudden stiff breeze wafting through the room.

"Papa, Maggie, *ça va?*"

"Dom, have a look at what Maggie found," Jean-Paul said, pausing before he dropped the asparagus into a sauté pan along with garlic and shallots. I put the still back up and turned the computer toward Dom. "Is that Ophelia Fouchet with Nabi?"

"*Oui.* That's her." His heavy book bag hit the floor at his feet with a dull thunk. "Not the best photo. Where was it taken?"

"At the train station Friday night," I said.

"Huh," was his only comment before picking up the bag again and excusing himself to go wash for dinner.

After dinner, while Dom and I were clearing away in the kitchen, Jean-Paul called Ari and asked if he wanted to see the CCTV footage. Ari said he did and would be right over. He was still crossing the lawn when both my phone and Dom's rang like doorbells. I startled at the sound; my phone had never chimed like that before.

"Front door," Dom said, reaching for his phone.

Dom had downloaded the home video security system into my phone over the weekend. This was the first time I had seen, or heard, it work. I pulled out the phone and there was Fabienne Simon, standing on our front porch.

Fabienne seemed quite agitated; she had come with a request. "Maggie, forgive me for interrupting your evening, but, well, if you don't mind, would you come with me? Some of the parents have gone over to Éric Aubert's house to challenge him about representing the little Arab–" She coughed to cover what she realized was a gaffe and started again. "The boy, Ahmad Nabi. I thought that what you said about him today at the bakery was something they should hear."

"Of course," I said, drawing her into the salon where Jean-Paul and Ari had their heads bent close over my computer's screen. "Jean-Paul, you know Fabienne. Fabienne, have you met Doctor Massarani?"

"*Doctor* Massarani?" she said, eyebrows raised as she extended her hand toward him. He dipped his head as acknowledgment, rose and gave her hand a quick press.

"Ari, Jean-Paul," I said. "Fabienne tells me some of the parents in the neighborhood have concerns about Nabi and have descended on Éric. She's asked me to go over to defend him, but I think Ari is the better person for that."

"Me? But–" Whatever Ari started to say, he held back. After a deep breath, he tried again. "If these people are upset, I'm afraid that my presence might only inflame them more. Nabi tells me he is regularly taunted for being a Muslim and being a refugee. Who am I, except the same?"

"Fabienne," I said, "Is Ari right?"

"I hate to think he is, but there are people–" A shrug filled in the words she did not or maybe would not say. For a moment, she seemed to study him, looking for what? He was tall, well-groomed, handsome, genteel in his manner, dressed in jeans and a cotton pullover, perhaps not the stereotype for a Muslim refugee she had in mind. Fabienne put her shoulders back and said, "To hell with them. Doctor Massarani, please come as well."

Jean-Paul put a reassuring hand on Ari's shoulder. "They should see Maggie's CCTV tape from the train station and get some good answers before they haul out their pitchforks, yes? Maybe you can answer some of their questions."

Ari looked at me. I raised my palms and shrugged; how could we say no? He smiled, did the same, and said, "*Bien sûr.* Of course."

"I'll text Éric that we're coming." Jean-Paul tucked my laptop under his arm, I smoothed my shirt, and we all followed Fabienne out the door.

The Auberts lived at the far end of our street in an older, more traditional house than most of its neighbors. There was a formal grace about the salon we were shown into by Éric's wife, a room that easily accommodated the eight or ten people who were there ahead of us. Ari and I were clearly objects of their curiosity when Éric introduced us. Fabienne made a point of introducing me to her husband and a few of the others, and Jean-Paul in turn introduced Ari, who was as much a stranger to them as I, another foreigner, even though he had been their neighbor for nearly two years. I found the *politesse* with which we were received to be excruciating. Though I would have liked for Jean-Paul to stay at my side as a sort of shield from the general scrutiny Ari and I were under, he went about the room greeting people, speaking with them quietly. I knew that there was a strategy in what he was doing so I stayed beside Ari until Éric asked me to bring the laptop and come with him. He wanted to see what I had found before sharing it with the others.

We stood in a little alcove off to one side of the room–a vignette, a decorator would call the space, a set with a pretty chair, a table, a lamp and no apparent purpose except to be pretty–where Éric viewed the clips, running through them a couple of times. I could hear snippets of the others' conversations in the larger room and felt uncomfortable. What I actually felt was defensive and angry as people who clearly had never met Ahmad Nabi and knew little or nothing about his history expressed concerns about his suitability to get an education among their own precious offspring. What really pissed me off was that I could have heard a very near version of that same heedless cruelty just about anywhere in the world. Certainly, I had heard similar narrow opinions about The Other, whoever that might be at the moment, expressed by the parents of my daughter's classmates in California. Why had I expected something better, more noble here? And worse, had I ever participated in conversations like this one about someone who was perceived as a potential threat before I knew enough to earn an opinion? Was I judging these people as unfairly as they seemed to be judging Nabi? Was I a version of them?

The doorbell rang and Detective Delisle was ushered in, a welcome diversion. She looked exhausted, all of her starchy trimmings abandoned. No tight bun, no tailored suit. Instead, she wore jeans and an untucked T-shirt with her hair falling loosely around her shoulders. Éric summoned her over and asked me to replay the footage for her. As she leaned in close beside me, I smelled alcohol on her breath, something a lot stronger than dinner wine.

"Where's your partner?" I asked.

"He's an old man. He needs a nap now and then." When she saw what was on the laptop, she looked up sharply at Éric. "This is CCTV footage. Where did you get it?"

He nodded at me. With a weary exhalation, she gave me a side-eye glance. "TV girl. Of course."

"You've probably seen this already," I said.

But she shook her head. "We haven't had a chance to get to it. We're the only two detectives assigned to this case. Believe it or not, a runaway teenager isn't our only concern."

"You're sure Ophelia Fouchet is a runaway?" I asked.

"I'm not sure of anything. But what I've seen here looks a hell of a lot more like a girl running away than anything sinister. I'm glad I saw it. I'll be very happy when these concerned citizens see it so they'll get off my back about the boy and let me do my work."

"With your permission," Éric said to me, holding out his hands for my laptop, "we'll show the others."

An antique cabinet in a corner of the salon hid a large flat-screen television. While Éric and a couple of the men struggled to establish a Wi-Fi connection between the TV and the computer, I edged nearer Ari, mother-hen-like, to eavesdrop on the conversation he was having with one of the women. He listened to her with full attention, arms folded across his chest, eyes cast toward the polished floor, nodding from time to time. When she finished, he said, "Now, remember that I am not licensed to practice medicine in France. Legally I can only give you my suspicions as an informed layman. But from what you have described, I wonder if your son has a simple case of contact dermatitis. Common enough in spring when the kids are playing outdoors. As a parent, I would try an over the counter two-percent cortisone cream on the rash area until you can get him in to see your family physician."

Another mother joined the conversation. I couldn't hear her question, but Ari's answer was, "Yes, except for his grandmother, all of his family perished when their boat went down." I heard murmurs of sympathy and edged away to leave Ari to charm and reassure the mothers, and went over to stand near Detective Delisle, who was leaning against a wall for support, so that I could keep an eye on the room.

Fabienne came over and, with the pretense that she was bringing the two of us glasses of claret, leaned in close to me to say, "Your

Doctor Massarani seems to have charmed the ladies. Good idea to bring him along." She left us and crossed the room to join the clutch of women hovering around Ari.

After some more fiddling, the Wi-Fi connection was made and the computer's home page graphic flashed up on the TV screen. Before he hit PLAY, Éric asked the group to pay attention to the date and time stamp in the upper right corner of the screen. When the grainy images of Ophelia and Nabi appeared, there was a gasp and then a susurrus of whispered conversation as the assembled recognized the kids. Afterward, no one had an answer to the first question asked: "Where did Ophelia go after that?"

Jean-Paul, who had come to stand beside me, spoke up. "All of us are concerned about the well-being of Ophelia. We showed you this security footage from the train station because we wanted to reassure you that young Ahmad Nabi had no role in Ophelia's disappearance other than to carry her cello for her the short distance between the school, where they had a concert rehearsal Friday night, and the train station. You saw Nabi give Ophelia her cello, say good-bye as friends do, and walk away. That ended his contact with her. Am I correct, Detective Delisle?"

"Oui," she said, managing with effort to push herself away from the wall to stand upright when she addressed the room. "You saw the two kids go off in separate directions. Ahmad Nabi told us where he went after he left Mademoiselle Fouchet at the train station, and his story checked out. He was in Arras with a sausage vendor until Monday noon. The girl was not with him. For Nabi, c'est tout, the end of his involvement with Ophelia. And I don't want to hear of anyone taking any action or saying anything that interferes with his well-being, understood?"

After looking at every face in the room, she went on. "I spent considerable time with young Ahmad Nabi this morning. He expressed two fears to me. The first, of course, to repeat what Monsieur Bernard said, was for the safety of Ophelia. The second was for his own safety. Without Ophelia to protect him, he told me he expects to be the target of schoolyard bullies, as he was before he met her."

"*Pfft*," a well-upholstered man sitting across the room uttered in the direction of the man next to him.

"What was that you said, Monsieur Roussel?"

"What is this kid? Some kind of a poof, he can't protect himself?" Roussel said, pushing out his chest. "I was a military brat, moved around a lot. Every time I started at a new school I knew a good beating or two was part of the initiation. The kid just needs to toughen up."

"Initiation, you say?" Delisle was at full attention now, a quiet fierceness about her tone. "I promise you that there are stiff laws against moral harassment, the legal term for *le harcèlement*–bullying. This includes verbal insults, racial or ethnic slurs, physical threats or action. Conviction carries from one to six years in prison and a very heavy fine."

There was a low murmuring in the room. After a pause, never taking her eyes off Roussel, Delisle went on. "I have had more than one occasion to meet your son, Louis, Monsieur. He is of an age now where he can be tried as an adult. I want you to consider what his initiation into a prison population would consist of, a young and attractive boy like Louis. Now, I hope you go home and counsel him accordingly. *Vous me comprenez, Monsieur?* Does anyone here not understand what I said?"

Roussel crossed his arms and glared at her, but he nodded.

She returned his nod and again addressed the room. "If you learn something of substance I want to hear about it before you discuss it with all of your neighbors. Let us not be party to spreading groundless rumors. Right now, I suggest you go home and speak with your school-age children about the village's zero-tolerance policy for *le harcèlement* and the consequences. I also hope you ask them if they have any information of substance that might help us locate Ophelia."

Among the mutterings that followed as people rose from their seats and gathered their belongings, I heard several iterations of "Prison for bullying, is that true?" and "How far could Ophelia carry that big cello?"

Good questions.

As everyone filed out, Ari went over to Detective Delisle. "Thank you for that caution about interfering with Nabi. He went to school today, but it was very difficult."

"I'll speak with *la directeur*," she said. "She's new. She should know the situation."

He looked less than reassured.

The detective turned to me. "Tell me, Madame, how easy is it for you to access CCTV?"

"Beyond what you saw, I don't know. Today was my first experience with it."

"How long did it take to find this?"

"Not long. I gave the video engineer a date, a location, and a fairly narrow time frame based on what Nabi told us. With that he pulled what you saw out of archived footage very easily."

"Maybe you can help me," she said. "Besides having no time, I don't have a video engineer to give me a hand, and I don't necessarily have a narrow date and time frame. Where did Ophelia go after that? Hell, I don't know where to begin finding out. Do you?"

"Want to take a walk?"

She scowled. "Now?"

"Just a short one. Have a flashlight?"

A wary and reluctant, "*Ouais*," the French equivalent of yeah, was the answer. So, yeah, she did, but she wasn't enthusiastic about admitting so.

We drove to the train station in her official little blue-and-white Peugeot, Jean-Paul and Ari scrunched into the backseat, and me fairly comfortable riding shotgun; it was a short trip. At a quarter to ten on Tuesday night the parking lot was almost empty. I asked Delisle to stand with me beside the pole closest to the lot's entrance to the platform, below a CCTV camera. With my telephone's camera turned on and focused toward the street exit, as the camera above was, I asked Jean-Paul and Ari to re-enact the movements of Nabi and Ophelia on Friday night. Together, they walked in from the street, stopped near us, then parted. Ari turned around and walked back to the street and out of view just as Nabi had. Jean-Paul followed Ophelia's route toward the left until he, too, disappeared from the little monitor screen in my hand. At that point he was only a few yards from the gap in the hedge I had walked through that afternoon. After calling Ari back, we went through the hedge, down the alley, and out onto the street beyond, retracing my earlier route. The shops were closed. There was very little traffic, no one else was on the sidewalk.

"I saw only two CCTV installations on this block," I said to Delisle. "And only at the intersections. How many shops have security cameras?"

With a weary sigh, she said, "I suppose I'm about to find out. Thank you, though. If Ophelia came this way, and there's a very good possibility that she did, we now have a time frame and a place to start looking, yes? You have saved me some effort."

Ari looked down the street both ways. "Maybe she was picked up. If not, how far could a petite girl carrying a cello go without help?"

"Not far." Delisle had her phone in her hand, tapping keys until she announced, "A cello in a hard protective cover like the one we saw on the tape weighs thirty-five to forty pounds. The girl can't weigh more than a hundred-five, a hundred-ten. If she got a ride, she could be anywhere. I'll work the shops tomorrow when I can. Maybe we'll get lucky and see something. But my *commandant* has already reported the girl as a runaway delinquent and handed her case to the Préfecture of Police in Paris, so I won't be able to spend much time looking."

"Delinquent?" I said. "That's harsh."

"There is some history," she said, an offhand remark before nailing me with a hard glare. "Now, Inspector Maigret, if we are finished playing detective, I will take you all home."

I thought we were finished for the night, but no. There was a car in our driveway, a black Audi. As Detective Delisle turned into our driveway behind it, the headlights of her little car hit Yvan Fouchet, pacing on the front walkway, lying in wait. He was even more disheveled than when I saw him the day before. No surprise there. I would be approaching apoplexy if my daughter had been missing for four days.

"*Merde*," Delisle muttered, bringing the car to a stop maybe ten feet from him. Fouchet rushed toward the car as Jean-Paul and Ari unfolded themselves from the cramped backseat. "Can't the man just go home and get some sleep?"

"Jean-Paul," Fouchet said, holding the car door as if that could hurry Jean-Paul's exit. "I knew you would find something, but why didn't you call me? I am so frantic for information."

"What are you doing out here, Yvan?" Jean-Paul asked, putting a hand on the man's shoulder.

"I heard everyone was *chez* Aubert, but they were already gone when I arrived. So I came here. Dom told me you would be back soon; I waited. Tell me what you know about Ophelia."

"I'm sorry you weren't called," Jean-Paul said, taking the laptop from under my arm and opening it. "And I'm sorry that whatever you heard got your hopes up. What we have clears Ophelia's friend, but it doesn't tell us where she went Friday night. Here, take a look for yourself."

When the first image appeared, the still shot of the two kids, Fouchet choked on a sob and reached his hand toward the screen as if he could pull Ophelia out to him. Weeping, he said, "My girl."

Twice he watched the CCTV footage, and became only more dejected when, twice, Ophelia walked away into the dark of night. And disappeared.

Monsieur Fouchet was in no condition to drive himself home. Jean-Paul took his keys from him and got him buckled into the passenger seat. Ari was enlisted to follow in our car to bring Jean-Paul home. After they left, I went inside, curled up in a big chair in the salon with my laptop and Google-stalked the Fouchet family.

Yvan Fouchet was an executive with a large international manufacturer of construction machinery, big stuff like cranes and earthmovers. His picture was on the company webpage. He was on the board of the local equestrian club and a national polo club. Now and then he still played a chukker or two of polo, and sometimes, according to photos in the online version of the polo club's newsletter, got knocked off his horse and came up smiling. His wife, Claire, was the secretary of the garden club, past president of the Peony Society, a member of the equestrian center, and was listed as a speaker at a meeting called by the Ministry of Education to discuss the issue of inequality in the national school system. There was no reference to what she had to say on the topic. In all, there wasn't much to be found. Except for one little nugget: Monsieur Fouchet sued the editors of a women's magazine for invasion of privacy and was awarded one euro. The details of the case, of course, were not revealed lest they invade the man's privacy doing so.

I looked up French privacy laws and learned that the definition of what constitutes a breach of privacy is very broad. Generally, it was illegal to investigate, make public statements about, or write about a person's sex life, friends, family life and home, leisure, health, religion, political opinions, and union membership without express permission. Suits for invasion of privacy, I read, were quite easy to bring and difficult to prevail against, but monetary rewards were very small.

The magazine had an online version, but my search to find any mention of Yvan Fouchet in back issues came up empty except for a one-sentence public apology made less than a year ago. The editors did not say that they had been incorrect, only that they regretted violating Fouchet's privacy in their April edition. The April edition had disappeared from the archive, but at the end of the March table of contents there was a thumbnail preview of what to expect the following month. Along with spring fashion news and tips for freshening the kitchen, the magazine would run Part Four of their series on workplace harassment, "What to Do if Outing Your Abuser Gets You Fired."

I read the first three installments and went on to the fifth, published in May. In my humble opinion, the author relied too much on anecdotal evidence, mostly interviews with woman who claimed abuse, and too little on hard evidence. But I had to admit that though they were little more than rehashings of the ongoing issue without offering any remedy, they were fast and interesting reads. I found that some of the follow-up letters to the editor were more revealing than the articles. Indeed, the most intriguing to me was in the May issue on the page after the April apology. Someone who signed herself as Déchaînée—Furious—wrote, "I reported my abuser. I was fired. I called his wife. She acted when no one else would. I feel pure *schadenfreude*. Try it."

My, my, my, I thought as I went upstairs to get ready for bed, that poor man got himself into big trouble. Now there were at least two angry women who gave him hell. I still didn't know what offended Yvan Fouchet enough that he sued the magazine, but my imagination was in overdrive. Whatever it was I was fairly certain it had nothing to do with the latest model of earthmovers.

] Five

D O YOU MAKE A HABIT of sticking your nose into other people's business?"

Monsieur Roussel, the tough talker from the gathering at Éric's house last night bellied up to me as I waited on the platform for my morning train into Paris. I was dumbfounded not only by the tone of this confrontation but by the way he used his bulk to intimidate me. I took a step backward and looked up to meet his narrowed eyes. I managed to say, "A missing child is every parent's business. So is abuse of any child, by anyone. And yes, I have made a career of sticking my nose into other people's business. It's called journalism."

"You're not one of us." He clearly had more to say but he was interrupted when a smaller man, similarly suited, carrying a similar briefcase, seemed to pop out from behind the big man.

"You're Maggie," the newcomer announced, smiling into my face. "We saw you on the *Jimmy* show last night. My wife told me that you had moved into our little neighborhood, and here you are. She'll be so excited when I tell her I actually ran into you." Then he turned enough to see the face of the man standing like a barrier between us. "Ah, *bonjour*, Roussel. Didn't realize that was you. Put on a few, have you? How is Adèle?"

"Not–" Roussel said after seeming to stumble over the question.

His voice quavered when he managed to finish the sentence. "It's not good, Claude."

I thought it was time for me to move along, but just then the approach of the Paris train was announced and the waiting crowd surged forward, pressing in around us. Roussel sniffled and I risked a glance at him. His face glowed red, his eyes had filled with tears.

"I am so sorry," the man he called Claude said, obviously uncomfortable about the other man's emotional reaction to what may have been nothing more than a polite question—How is Adèle?—to an old acquaintance. "She looked well last I saw her. Still hopeful, yes?"

"Not hopeful, no. The chemo that worked last time does nothing this time," Roussel said. "The doctors offered her something new, a medical trial, but it has made her so sick. She has refused it. She says, enough. No more."

I thought he might keel over, so as a reflex I put a steadying hand under his elbow, pulled a tissue from my bag and handed it to him; tears coursed down his cheeks. After he blew his nose and took a few shuddery breaths he managed to gain enough composure to see that it was I who offered him succor. The look on his face, was it shock? No, it was chagrin.

"My train is here," I said, and moved into the flow of humanity surging toward the train as soon as the doors opened. Once inside, I spotted a window seat halfway down the car and managed to claim it. A woman took the aisle spot beside me but when a friend passed by my seatmate immediately got up to join her. While the other passengers shuffled in, I watched the platform, looking for patterns in the movement of people, trying to decide between the benefits of rushing aboard in the vanguard or hanging back for a more leisurely entry; there was room enough for everyone. The seat next to me was claimed just as the train began to move. I settled back and looked over to see the once again composed face of Monsieur Roussel looking back at me.

"*Merci,*" he said.

"*De rien,*" I answered, because I had done nothing but hand him a tissue. And keep him from falling over. I definitely did not want to hear an apology for his boorish behavior earlier so I said, "I'm sorry about your wife."

"*Merci*, but you can't know what it is like to watch and be helpless."

"I lost my husband to cancer," I said. He sighed and dropped his head, chagrined yet again. I told him, "Like your Adèle, my Mike came to a place where he refused further treatment. I think that was the last piece of his life he felt he had control over."

"Was the end–" He needed a moment to compose himself before he could make another attempt at the question. "Was the end hard?"

"For everyone who loved him, yes, it was brutal. But he was at peace." I left out the part where Mike, knowing what was ahead, sat down in the backyard with a glass of very good wine and his police sidearm, a Beretta, and kissed the world good-bye. Instead, I said, "Nothing can make what you're going through easier, Monsieur. Sometimes I just wanted to hit something."

At that he smiled. "After that girl *flic*'s warning last night, I did speak to my son, Louis. The situation with his mother has been difficult for him. He doesn't know how to handle what he feels. Nor do I."

"Understandable. Did you know that Ahmad Nabi lost both of his parents and his three siblings during their attempt to find a safe place to live? I think his music helps him continue on."

"I didn't know anything about him until last night." This time, no doubt, he was past chagrin and suffering a full dose of the bile of shame about what he had said the night before, and probably that morning as well. He had to look away from me to gather himself. When he turned back, he said. "I am an ass, aren't I?"

I laughed. "I don't know you well enough to answer that, Monsieur."

The retort caught him by surprise and made him laugh. After a moment, and with the hesitation of a man who knew he was about to say something that maybe he shouldn't, he said, "It's just that the boy is so very different from us. How can he fit in?"

"Other than, his skin is half a tone darker than yours and he apparently has a real gift for music, what is so different about him?"

With a sidelong glance, and a wry little smile, he said, "You are going to make this as difficult as you can for me, aren't you?"

"I'm trying to, yes. Look, all I ask is that you don't do anything to interfere with the boy. Isn't being a pimply-faced teenager punishment enough for him?"

He chuckled. "Oh, God, how did we survive those years?"

"I still have nightmares," I said.

"*Zut alors, eh?*" he muttered, leaning back in his seat, arms crossed over his barrel of a chest. For a moment we didn't say anything. But after a quick glance at me, he said, "I understand that Ophelia Fouchet is quite serious about her music, as well. Last night, on that bit of security film we could see that wherever she was going she took her instrument with her."

"Interesting, yes," I said. "Do you know her well?"

He toggled his head from side to side, an answer I interpreted as maybe yes, maybe no. "I know her parents from school committees. The girl was always one of the general pack of kids around; I never spoke with her. My boys are all football, football, and she runs with the equestrian crowd. Her father is a big horseman, anyway. That group is, well, *très snob*, if you know what I mean."

"I think I do."

"The girl was always done up just so, looked like she fell off a magazine page. Just like her mother, for that matter. My family thinks that I am strict, but next to Yvan and Claire Fouchet I am a cream puff. And then, one day I see Ophelia with black-dyed hair and torn stockings and makeup like a ghoul and I think, *oh-là-là*, look out, the teenage revolution has begun *chez* Fouchet. I wondered how old Yvan was taking it."

"How do you think he was taking it?" I had seen for myself that the man was currently a wreck. But I wanted to hear what Roussel had to say about Fouchet before Ophelia took off.

"*Qui sait?* Every time I see him, he looks worn out. But he always says everything is good, life is perfect. But how good can it be, eh, if his daughter keeps running away?"

"She's run away before?"

"*Ouais.* Hanging out overnight in the *haras* with dope-smoking friends; who knows where she goes? But not like this time. Maybe she's finally figured out how to do it right."

"Maybe so," I said. "I hope she's safe."

"Yes, *bien sûr*, of course. We all do."

During the little time remaining until I had to change trains, Roussel asked about what I had done that I was on Jimmy Jardine's show the night before. His friend Claude seemed excited about it. I told him, in brief, and in turn he told me he worked in securities at a big firm in La Défense, the financial district of Paris. Nothing interesting, he said. For a long time, whenever I asked Jean-Paul what he did before he was appointed consul general to Los Angeles, he told me he was just a boring businessman. I learned soon enough that nothing could be further from the truth. I was beginning to suspect that saying one's work was *très ennuyeux* could be cover for some version of "If I tell you I'll have to kill you."

When we reached my transfer stop, we said good-bye and headed off in separate directions. I went from the train to the studio for a meeting with Diane Duval about air dates for the Normandy piece, followed by a discussion of possible topics for the films Guido and I would follow with.

Diane greeted me by handing me a box of freshly minted business cards, stiff little cardboard rectangles with the network logo, my name, and my title, *Cinéaste d'investigation.* I thought they were grand. I put a couple in my pocket and stuffed the box into my bag.

"I know the production schedule is tight," Diane said, leading me to an arrangement of chairs by her office window. "So we need to begin hiring your crew and support staff right away. Who do you need first?"

"A researcher," I said. "Guido and I worked with a very capable woman in Los Angeles. If immigration and union benefit packages weren't issues, I would buy her a ticket and get her here now. But, assuming we're stuck with reality, we need someone who is not only an experienced researcher but who is a relentless and fearless snoop. We never know what we might get into, so this person needs to be flexible as well."

She laughed. "I was hoping you'd adopt Bruno. You might go down to the studio morgue and ask around. Now, tell me what you're thinking as follow-up, just in general."

I did, in general, because that was all I was prepared to share. Diane was so agreeable to my ideas, as amorphous as they were, that I wondered if Guido and I were being given a honeymoon period while we settled in. We had come from such a mercurial situation at our last network that both of us were conditioned to keep one foot out the door. Maybe here it would be different. Or maybe not, once we had settled in.

After our meeting, and after getting lost in the maze of hallways only once, I walked into live studio operations to speak with Zed. He was intrigued enough by the mystery of the missing girl that when I asked him to pull up some Friday night CCTV footage from the street behind the train station, he agreed. When he had time, he would collect it and send it to my studio inbox. Zed also helped me figure out the Paris Métro schedule so that I could get across the city from Issy-les-Molineaux to meet Guido at Isabelle's apartment on rue Jacob in the sixth *arrondissement* without going too far astray or spending the rest of the morning getting there.

Because my meeting with Diane was shorter than I had expected, I had over an hour and a half to fill before Guido expected me. I was in Paris, so filling an hour was hardly a problem, however, it occurred to me as I walked outside and looked around that the studio, on the edge of a densely packed media company district, was only a short distance from the editorial offices of the magazine that published an apology to Yvan Fouchet almost exactly one year ago. I knew this because the night before, more out of habit than plan, I looked up the address of the magazine. And there they were, the third giant complex on the right. With a half-formed plan and no great expectation anything would come of it, I walked into the vast, shiny lobby below the magazine offices, handed one of my brand-new cards to the security desk and said, "I have an appointment with Roni Pascal."

He read the information on the card into the phone, listened for a moment, and then walked me to an elevator, used an electronic fob to open the door, pushed a number inside, and sent me on my way. I came out of the elevator into another shiny lobby. A young woman, simply dressed and *très chic*, with a pink sticky note stuck to her index finger like a flag waited for me to step out. After glancing at the note, she said, "Maggie MacGowen?"

"Yes." I handed her one of my cards. "I'm here to see Roni Pascal."

"I'm Roni," she said. "I'm sorry, I didn't remember we had an appointment."

"We don't. I lied to Security downstairs because I want to talk to you about a series you wrote last year on workplace harassment."

She shrugged as she thought that over, then she said, "Sure. Let's go in here."

In here was a small meeting room that hadn't been tidied after its last use. Roni pushed coffee mugs to a corner and offered me a seat. As she settled into her chair, she said, "I know who you are, Maggie. I read in the trades that you are working over here now. How can I help you?"

"A year ago, in May, your magazine published an apology to a man named Yvan Fouchet for something that was said about him in April. I haven't read the April issue, but I would not be surprised if what he thought was a breach of his privacy was a reference to him in the fourth installment of your series on workplace harassment."

As soon as I said Fouchet's name her face screwed up as if a sudden stench had wafted into the room. "I can't talk about him."

I chuckled. "The expression on your face already answered part of my question."

"Good thing I'm in print journalism, *oui*? I wouldn't last on television. So, yes, the man's name came up in the April installment. He was angry, he sued, he won. For me, the story of Yvan Fouchet is done, *fini*."

"Did you know his daughter has gone missing?"

"Fouchet's daughter? No. Tell me."

"I don't know much to tell," I said. "On Friday night she got permission to go to a pizza party with a school group. But there was no pizza party. She simply disappeared into the night."

"Hmm." Chin resting on her fist, she studied me for a moment. "You think there's a connection between the missing girl and my article? It came out a full year ago."

"The only obvious connection between Ophelia Fouchet and whatever you wrote is Monsieur Fouchet. Who is he? What is he? I hear he's strict, I hear he fights with his wife. At the moment he looks like he's on the edge of a nervous collapse."

"Fighting with the wife is no surprise, but if you quote me saying even that there could be another suit for breaching his privacy. You need to be careful or he could sue you, too."

"French privacy laws are very different from American laws. They are so broad they must make your work difficult."

She nodded. "I hear Americans say that the French are not scandalized when prominent people, or even ordinary people, I suppose, get involved in sexual escapades. A prime minister has a child with a mistress, a powerful economic figure screws any woman he can trap, whether she wants it or not, and the French press says nothing. Believe me, we are also scandalized, but in France a person's privacy is more important, more powerful, than freedom of the press. If you reveal that a man has a mistress, you are interfering with his family because you are creating discord between him and his wife or causing the disrespect of his children, or, heaven forbid, snooping into his sex life. He has the hammer of the courts on his side. So, we journalists tread a fine line."

"The lawsuit and the apology come after the fact. If a man's name shows up in a national magazine, I'm certain that someone will make sure the wife knows about it long before he gets his grievance into court. Your magazine paid him one euro in reparations?"

She wagged a finger at me. "I can say nothing to you about Yvan Fouchet."

"Of course." But she had already told me plenty, and I thought she was ready to send me on my way. Before she did, I said, "In your series on workplace harassment, you were very circumspect about identifying the women you interviewed. Do you ever follow up with them, stay in touch?"

"The ones I knew before I wrote the series, of course, yes. It was not difficult to find friends with stories to tell. But the women my research led me to I rarely hear from."

"You have my card. If you happen to speak with anyone who might have something she feels like telling me about Monsieur Fouchet, I would be very grateful if you shared my contact information with her."

"You realize how risky that could be for her."

"A girl is missing. Maybe your source knows something that would help find her."

"No promises." She picked my card up off the table as she rose from her chair. Offering her hand, she said, "I'm happy to have met you, Maggie. I hope to see you again."

"Thank you for speaking with me," I said, taking her hand.

"Sorry I couldn't help you."

"But you have," I said. "You have."

Even with Zed's good instructions, I had so much to think about after I left Roni Pascal that I missed my first train transfer and had to double back. When, at last, I walked through the front door of Isabelle's apartment, except for a fine layer of dust coating every flat surface, everything looked very much as it had when I handed the keys over to Guido. I ran my finger through the dust on the bare dining table and held it up to Guido. "I asked the cleaners to come in last Friday."

"Yeah, well." Guido looked around. "They didn't. Barry downstairs said there had been an incident between the cleaning ladies and one of your nephews—he pulled a hijab off one of them?—so when they saw I was here alone they wouldn't come in."

"For the record, it wasn't my nephew who did that, it was one of his friends. Anyway, if you want someone in to clean, ask the concierge. Madame Gonsalves likes to be helpful."

"I tried talking to her, but hand gestures only convey so much. Don't worry about it. I can clean up after myself. I've just been so busy since I got here," he said. "Come down and take a look at the work room. That's where I've spent most of my time since we got to Paris."

Isabelle, my bio-mother, was an odd and complex woman, prone to whims fueled by manic episodes. At some point, without informing her investment partners who included Jean-Paul, during the renovation of the long-abandoned convent they acquired and its conversion into modern apartments, she had workmen build a private stairway that led from her own apartment down to two rooms she partitioned off from the rest of the cavernous cellar. On one side of the landing at the bottom of the stairs, she installed and stocked a wine cellar. On the other, a hidden door opened into a temperature-controlled space that housed a small library of rare and precious books that was left behind, probably forgotten, when the religious order was shut down by the Vatican and the last of the nuns was sent into retirement. When I inherited the apartment, along with Isabelle's half of the entire building, after some righteous controversy, mayhem, and attempted murder, I sent the books away for safekeeping, freeing up that very comfortable library room for Guido and me to work in.

"I met with Diane this morning," I told Guido on our way down the narrow stairs. "Part One of the Normandy project will air in June at the end of the regular season, and Part Two will open the fall season in September. She wants us to give her a tentative outline for the four films to follow, one a month through January of next year. And then we'll reboot, I guess, if ratings are good."

"Finishing one a month will be brutal," he said.

"If we had to do one a month, yes, it would. But from next week, when we hand over the finished Normandy film, we'll have until October before the next one goes on the air. We aren't making feature-length films, Guido. I think we can fill an hour time slot without too much grief once we come up with, in Diane's words, good hard-hitting topics. If we're very good children, we can have the entire remaining handful finished well before December."

When we reached the small landing at the bottom of the stairs, he opened the library door, now the work room door, and ushered me inside. Film topics and content were my area, the mechanics of filmmaking were his. While I worked out what we would focus on next he had been setting up a workplace.

The four heavy library tables were now end-to-end down the center of the room with a power strip running along the entire front edge. On top of this expanse of tables was an array of the equipment Guido called his junk: three wide-screen computers, external data storage units, a videotape-to-digital converter, a film-to-digital converter, a CD reader, Wi-Fi boosters, emergency power backup, and a heavy-duty printer. His cameras, lights, cords, reflectors, tripods, tools and gaffer's tape—duct tape—and a variety of whatevers were stowed in the glass-fronted shelves along the walls where books had once been. And attached to the far wall was a fifty-inch television.

"Isn't this great?" he said, grinning, holding his arms wide as if to embrace the entire space. "So much better than anything we've had before."

"Looks like home," I said. "If home is a digital film lab."

"Sometimes I feel like I live in the work room," he said, still smiling happily. "Gets a little lonely, though."

"Diane is ready to hire a staff and crew for us. Ask her for an intern or two, and maybe an assistant. I'm on the lookout for a researcher."

"We're going to miss Fergie. Any chance you can talk her into coming over?"

"I don't know how," I said. Fergie had been our general gofer and third pair of hands for about five years at the American network studio where we worked in Los Angeles. Talking her into, or even asking her to, abandon a union benefits package would be hard. The other little detail would be getting her a French work visa; there were plenty of available and willing hands in the country.

"Anyhoo," Guido said. "Any ideas about what we're going to do for Diane after Normandy?"

"Some." I gave him more detail than I'd given Diane. He made some suggestions, but topics were generally left to me. He was more interested in where we would be shooting and what he would aim his cameras at than in why he was doing it. After we had a broad notion of what was to come next, we pored over the notes Diane had sent with me that morning and talked about final edits and cuts on the Normandy film. Some of Diane's comments were impressively insightful. Others we debated before crossing out. Once the decisions were made about what to cut and what to keep, I left it to Guido to figure out how to implement them. Every television production needs to be tailored to fit certain time signatures with precision; never a second over, never a second under. Making that happen is an art form all its own, and Guido was the maestro.

While Guido began finessing images against time restraints, I was superfluous except now and then when he asked for input about where to lose a few frames, where to extend. For something to do, I booted one of the other computers and pulled up several online personal sales sites. Unless Ophelia ran away to join a gypsy orchestra or had found some sort of Svengali, that cello would be cumbersome to travel with. It could also be a source of cash if she needed it. Or if someone else did. I searched the listings, looking for a cello. First, I looked for cellos in big red cases, and found one, but the listing was a month old and it came from Prague. I didn't know the maker of Ophelia's instrument, so all I could do was go through recent listings and look for possibilities. There were two. I left my contact information with the sellers, and before I logged off signed up for text alerts for any new listings from the three sites that had the largest number of musical instruments on offer.

When I came up for air I found Guido watching me.

"How are we doing?" I asked.

"I'm going blind from looking at this monitor. How are you doing?"

"Just peachy."

He shook his head. "I don't think you are. What's up?"

"Guido, did you ever run away from home?"

"Oh hell no. I knew that if I did my mother would turn my bedroom into a sewing room and my dad would change the locks before I got to the end of the block. Why? Did you?"

"I didn't need to. My folks packed me off to a convent school and then they ran away on a sabbatical."

"It's that girl, isn't it?"

"I'm afraid it is. The detective on the case called her a runaway delinquent. She said Ophelia had a history. I learned on the train this morning that she had run away before. I have a feeling that because of that history the police aren't looking very hard for her. Other than running away, I wish I knew what she did that got her a bad reputation with the police. And I'd like to know what happened in her home that made her so angry that she would punish her parents this way."

"I seem to remember that Jean-Paul is good buddies with the Paris police chief, or whatever they call him."

"Oh sure, like I'm going to call David Berg and ask him to look up a juvenile's record just because I'm nosy as hell." Truth was, I was sorely tempted to do just that. "I would probably get better information out of the local cop than I ever would out of David. By the way, the local cops found the CCTV footage we pulled up helpful. Doesn't lead to the girl, but it clears the boy."

"That's good."

"Yeah. It is. So, what now, partner?"

"For today? *Je suis fini.*"

"I think you just said you're dead, Guido. But I'm proud of you for working on *la belle langue*. Soon you'll be speaking French like a native."

"Don't hold your breath. I'm going to the movies tonight with my tutor. He says movies are the best way to learn how to talk dirty."

"Enjoy." We stopped in the wine cellar where I pulled out a couple of bottles of Jean-Paul's favorite Bordeaux to take home and Guido chose a very nice *eau de vie*, an aged apple brandy my cousin produced on the family farm in Normandy. Guido had developed an affection for the potent stuff during our summer of filming.

On our way back upstairs, he asked, "What are you doing tonight?"

"I'm hoping for a quiet evening at home with my true love. But one never knows." I grabbed a shopping bag from the hook where Isabelle kept them, wrapped the wine bottles in a kitchen towel and carefully laid them inside the bag to carry home. "Guido, I

almost forgot. My brother Freddy may call you. There are a few of
Isabelle's things that he and his sons would like to have. They'll be
in the city over the weekend, and if it's okay with you, they'll call
and find a time with you when they can come fetch stuff."

He scowled. "What kind of things?"

"My nephew Robert would like Isabelle's computer and printer.
We don't need it. When they stay in Paris with Grand-mère Robert
has to share with his father, and that isn't working out. There's
an armoire in the smaller bedroom that is from Freddy's father's
family and he wants it. They also plan to box up Isabelle's books
on math, physics, and agronomy for the library at Robert's school
in Normandy. I already sent her clothes to the charity shop and
Grand-mère claimed the family photos and mementoes, so I've
just about swept the last of Isabelle out of the apartment, but I told
Freddy that if there's anything he wants he can take it as long as
he doesn't cart off all the furniture and leave you nothing to sit on."

He looked horrified. "Is there a danger of that?"

"No," I said, confident in the answer. My half brother, Freddy,
and his sons, Robert and Philippe, had been living in Isabelle's
house at the family farm estate in Normandy since he began his
construction project there. That house was fully furnished. His own
furniture was put into storage when he had to sell the family house
to pay his wife's, now his ex-wife's, legal fees. He didn't need yet
another sofa.

"Whatever. Want to grab some lunch?"

"I'm meeting Jean-Paul. He came into the city early for meetings. With luck he's finished for the day and we can go exploring
after lunch."

"You kids have fun," he said. "What's on the schedule for
tomorrow?"

"Unless you have other ideas, I'll leave you to work on the final
edits and I'll start work on a shooting script for the next blockbuster
in the pipeline. When I have a draft to show you, we can work on
the shot list."

"Dandy," he said, showing me to the door. "I'll call if I get
lonely."

"Do that. You know, you can use the studio facilities if you want to be around people."

"I might do that at some point, but I like it here. Hell, I'm on the Left Bank in Paris. Any time I want to come up out of this hole in the ground, guess what? Paris is right outside. What's not to like?"

He walked me down to the front door and waved good-bye as I set off across the cobblestone courtyard. I stopped at the concierge's apartment next to the street gates to say hello, but Madame Gonsalves wasn't home. If she were, I would have heard her television. I went out onto rue Jacob and walked the few blocks to Le Procope where I was to meet Jean-Paul. The restaurant was the oldest in Paris. My first impression when I walked inside was red leather and white linen and the subdued murmur of many conversations, punctuated by the clink of glassware and silver. The maître d' bowed slightly when I gave him Jean-Paul's name and he escorted me down a hall to a smaller dining room in back. Jean-Paul was watching for me. He rose from a side banquette and came around the table to claim me. The man seated across from him rose as well.

"David Berg," I said, leaning toward the other man for *les bises* after exchanging same with Jean-Paul. "What a nice surprise."

"Isn't it?" Jean-Paul said, the picture of innocence as he took the shopping bag with wine from my hand and seated me on the banquette next to him. He knew very well that there were questions I would love to ask David, and I knew that's why David, the *Préfet de Police de Paris*, the head cop, with jurisdiction over not only the city of Paris but also the nearby suburbs including Vaucresson, had been asked to join us. Jean-Paul's explanation was flimsy: "I was at a meeting at the Palais de Justice, so I dropped by Davey's office to make sure he was staying out of trouble. He looked hungry, so what could I do but bring him along?"

"It happened just like that?" I said, aiming the question at David.

"Wouldn't hold up under cross examination, but close enough," David said, spreading his napkin on his lap. "I suggest we start with the oysters. They're famous for oysters here."

"Well, well." I looked from one man to the other and saw only innocent smiles. The two had been in school together. Not just any school, but one of the nation's *Grandes Écoles*, the elite universities that produce the experts that go on to staff the upper tiers of the French bureaucracy or became leaders in commerce and politics. Dom was preparing to enter just such a university. If he did well, his future would be set. Because of his university affiliations, Jean-Paul seemed to know every person in a position of authority in France because it was likely that they were all alumni of the same school, or their professional colleagues were. Forget six degrees of separation. Among them there was rarely more than one degree of separation before they could connect with exactly the person they needed, whatever the situation. At fifty, Jean-Paul and David had successfully risen through the ranks to have reached if not the top positions in their fields, then the rungs immediately below. Their network ranged broadly, reached high.

"After the oysters," Jean-Paul said, "what looks good?"

When I saw the prices on the menu the waiter placed in in front of me I had to swallow. Under the table I squeezed Jean-Paul's hand. "Do you eat here often?"

"No, but I thought you should, if only once. Can you imagine how many revolutions, coups, and wars were plotted in this room? Here Franklin and Jefferson squeezed Jacques Necker until he released enough cash out of the French treasury to finance the American Revolution and bankrupt France in the process. Napoleon left his hat here once to cover a bar tab. I'll show you on our way out; it's in a display case."

"I'm surprised they let riffraff like that through the door," I said, glancing at him over the top of my menu. "What do you recommend?"

"After the oysters, I'm thinking about a salad *au poire* followed by a piece of beef, the *onglet* or a filet. What looks good to you, Davey?"

They worked it out, consulting me about my preferences for each course before we each made our choices. This discussion around the table about assembling meals out of the available components was, I had discovered, part of the culture of dining out in France. When, at last, all was decided, we went on to the next topic: which wine? Jean-Paul patted the shopping bag on the bench beside him.

"You visited Isabelle's cache on rue Jacob?" he asked.

I told him what was in the bag. Smiling, he planted a kiss on my forehead, an unusual public display for him, and summoned the waiter as he freed one of the bottles from its wrapping and set it on the table. The waiter saw what it was, bowed, and carried it off somewhere. When the bottle reappeared, it was in the custody of the restaurant's elegantly garbed sommelier. With ceremony, he pulled the cork and sniffed it before pouring a soupçon from the bottle into the little silver cup he wore on a heavy chain around his neck. After he swirled it in his mouth and swallowed, he poured a similar amount into Jean-Paul's glass. Jean-Paul sniffed it, swilled it, declared it potable, and we were served at the very same moment that tiny forks and small plates were set before us and a platter of raw North Atlantic oysters and lemon wedges was placed center stage, that is, in the middle of the table. Such an impressive feat of choreography would be expected, as dining in France generally does have a bit of theater to it.

Helping himself to oysters, David opened the conversation after catching Jean-Paul's eye. "Maggie, my friend, Jeep, here, mentioned on the walk over that you had some interest in the case of a missing girl. Sounds to me like an ordinary situation where an adolescent, as an act of rebellion, does a runner. What intrigues you about it?"

"I think the girl didn't intend to run. If we believe Ahmad Nabi, the boy she was last seen with, she lied to her parents to get permission to stay out a few extra hours because she had something to talk over with a person she did not name. I have a bad feeling that the meeting didn't go as planned."

"And you don't trust the police to handle the situation?"

"I do. But when Nabi showed up in our backyard we were suddenly put into the middle of the drama," I said, squeezing a lemon wedge over my oysters. "He's a very sympathetic kid. When he told us that he was a target for bullying, my heart went out to him."

"The mother instinct, yes?" he said, smiling. Next to me, Jean-Paul slid an oyster off its shell into his mouth and declared it perfect.

"Some parental feelings, sure," I said. "But I think it was when I met the boy's grandmother that I became more interested. There she was, a cultured woman, obviously a member of the Afghan elite before her family was targeted by the Taliban, now working as a nanny and housekeeper. Her grandson, the only family she has left, is allowed by her employers to live with her in the servants' quarters, but she can't get away from her duties to participate in most of his school activities and he is not allowed to bring his friends over. On weekends, when I imagine her employers are around, Nabi goes away to work. The grandmother seems to feel very tentative about the security of her situation, and I wonder if she thinks she needs to keep the boy as invisible to her employers as possible. At the same time, she worries that he could become angry enough or feel alienated enough that he might succumb to extremism, as other Muslim refugee youth have. The two of them fled from one sort of hell into another."

David dabbed his lips with his napkin. "Smart of her to keep an eye out for the boy."

"It struck me that at the same time Nabi and his grandmother accept their less-than-perfect situation so that they can have a roof over their heads, a girl, his only friend, is in full rebellion against her own materially comfortable circumstances. I can't help wondering what her issues are."

"Drugs, a boy, parental rules?" David said. "By the way, the wine is exquisite."

"Happy you approve." I turned to Jean-Paul. "Have you heard anything like that about Ophelia?"

He shook his head. "Drugs or boys? No. But both are possible. Don't forget, I've been away."

"Sure, but you've known the Fouchets for a while. I hear their household is, well, stormy, and that they are very strict with Ophelia."

"Marian mentioned once that it wouldn't surprise her if Ophelia rebelled one day," he said. "She thought that Yvan and Claire, the parents, expected too much from the girl. And maybe too much from each other. Not a cheerful pair, on the whole. So, here it is, unhappy Ophelia has run away, and not for the first time."

I turned to David, who was heaping yet another empty oyster shell onto the neat pile on his plate. "The detective on the case, Fleur Delisle, referred to Ophelia as a delinquent. Does running away make her a delinquent?"

Again, he caught Jean-Paul's eye before he spoke. "Possibly. I cannot speak about a specific case, you understand, but there are all sorts of status offenses runaways commonly commit, such as shoplifting or panhandling, or perhaps squatting in a vacant building. It is common for squatters to build fires to cook or keep warm and the fire gets out of hand. At the more serious end of the spectrum are drugs, prostitution, and so on. It's possible that your Detective Delisle merely made an offhand remark and the girl has no actual history of offenses, other than running away."

"I thought of that," I said, looking up as my plate of empty oyster shells disappeared; we had eaten all of them. "Delisle is hardly forthcoming with information."

"Good. A discreet cop."

There was no hurrying about the meal. Soiled plates were removed right away, but we were given a little time to relax between courses. One after the other, a salad of fresh green beans and hazelnuts appeared in front of me, followed by coq au vin. Wineglasses never went completely empty. And the conversation moved on from missing teenagers to the problem of bullying, not only among children at school, but in the workplace. I picked up my knife and fork and turned my attention to the bird in front of me, but before cutting into it I glanced at my lunchmates. Their heads were bent over their plates, beef filet for Jean-Paul and fried calf sweetbreads for David. He raised his eyes and caught me watching him.

"All is well?" he said.

"I'm missing something here," I said. Jean-Paul looked up and exchanged a told-you-so look with David. "And you two know what it is, yes?"

"I can't talk about juvenile cases," David said, forking his first bite of sweetbreads. "But–"

I waited, but he didn't go on. But what? Jean-Paul, chewing, was watching me as if waiting for me to do or say something. David couldn't talk about juvenile cases, but he could talk about what? Jean-Paul had a purpose in bringing him to lunch. It was up to me to ask the right question because maybe David could not volunteer information. I cut into the chicken breast.

"Can you answer questions about adult cases?" I asked.

Smiling, David toggled his head in that familiar maybe yes, maybe no response. "Depends, of course, on the nature of the case and the stage of a case. Once a criminal case has been presented in court, the pertinent details may enter the public domain. Issues relating to family and private life, however, remain private."

"Even when a child is involved?" I asked.

"Depends on the nature of the situation," he said. "How is your coq au vin?"

I took a bite, declared it good with a nod, and turned to Jean-Paul. "A neighbor compared the Fouchet household to thunder and lightning. I discovered that Yvan Fouchet was mentioned in a magazine article about workplace harassment. I haven't been able to find the article to know what he was accused of because he sued and the online edition was removed, but it suggests to me that he didn't get along with everyone at work, either. The two times I've seen him he was in a state of great distress, which I would expect in the circumstance. I have never seen Madame Fouchet. Tell me about her."

"Claire?" Jean-Paul sipped his wine while he considered his answer. "Quiet. Nervous. Careful about appearances. I have never heard her say very much."

"Hmm," I said, and turned my attention back to my delicious meal with the words *quiet, nervous, careful about appearances* running on a background loop through my mind. After a while, at about the time I had done all the damage to the chicken I could manage, I turned to Jean-Paul. "Cowed by a domineering husband? Or is she maybe a dominatrix in private?"

"Can we know what happens behind closed doors?"

"Yes, if it spills outside the doors," I said. "Or someone gets hurt. Right, David?"

He touched the end of his nose with an index finger; the answer was Yes.

The waiter appeared just then to clear away the empty wine bottle and finished plates. Coffee and a variety of cheeses and tiny chocolates arrived not long after. I declined a digestif. I was not accustomed to drinks at lunch and was already feeling sleepy. When I decided that one more bite or sip of anything would be the tipping point between happily satisfied and stuffed, I set my cheese knife on the plate, leaned back and looked across at David.

"I have learned a few things about your privacy laws. Now, what can you tell me about domestic abuse laws in France?"

"Ah," he said, and reached down for a slender attaché case on the floor under his chair. He pulled out a sheaf of maybe a dozen pages stapled together, turned to an inside page and handed it to me. A passage in the middle of the page was highlighted by yellow marker: "Harassment of one's spouse, partner, or co-habitant by repeated acts that degrade the other's quality of life and cause a change to the other's physical or mental state of health is punishable by a maximum penalty of three years in prison and a €45,000 fine."

I flipped to the first page to see what he had handed me. It was an informational pamphlet titled "Frequently Asked Questions about Spousal Rights under Law," a document available to the public. I turned back and read the second marked passage. "Under Article 22 of the Act of May 26, 2004 on divorce, a violent spouse may be evicted from a conjugal home when the violence places a spouse or children in danger. Additionally, the Act of December 12, 2005 facilitates the eviction of a violent spouse prior to a judgment or following a court judgment, when it is a repeat offense."

Jean-Paul took my hand and held it under the table. He said, "You see?"

"I see more questions in your immediate future, unless David is giving me a premarital warning, *mon amour*."

He laughed and brought my hand up to kiss before setting it back on his leg under the table.

David took a quick glance at the tables nearby, perhaps checking to see if anyone was eavesdropping before saying, in a low
voice, eyes holding mine, "If a teenager brought an accusation
against a parent for domestic abuse by harassment, using the definition I showed you, there would, one hopes, be an inquiry. If the
inquiry did not find that the home situation was serious enough
to remove the child or the accused parent, you can imagine the
quality of his or her home life afterward, yes?"

"*Bien sûr*," I said. "The kid might decide to run away. Is that what
happened *chez* Fouchet?"

David held up his hands, giving a little noncommittal shrug.
"We are speaking only in hypotheticals. How many adolescents, do
you think, believe that ordinary parental rules about dyeing their
hair or staying out late amount to harassment and a degradation
of the quality of their lives? At least, the lives they would prefer to
live. Did you ever feel your parents' rules got in your way or drove
you crazy?"

"No," I said, laughing at the thought; my parents were very
permissive, up to a point. "They sent me away to school and left
rules and enforcement to the nuns."

David, smiling, shook his head. "Wish I'd done that when
my son was fourteen. *Merde*, what misery kids can put a family through. But I'm happy to report that at about eighteen a fine
human emerged from the belly of the adolescent monster. Now
that he's twenty I am no longer seen as the *bête* he once thought
me. In fact, we are friends again."

Jean-Paul smiled, but didn't say anything. During much
of Dom's adolescence, he and his father were grieving Marian.
Jean-Paul told me more than once that he worried that Dom was
overly careful not to cause his father any more stress than that
created by simply getting up in the morning and putting one foot
in front of the other. Three years later they were still very careful
with each other.

A saucer with the meal check face down on top was quietly
left on the table halfway between Jean-Paul and David. Before
looking at it, the two men had a brief but friendly verbal tussle

over whose turn it was to pay. Jean-Paul won. He slipped a gold credit card out of his pocket, gave the tab a very brief glance, and put his card on top.

After a quick visit to Napoleon's hat, we said good-bye to David outside, with promises that we would get together again soon. He told us that, alerted by Jean-Paul, he and his wife had watched my brief turn on the *Jimmy* show. She was curious to meet this woman who was brave enough to take on Jean-Paul Bernard as a project. If the weather stayed warm, Jean-Paul said, we would have them over for a swim and barbecue. Cheeks were smooched all around, and we set off in different directions.

When I saw that David was out of earshot, I asked Jean-Paul, "What did he tell you that you aren't telling me?"

"Nothing," he said, pulling my arm through his. "But he reminded me about a school acquaintance, a terrible bully when we knew him, whose son was a habitual runaway. One night the boy stabbed the father while he slept."

"Killed him?" I asked.

"No. The *ambulanciers* arrived in time; it was the son who called them. There was a great scandal because the father was a minister in the government, a very powerful man. The boy's defense was exactly what Davey showed you at lunch. Abuse by harassment to the point the boy's mental state was altered. The son got off. And immediately the wife sued for divorce using the same grounds. That happened around the time a new law was passed against bullying in the workplace. Our poor classmate, after being stabbed and divorced, was then tried for being such a workplace bully that three of his staffers committed suicide in despair after months of endless haranguing and harassment."

"He went to prison?"

"Briefly," he said. "He had very good lawyers."

"Should Yvan Fouchet be sleeping with one eye open?" I asked.

"I wonder."

"What are your plans for the rest of the afternoon?" I asked, raising my face to the sun.

"That was my question for you."

"Other than walking you wherever you have to go next, nothing."

"Perfect." He put his hand over mine where it rested on his arm, we turned left and headed down the street.

"Where are we going?" I asked.

"It's a beautiful day," he said. "I thought maybe, after that lunch, a nice walk in the Luxembourg Gardens is called for. You disagree?"

"Lead on."

We crossed Boulevard Saint-Germain and continued along rue de Condé past the great stone Senate building and into the palace gardens. The flower borders were in full color, the lawns lush and green, at last. And there wasn't a cloud in the sky. In other words, a perfect day for strolling arm in arm in the park with one's lover.

He asked about my morning and I told him about my run-in with Monsieur Roussel at the train station and the conversation that followed. We agreed that people are not always what they seem on the surface; maybe there was hope that Roussel had a kind heart beating inside that large chest. There was also, it seemed, a chip on his shoulder where the horsey set were concerned.

"Jean-Paul," I said. "You belong to the riding club, don't you?"

"*Oui*. Do you want to go for a ride?"

"Sometime, sure," I said. "Roussel mentioned that the Fouchets hung out with the equestrian crowd. Is there a clique?"

"*Bien sûr*, of course. Like Marian's parents and the golf club, there are people who center their social life around other riding club members to the exclusion of others. I am a member, as my father was before me, because I enjoy riding and there is no comparable equestrian facility anywhere near the city, and not because membership allows me the privilege of drinking with other horse owners. In fact, I find some of the members to be *très snob*."

"Roussel used exactly those words," I said. "Did you ride with your father?"

"Oh yes. From the time I was very young. He trained me in the rigors of *haute école* and when he was confident I could manage my mount, we spent many holidays riding together. When

Dom came along, I trained him as I had been trained and he rode with us."

"*Haute école* is dressage?"

"Yes, but generally we rode just for the pleasure of it, the way you ride your horses up into the Santa Monica Mountains in California," he said. "Papa was a stickler. He would say that if you are to study music, you learn piano first. To dance, you must know ballet. Before I could ride off into the woods with confidence, he believed I had to know the classical forms of horsemanship just as your father grilled you on the physics of light and color, and now you are a filmmaker."

"I don't know that Dad was that prescient," I said. "I fell into filmmaking; it wasn't something I trained for."

"Perhaps you didn't train formally, my dear Maggie, but when the opportunity presented I believe you already had the essentials well in hand. Otherwise you would not have succeeded," he said. "Speaking of films, have you settled on topics for the fall season?"

When I told him my ideas for fall film projects he listened with intensity and asked good questions. His last question was, "How much leeway do you have? For instance, can you film outside the eurozone?"

"I haven't asked," I said, brushing my cheek against his shoulder. "Why?"

"Just thinking about possibilities," he said.

"I'll ask Diane Duval. Now, tell me about your morning."

"It was interesting." He paused, seemed to be deciding what to say, or maybe where to begin. "You know that after Marian died so suddenly, my friends arranged for my appointment as consul general in Los Angeles so that Dom and I could heal, get a fresh start. My work had always required me to travel, sometimes for months at a time, while Marian managed the household and watched over Dom. The posting to Los Angeles let me stay put, with Dom, in one place for more than two years. I cherish the time we had together in California without the constant good-byes before flying off and away from the daily routines of his life. Now we are back in France and it is Dom who is preparing to fly away. I have him as a child under my roof for only one more year. I know he is eager to move on to the next, but am I?"

"Trust me," I said, speaking from experience. "It will be more difficult on you than on Dom when he goes away to university."

"Because I have only that one year left, when we returned to France from Los Angeles last fall, I dragged my feet about accepting any position that is more permanent than a short-term consultancy or a fact-finding mission. And now, there is you."

"Don't let me get in the way of your work," I said. "We've managed so far to juggle and figure things out."

"But I don't want to juggle anymore," he said, putting his hand over mine where it rested on his sleeve. "Since we've been together, we have never managed to be on the same continent for longer than a month or two at a time. You were here last summer, I was in California. Then in October we switched, you were there, I was here. All winter you were globe-trotting from war zone to war zone while I was examining refugee camps in Greece and Turkey. We were only able to spend time together during holidays and transitions from one place to another." He took a breath. "Maggie, this morning I was offered a wonderfully interesting post with our trade mission to Singapore."

I doubt one's heart actually does leap into one's throat when hit with scary news, but that's what it felt like. I managed to ask, "Did you accept the offer?"

"No, of course not. But that's what I want to talk to you about." He led me into the great green bower around the Marie de Médicis Fountain and found a bench where we could sit and feel alone beside the reflecting pool. As he relaxed against the back of the bench, he removed his tie, rolled it up, stuffed it into a jacket pocket, and undid the top shirt buttons. "Maggie, *ma chérie*, now that we are, at last, in the same time zone, in the same house, I want us to enjoy as much of that time together as we possibly can. But there is still a great big beautiful world we have yet to explore, you in your work and me in mine. So, how can we manage for both of us to brush our teeth together every morning and still get out into the world in a meaningful way?"

"Experience tells me you had an answer before you asked the question."

"A possible answer. At least, one that might be worth considering."

"I'm waiting."

"Your contract is for one season, yes? Six films."

I nodded. "So far."

"Your television friend, Roddy Combes, the talk show host, was so in love with the Laotian segment of the unexploded bomb piece you recently finished that he offered to partner with you on a future project, meaning he would bring his checkbook if you let him come along to, as he says, play. I am making you the same offer."

"With or without Roddy?"

"He's good company, he can come, too."

"After the last film on this contract airs in January?"

"Yes. Or, until you complete the last film on the contract."

"To be clear, you're talking about going independent. No contract, no salary, no benefits."

"I am. Unless your new employer agrees to come aboard."

"And Guido?"

"We'll ask him what he wants to do."

"I am intrigued, Jean-Paul. But there are these little details to think about, like paying the mortgage and keeping the lights on. Dom starts university in a year, and that will be expensive. I know there is no tuition here, but room and board and books—"

He smiled. "To begin, Dom will have no university costs. As a student at one of the *Grandes Écoles* he will have the same status as a military recruit and will be paid a small salary until he completes his degree. Next, I have no mortgage and I am fairly confident that income from investments will be sufficient to keep the lights on and put food on the table."

"But I have a mortgage on my house in Los Angeles," I said. "And a daughter at a very expensive public university with plans to go on to medical school. Health insurance to pay for."

"My dearest Maggie, you do realize that your share of the

income from the apartments at rue Jacob will more than cover those expenses, yes?"

"Oh" was all I could manage, because I had not factored in the rents from rue Jacob. Shortly after Isabelle died, I was told that I had inherited her share of a "residence" she owned on rue Jacob. With my imperfect understanding of French and my *notaire's* sketchy English, I gathered that I had inherited an apartment. Just one, though that was amazing all by itself. But recently I learned that I now owned not only Isabelle's apartment but a half share of the entire apartment building on rue Jacob, and that Jean-Paul owned the other half. The fact of that seemed more like something out of a Gothic novel than a reality in the life of Maggie MacGowen who for years had lived and supported a daughter from paycheck to paycheck. I knew it was going to take a while for me to adjust to the reality, or the unreality, that I did not have to worry anymore about where the next paycheck would come from if I was careful.

For a while, before we were rescued by a television network contract, Guido and I had made independent films and nearly starved. I doubted Jean-Paul knew the extent of the economic perils of his proposal. After running through a mental checklist of what would likely be involved, I said, "Filmmaking can be expensive."

He shrugged. "Let me and Roddy worry about that."

What he proposed was huge. I had not been financially dependent on anyone since I graduated from college and left the shelter of the Bank of Mom and Dad, and I was proud of it. Adamant about it, in fact. So much so that I had avoided talking with Jean-Paul about financial arrangements once we married. Maybe the time had come. I said, "I've never asked to look at your bank statements."

"I have offered. My current financial statements are still in the top left-hand drawer of my desk," he said. "The drawer isn't locked. When you're ready to talk about it, you know where to find me."

"Jean-Paul, this is huge. Before we go any further, I have to know why."

"Why." He gripped my hand and sighed. "There is so much hate, so much danger out in our big beautiful world right now. For all of my working life I have believed that quiet, reasoned conversation among reasonable people with authority–diploma-cy–would resolve most global problems. You give some, you get some, we find a way to co-exist. But without reasonable people in authority, maybe I can be more effective if I stop talking to leaders and start showing to people."

I said, "From diplomacy to propaganda?"

He laughed. "I prefer the term huckstering. All media are sell-ing something, yes? So, is it wrong to want to sell compassion for our fellow man?"

"I suspect you have some very particular men in mind."

"And women and children, yes," he said. "I want to show the world the conditions in refugee camps. But more importantly, I want to show who the people are and let them explain why they are there."

"Unfinished business?" I said, looking into his eyes. What was there, lurking behind the little smile? With a finger I traced the fine scar line that coursed down the left side of his face from his hairline, around his eye socket, ending in the middle of his cheek, a reminder of the last time he inspected a camp. The plastic sur-geon who worked on him the day the bomb hit the road in front of his car did a brilliant job of putting him back together. In another six months, or maybe a year, the scar would be nearly invisible. At least, the scar on the outside would no longer be apparent. But the scars inside, the ones we cannot see, what about them? When would the nightmares go away? He took my hand and kissed the palm.

"What happened to me in Greece, *ma chérie*, had nothing to do with the refugee camp I was visiting," he said. "But yes, unfinished business. Everything about the camps is unfinished business."

I said, "What will be your role be in this filmmaking enterprise, other than signing checks?"

"Logistics and contacts. You know I have contacts."

"You'd share a tent with me in a snake-infested jungle?"

"I'd share a tent with you anywhere."

"I can be very bossy and very exacting."

"I am a trained diplomat."

I laughed and extended my hand to seal this deal. "If you're game to explore the idea, I am."

He shook my hand. "We'll call Roddy tomorrow."

We spent the rest of the afternoon being Paris tourists, talking over some of the details of this possible filmmaking joint venture while we walked. After strolling through the Luxembourg Gardens, we stopped at the fifteenth-century shrine to Saint-Étienne du Mont to gawk at the Gothic structure. I was walking up one of the flamboyant lacertine staircases to the loft above the chancel to get a better look at the stained-glass clerestory windows when my phone vibrated. For just a moment, against logic, I hoped this was a call from Roni Pascal's source about Yvan Fouchet ready to spill some bit of information that would help to find Ophelia, but it was way too soon for that call to happen. Likely it never would happen. That doesn't mean that hope will cease to trickle even when it's clear it won't spring eternal. Still, the text that set off this flutter was plenty interesting.

During his lunch hour, Zed had looked at the CCTV tapes from the street behind the train station Friday night and found the girl carrying a cello case. He parked the footage in my cloud account because Bruno wasn't around to give him my inhouse mailbox information and I wasn't listed in the studio directory yet. I found Jean-Paul studying the pipe organ and showed him the text. We waited until we were outside to open the file on my phone.

With a stone effigy of the martyred Saint-Étienne du Mont looking over our shoulders, on my telephone screen we watched a dark blur emerge out of the general haze beyond the range of a CCTV installation at an intersection. The blur took form and become identifiable as Ophelia, still carrying her cello in its hard-shell case. She passed below the camera and out of view. Zed then cut to the camera above the next intersection. We could see her approach, but the second camera was installed on the opposite side of the street so we lost sight of her whenever a car passed between her and the lens. A slow-moving service van went by followed by two cars trapped behind, unable to pass. When we could see the far sidewalk again, Ophelia was again a gray blur walking out of range until she disappeared into the night. The entire sequence took just over three minutes. The time signature on the last frame was 21:35:18, a little less than fifteen minutes from the time Ophelia and Nabi walked into the train station's parking lot.

"Vanished," I said as I forwarded the footage to Detective Delisle with a brief note. "I wonder if anyone in those vehicles remembers seeing her."

"The image isn't very sharp, but maybe our fine detective can get registration numbers off the vehicles. Someone may have seen something after the cameras lost her."

"If Delisle has time to look," I said. "Officially, she isn't on the case anymore."

"Ah, there is that. Maybe we can find her some help," he said, holding out his hand. "May I?"

I gave him the phone and he tapped in a text before forwarding the video somewhere. Within moments a reply came to his own phone.

"Who was that?"

"A friend at vehicle registration. He'll work on it."

I laughed, taking his arm. "The people you know."

"You see? I can be put to good use. Now, what would you like to do?"

"I want to go home," I said. "It's getting late. We need to pick up something for dinner on the way, but something light after that lunch. Isn't there a big marketplace near here?"

"Yes." His face brightened. "*Le Marché Mouffetard.*"

Rue Mouffetard was a street lined with food shops and outdoor stands, a food lover's paradise. We picked up some interesting cheeses, thinly sliced ham from Savoy, fresh cherries from Vaucluse in the south, spring peas from Normandy, lemons from Calabria, and beautiful dark chocolates made on the premises from African fair-trade beans. There was still room in the shopping bag I had brought from Isabelle's, so we added some whole-grain rolls, several bunches of fresh herbs, and a tub of Greek yogurt.

Arm in arm, we walked toward the closest Métro station, just a block away. It was the evening rush hour and the one-way street was packed with cars creeping forward in fits and starts, and pedestrians, many with laden shopping bags and sometimes also briefcases, school children lugging backpacks, little family clutches of parents and children; end of the work day, everyone headed home. I leaned into Jean-Paul, thinking how lovely it all was, how happy I was to be there, at that moment, with him.

Car horns came first, then screams and an unfamiliar dull thump. Everyone turned toward the noise, as people do, curious and alarmed at once. Just as I realized that a small van was on the sidewalk speeding toward us, plowing through people, the van seemed to take flight an instant before a ball of fire and black smoke erupted inside and blew it apart. I felt the explosion before I heard it, a push of pressure that stole the air from my lungs and deadened all sound for just an instant before shards of burning metal, glass, stone, asphalt, and people rained down around us. I reached for Jean-Paul as I turned to run but he grabbed me around the shoulders, pulled me down tight beside a stone wall and crouched over me. Because it's what I do, it's who I am, I had my phone out and, because he would know where to send it, I streamed video of what I could see sheltered under Jean-Paul to Zed at the studio: the feet of people running into traffic, climbing over cars stalled in the street, desperate to get away, a cacophony of car alarms and screams. And blood. Arms, chests, legs, faces washed in blood.

Jean-Paul's face was next to mine, his phone in his hand. My ears buzzed from the blast so the only words I understood were *car bomb*, *Mouffetard Métro*, and *come*. Panicked people surged around us, bumping us as they tried to push their way through the mass of souls in their path. Through the buzz in my ears I heard the two-tone claxon of police and fire sirens, adding another layer of noise to the confusion as they approached. Sharing the feeling of panic, I shoved against Jean-Paul to get up, to run. But he held me tighter and said, "Wait for the gas tank to blow."

I saw on the video later that hardly a minute elapsed from the time we first saw the van careen into the crowd until the second explosion sent a second wave of fire and debris flying into the crowd. I felt Jean-Paul flinch and knew something or someone had hit his back, but he stayed in place, a shield around me.

His phone buzzed; he looked at the screen, said, "Now," and pulled me to my feet. Traffic was at a standstill; the blast set at least two cars aflame and now they blocked the street. Moving against the flow of humanity, we wove our way through stalled cars and rushing people, headed toward the fires. The closer we got, the thicker and more rank the air became with burning oil and rubber and I didn't want to know what else; people had been trapped under the van. The heat grew nearly unbearable as we ran past the flaming cars, but we kept running forward, into the zone of conflagration, fighting against the tide of people moving away.

A big black Peugeot pulled up just as we emerged through the curtain of smoke and out into nearly breathable air on the far street. Jean-Paul opened the car's back door, dove in and pulled me with him. The door was still open when the driver took off. Reaching past me to grab the handle, Jean-Paul told the driver, "Vaucresson, Charles, s'il vous plaît."

Stunned that a rescue car had suddenly appeared, I said, "Jean-Paul, who are you?"

"I couldn't be seen there," he said, struggling out of his suit coat. "Delicate negotiations are underway."

"Do you think that car bomb was aimed at you?"

"Of course not." He put his finger through a hole burned through the back of his coat by flying debris. "Look at that."

I nudged him forward and pulled out his shirttail so I could get a look at his back. The shirt had a charred spot and there was a red mark on his skin about the size of an American quarter, but no blister. I kissed the spot and said, "All better now."

He laughed and wrapped his arm around me. "Forgive me if I handled you roughly, but things were flying about, yes?"

"Yes."

"We were very lucky. And this is very important: We were not there, d'accord?"

"I don't know." I looked at the video I shot. When I had shifted the angle of the phone to pan up, a bit of Jean-Paul's sleeve covered the top of the lens. But that second of dark blur was all of him I captured. I texted Zed again and told him that if the news division used the footage I sent him, it was important that I not get credit. He texted back a thumbs-up emoji.

"May I see?" I handed my phone to Jean-Paul. He ran the first few frames a couple of times and handed it back. "Did you get a look at the driver?"

"No. I didn't pull out my phone until after the explosion."

"Someone is sure to have gotten a look at his face. Not that it matters; we know who he was, do we not?"

"Do we?"

His left shoulder rose slightly. "Young man, probably between eighteen and thirty-five, feeling disaffected, alienated, became angry enough or felt righteous enough about a cause or his own rage that he sacrificed his life to make his point known. We'll learn his name soon and forget it soon afterward."

"You haven't answered my question, Jean-Paul," I said. "Who the hell are you? There's a car bomb, total chaos, you make a call, and boom, within minutes we're in the backseat of a big black car. How does that happen?"

"The Palais de Justice is very close by, *ma chérie*. I called my friend Davey, who is always in his office until late. He sent his driver, and we are *extrait*."

"Extracted like a bad tooth, or like a spy, by David Berg, the chief of police?"

"A spy?" He chuckled. "No, never that."

"Tell me what it is, exactly, that these delicate negotiations you're involved in are trying to make happen?"

"Trying to *make* happen? Nothing," he said. "Maggie, I am the Dutch boy with his finger in the dike, trying to hold on to the status quo in a very volatile situation. We may not be happy with things as they are, but if I, if we, fail, then the dike breaks and the results will be catastrophic. What do I do? I make nothing happen."

"Next time you tell me your work is boring, I won't believe you."

"Believe me," he said. "It's very boring. I work hard to maintain boring." He leaned forward and tapped the driver's shoulder. "Tell

Maggie, Charles, what does the head of the Paris police prefer, a boring day, or an exciting day?"

Charles laughed. "Better to keep the finger in the dike, sir. Much better."

When I was considering the offer to work at a French television network, Jean-Paul warned me that commuting by car between Paris and the suburbs was grim; better to take the train, he said. The traffic was not as grim as Los Angeles, but awful just the same. That Wednesday night, however, nestled together in the backseat of David Berg's big car with the capable Charles at the wheel, I was grateful for the time it took for the short trip between con-flagration in Paris and the leafy quiet of Vaucresson. By the time Charles let us out at the train station car park, the initial rattle of shock had morphed into a dull unease and wariness. I won-dered, did people who lived in war zones, under regular bombing raids, ever become inured, numb, to danger? I decided that wasn't possible.

On Wednesdays, Ari taught several after-school remedial math and science sessions at the Islamic Community Center. The routine he and Jean-Paul worked out was for Ari to drive to the train when he left in the afternoon, leaving the car in the lot for Jean-Paul to drive home again in the evening. I was happy that evening that I would be spared the walk home because I felt safer within the flimsy armor the car provided than I would out in the open.

Charles parked behind our car, got out and opened my door. I accepted the firm hand he offered to help me out and thanked him when I was again on solid ground. He and Jean-Paul exchanged a quick embrace and a back pat or two, and we turned toward our car.

"Monsieur Bernard, Madame," Charles called. We turned and watched him pull our shopping bag off the floor of the backseat. I hadn't realized until I saw the bag that during all the chaos I had held the damn thing tight against me until we bailed into the car, where I dropped it unaware that I had it. Odd what we do in a state of absolute panic. Jean-Paul laughed when he saw it, and I began to cry.

For a few minutes, we sat in our car, clutching each other, until we were able to breathe normally again. When we had ourselves at least outwardly composed, we started home. The evening was warm and wonderfully fragrant. I rolled down my window to let it in. As we approached our driveway, I heard music, a plaintive violin so far away that it floated on the air as softly and subtly as the scent of flowers in the yard. And then Jean-Paul pushed a button and the garage door rolled up and both perfume and music were gone.

First thing, we went upstairs and showered away the oily smudge and bits of debris from our hair and bodies. In fresh clothes, looking somewhat normal again even though we felt anything but, we went back downstairs. We were still in the kitchen unloading the shopping, marveling that everything except for the bread was intact, when Dominic came in with the usual burst of energy. He told us that he heard there was another car bomb in Paris, this time outside the Mouffetard markets. So far, he said, there were five confirmed dead and many casualties. Were we anywhere near there? Jean-Paul paused from opening a bottle of wine to shoot me what I took for a warning glance and said, "We saw the smoke."

Relative quiet returned when Dom, glass of wine in one hand, book bag in the other, went upstairs to wash before dinner. In the quiet left in his wake I heard the music again.

"Where is that coming from?" I asked Jean-Paul as I headed for the salon to open all the doors. There was Nabi, sitting on the patio in the gathering dusk with his back to us, playing his violin. Azadah Diba, his grandmother, was stretched out on a chaise beyond the pool, eyes closed, maybe listening, maybe napping. A pile of stuffed duffel bags next to the guest house door let us know that something had gone terribly wrong for them, yet again. Jean-Paul came up beside me and handed me a glass of wine. We looked at each other, shrugged, and stayed where we were to hear the boy play. I did not recognize the piece, I only knew it was beautiful and sad, and that Nabi was very talented. At the end, Nabi sat still with his violin under his chin until the last notes faded to

nothing. When he put down the bow and rested the instrument on
his knee, we stepped outside.

Jean-Paul broke the silence. "Nabi?"

Nabi turned, saw us and rose. With our first look at his face I
gasped, Jean-Paul groaned, or maybe he growled. Someone had
pummeled the kid, leaving his left cheek so battered and swollen
I doubted he could see much out of that eye. And then, for good
measure, it looked as if someone had dragged him across a pavement face down. A large adhesive bandage covered the back of his
right hand, his bow hand; a defensive injury?

"Oh, Nabi," I said, walking to him. Azadah Diba rose as soon
as she heard our voices and came to her grandson's side.

"Monsieur Bernard, Madame MacGowen." Nabi, clearly embarrassed and uncertain, took a small step toward us. "Ari told me we
could wait here until he finishes at the center. I hope it's all right."

"If Ari invited you," Jean-Paul said, "of course it's all right. Is
this your grandmother? We've not met."

Nabi made the introductions in French. Jean-Paul responded
in English, remembering that the woman did not speak French,
offering her his hand and giving her a little bow when she accepted. She then offered me her hand and said she was happy to see
me again.

"Come inside, please," Jean-Paul said, gesturing for them to
lead the way in. "Tell us what happened."

First things first, both of our guests visited a bathroom, Nabi
to the hall bathroom upstairs and Azadah Diba to the powder
room off the entry. In the meantime, I filled the kettle for tea,
made an icepack for Nabi's shiner, found the acetaminophen,
and carried it all out to the salon on a tray along with a plate
of sliced *poulaine* bread and Camembert from my grandmother's
fromagerie. When everyone had assembled in the salon and had
a drink in hand, Nabi told us about his very bad day, a day that
was exactly what he expected it would be without Ophelia there
to protect him. The harassment began early, he said, and esca-
lated as the day progressed, more kids joining in, girls as well
as boys. He was accused of doing something to Ophelia, kicked

and taunted for being Muslim, and then before his last class of the day, beaten by some footballers—soccer players, that is—just because he was Nabi. The new principal—la directeur—was summoned to restore order. She took Nabi to the school nurse, who, at the insistence of la directeur, called the police. And then things only got worse.

"What did the police do?" Jean-Paul asked, sitting forward.

"They drove me home," he said. "But my grandmother's employer was already back from work. When she saw me get out of the police car looking like this she went crazy. She said we had to go. Now! She didn't want a troublemaker near her family."

"She said 'terrorist.'" Azadah Diba interjected. "She called my Nabi a terrorist. Can you imagine? He's not the terrorist, it's those horrible boys who harass him who are."

"She fired you?" I asked her.

A deep sigh. "Yes. What do we do now? It was difficult to get that job, but without a good reference, who will hire me? How will we live?"

"First," Jean-Paul said. "We'll have some dinner. Madame Diba, Ari strictly adheres to halal dietary rules. Do you?"

"No," she said after taking a moment to calm down. "We do not eat pork, of course, and other haram foods, or drink alcohol. Please, may I help prepare the meal? Nabi and I do not want to burden you."

Jean-Paul and I exchanged nods because letting her help simply made sense; I had no idea what we had to offer that might be haram and therefore forbidden. The ham we dragged home from the market was absolutely forbidden, but other than that I was uncertain. Azadah Diba and I repaired to the kitchen while Jean-Paul spoke with Nabi in the salon. I heard Éric's name mentioned, and Detective Delisle's. I opened the refrigerator and invited Diba, as she asked me to call her, to take a look.

"Oh, yes," she said when she saw the roast chicken left over from last night. The chicken was followed to the counter by a variety of salad vegetables and a plastic tub of feta cheese. The fresh herbs we bought that afternoon were in a jar of water next to the sink. As she snipped sprigs of dill and oregano she asked, "Have you an onion, garlic, olive oil?"

I opened the pantry for her and she began pulling out ingredients to make an Italian-style soup from canned tomatoes. Dinner, then, would be salad with cold chicken and soup, followed by cherries and cheese, always cheese. My part in the enterprise was to chop, slice, and mince as instructed, and to hold up one end of the conversation. As she relaxed, Diba began to open up to me. She liked to cook, but her now-former employers, the Australians, stuck to a strict Paleo diet, meat and raw vegetables, which made no sense to Diba. No bread, no rice, no potatoes? No wonder they were so skinny and so ill-tempered. Most Australians she knew were such happy people. How did she have the misfortune to draw these two? There was no bitterness in her tone when she spoke about them, only a sort of mystification about people who refused to even taste her famous honey cake when she made it for the toddler. At least they let the children eat real food.

The conversation moved from there to concert tours with her violinist son until an injury put an end to his career. And then he taught. Nabi, she said, was his best student. So eager to please his father. I told her my mom, the mom who raised me, had once been a concert pianist and still taught. I was her worst student; Isabelle, I was told, was tone deaf. It was a friendly conversation, and in short order the meal was ready.

"Oh, I made too much food," Diba said, watching me place serving bowls on a tray to take outside. "I was once accustomed to cooking for a big family. Talking with you I must have gotten carried away. On autopilot you could say. But thank you. It felt so wonderful to remember how it was with my family, if just for a moment." She dabbed at her eyes, picked up the salad bowl and quickly left the room.

We ate on the terrace under an arbor strung with lights. Dinner conversation was a bit stilted at first, but when Dom and Nabi began to talk about school and plans for university everyone relaxed and joined in. Nabi, who was three years behind Dom, hoped to be admitted in the fall to one of the regional conservatories of the arts to study music. He had requested the school in Paris where he thought there might be more tolerance than in the suburbs. I glanced at Jean-Paul, remembering what one of Jimmy Jardine's guests had said about anti-Semitism in Paris schools. Could music overcome bigotry? Besides, in our suburb, so far at least, no one had detonated a car bomb.

When Ophelia's name came up, I asked Nabi, "Why does your friend run away?"

"When she can't take it anymore at home, she goes," he said.

"What is it she can't take any more of?"

"The fighting," he said. "Her parents hate each other. She says they hate her, too. They want a puppet, not a real girl. At least, she says, not one who can think for herself. So, sometimes she just has to get away."

"Where does she go?" I asked.

"She used to go to her friend Ambre's house, just to cool off. But one time she lied to Ambre's mother and told her she had permission to stay overnight, but she got caught and Ambre got in trouble, too. They weren't friends after that. Without Ambre, she didn't have anywhere to go. At least, nowhere she felt safe; scary people come out at night. One time—" He paused to glance at his grandmother. "There's an apartment over the garage in that big house where Grandma and I have been living. No one goes up there. One time, I gave Ophelia the key." He glanced at Diba again. "For one night, that's all, I promise."

"Oh, Nabi," Diba moaned. "I could have lost my job."

He reached his hand across the table toward her. "I'm sorry."

She took his hand and drew a breath and forced a smile. "It doesn't matter now, does it?"

Jean-Paul asked, "Could she be in the apartment now?"

Nabi shook his head. "I looked when I got home yesterday."

"Where else would she go?" I asked.

"I keep trying to think, but I don't know."

"No boyfriend?"

Again, he shook his head. "She hates boys."

"Except you?" Dom asked.

"Well, me and our music teacher. And her calculus teacher. Sometimes she pretends she needs help with an assignment so she can go after school to talk to Monsieur Gold."

We were still at the table, picking at cheese and cherries after the meal, when Ari arrived home and saw that everyone was taken care of. He caught Jean-Paul's eye, put his palms together and made a little bow, a small gesture that said volumes about his gratitude. Jean-Paul's response was to pull up another chair. But before he sat, Ari went over to Nabi, took his face in his hands and examined the shiner. Gently, he palpated the cheekbone under his eye, raised the boy's chin and studied all the scrapes and scratches, lifted the bandage on his hand and looked under it. When he pressed his palm against Nabi's ribcage Nabi flinched and paled but said nothing.

"Show me where it hurts most," Ari said.

Nabi put a hand on his back just at his waist.

"You were kicked there, perhaps?"

"Yes."

"Are you pissing blood?"

"Some."

"Have you seen a doctor?"

"No, sir."

"Who patched you up?"

"The school nurse."

"You should have been sent right to a doctor. After you finish your meal, we are going to the hospital for X rays."

Ari was quietly furious. Jean-Paul rose and started toward him when the telephones in our pockets chimed.

"Doorbell," I said, pulling out my phone to see who was there. "Detective Delisle. Excuse me."

Our detective looked even worse than she had the night before. She wore her work clothes, a tailored suit and low pumps, and she had her hair in its bun again, but all of her sharp edges seemed frayed.

"Is Ahmad Nabi here?" she asked in lieu of Hello.

"He is." I ushered her inside.

"I thought he might be. I want to talk to him about an incident at school today, but the people at the address I have for him said that he and his grandmother left in a taxi without saying where they were going. This seemed the likely place."

"Everyone's is out on the terrace, eating."

"*Merde*," she muttered. "Sorry. It is the dinner hour, isn't it? I hadn't thought of that."

"Have you eaten?" I asked.

"Eaten?" She gave a sad little chuckle. "What's that?"

"You might as well join us. Nabi's grandmother made enough to feed the multitudes," I said, gesturing toward the doors. "What will you drink, water, tea, or wine?"

"Kind of you, but–" She shuffled her feet, looking anywhere but at me before she pursed her lips and let out a puff that sounded like Pooh, as in Winnie the, with a lot of air behind it. "Oh, what the hell. Sure. Yes. I'm starved. And wine. Plenty of wine, please."

"Go outside and pull up a chair. I'll get you a plate."

I went to the kitchen for two place settings, one for Delisle, the other for Ari. Just as Ari had, Delisle examined Nabi's face. She pulled out her phone and took pictures.

"Who did this to you?" she asked, looking into that swollen eye. When he stubbornly shook his head, refusing to answer, perhaps afraid to snitch on the bullies, she said, "Was it Louis Roussel?"

Reluctantly, he nodded.

"And who else?"

"Maxime and Octave."

"I know who they are. Who was the girl?"

"Ambre."

"This was in the schoolyard between classes?"

"Yes."

"And it was the *directeur* who broke it up?" When he nodded, she gave his shoulder a gentle pat and walked around the table to take the chair between Diba and Ari that Jean-Paul held out for her. Accepting the salad bowl from Diba with a little bow of the head, she glanced over at Nabi and said, "Don't go to school tomorrow. The *directeur* is holding an all-school meeting and she thinks it would be wise if you weren't there. She promises things will change and I promise I will help make that happen."

While Ari translated what she'd said for Diba, I handed the detective a bowl of soup and asked, "What happened to the old *directeur*? He seems to have simply disappeared."

"That's a question for the education ministry." She took her first spoonful of soup and smiled for the first time. "This is delicious. Reminds me of a visit to Italy."

There was nothing on Ari's plate. Jean-Paul set the bowl of cherries in front of him. "The season is short, enjoy them while you can." Ari helped himself.

"Nabi," I said, "how is Ophelia able to protect you from these kids? Are they friends of hers?"

"Not the boys. I mean, Louis has this thing for Ophelia, you know what I mean?"

"He has a crush on her?"

He nodded. "His mother is sick so Ophelia is nice to him. I mean, she isn't openly cruel to him, but she avoids him. He follows her around sometimes and that annoys her. Ambre was her best friend until that thing happened between them. Ambre wanted to talk it out, be friends again, but Ophelia blocked her."

"Are Louis and Ambre jealous of your friendship with Ophelia?" I asked.

"That's what she said. I think they are a little afraid of her."

"Kids," Dom said, as if at the ripe age of eighteen he was past all that sort of nonsense. "What can you expect?"

The adults chuckled, and he grinned.

"With your permission, Diba," Ari said in English after discreetly spitting a cherry pit into a napkin. "After we get Nabi checked out at the hospital, I want him to stay with me overnight so I can keep an eye on him. I'm worried there may be a mild concussion and a broken rib or two, and the blow to the kidneys didn't do him any good. But for you, maybe a hotel?"

"Oh, I can't–" Diba got no further. "I lost my job today, Doctor Massarani. I can't afford a hotel, and I won't let you pay. But if you'll keep Nabi tonight I can go to a shelter, and I will be fine."

"Nonsense," Jean-Paul said. "The two of you have been through enough for one day. You'll stay here tonight, Diba. Tomorrow we'll try to sort things out, yes?"

"Thank you," she said, tears filling her eyes. "Thank you."

"Okay, then. Everyone's set." Detective Delisle drained her glass for the second time and stood. "The meal was lovely, thank you very much. I needed the fortification because now I get to go beat up a bunch of toughs, in a legal sense anyway. Nabi, you aren't the only kid who will be missing school tomorrow."

"I'll walk you out," I said. On the way I asked, "Did you see the footage I sent you this afternoon?"

"I did, thank you, but I'd already seen it. We do have resources, you know. I saw nothing that looked like an abduction, did you?"

"What I saw were potential witnesses slowly driving by, as well as the general direction Ophelia was headed."

"Witnesses to what, exactly, Madame MacGowen? A girl running away, perhaps to earn a few euros playing cello in the Métro? To hide at a friend's house? Meet a boy?" She raised her palms—Who knows? "I'm confident Ophelia will turn up. My concern is for the condition she'll be in when she does. In the meantime, she is a case for Paris police in the juvenile section, a runaway. At this moment I am working on the assault of a student at our local school, one Ahmad Nabi. So, unless you have further questions, I will thank you for feeding me and for taking in our displaced family, and I'll get back to my job."

"One question," I said. "What time is this school meeting tomorrow?"

"Two o'clock, immediately after lunch. Why?"

"I want to be there," I said.

A little shoulder lift as she thought that over. "Not my call. Talk to the *directeur*."

I opened the door for her. "Maybe I'll see you there."

Jean-Paul had been eavesdropping from the end of the short entry hall. I went over and kissed him. "You are one of the good guys, you know?"

He wrapped me in his arms. "How does that song go, the one

from that American musical? Oh yes, 'I'm just a guy who cain't say no.'"

"From *Oklahoma!*, and it's a girl who cain't say no, but you do a pretty decent cornball country accent. Any time you want to sing in my ear, you just go right ahead."

"I'll remember you said that." He kissed my neck and released me. "You really want to go to that meeting tomorrow?"

"What I really want to do is go in with cameras."

"Good luck getting permission."

"I have a friend, a trained diplomat with contacts. I could appeal to him. I could also go to this giant television network that drops a paycheck into my bank account and ask them to send over a news team. But I'll have to think about it before I call on either. The situation at the school is already flammable. I wonder if having a camera crew show up will set something off. Or would it put the kids on their best behavior?"

"Could go either way."

"Could," I said. "Now what?"

"I'm going to the hospital with Ari, Diba, and Nabi. Will you get the guest room ready for Diba?"

"Of course."

"I'll call if we'll be late."

"I'll keep the home fires burning."

The house felt oddly empty when they were gone. Dom, as usual, had retreated to his room to study as soon as we had the dishes into the dishwasher and the counters wiped down. I put fresh sheets on the guest room bed and a set of towels on the chair next to the dresser. There were water glasses in the bathroom. After that, I wandered back downstairs to my office, looking for something to keep me busy until Jean-Paul returned. I was still unnerved by what we had seen that afternoon. And now Nabi. Without the violin, and without Diba and Ari, and probably Ophelia, who might Nabi become?

Feeling restless, powerless, I looked for something to do, a distraction. There was film research I could do, but first I needed to set up my home office. Marian's furniture had been hauled away that morning, leaving the room bare except for the mass of unopened boxes full of office things I had ordered. The long work table came in a flat pack and was too heavy for me to easily assemble alone, so I left it until I could recruit some help. Without it, I set up the new computer on the floor. I began downloading files Zed dropped into the cloud but stopped to take another look at the various clips of CCTV footage he had left there for me.

When we saw Nabi and Ophelia walk into the train station off the street, I had asked Zed to run the tape in slow motion as the kids came toward the camera placement. I ran that clip twice because on the first go my eye went past the kids to the street. After nine o'clock, there was very little traffic on the street beyond the driveway. A large dark car came into frame and seemed to slow before it moved out of camera range. I opened the same sequence in real time just to make sure, and could see that the driver had, indeed, slowed significantly as he, or she, passed the driveway apron, as if he was watching the two kids. Before the end of the clip, the same or a very similar car, traveling from the opposite direction, passed the driveway and slowed again. Had the driver made a U-turn and come back for a second look? Or was this a different car altogether? I couldn't identify the make.

Curious, I pulled up the footage from the street behind the station and paid attention to the cars on the street instead of to Ophelia. The first sequence picked up Ophelia after she turned onto the street from the alley that led from the car park. She was walking away from the camera, toward the intersection with the street that fronted the train station. All I could see of the intersection in the distance was the headlight beams from cross-traffic as they creased the dark. One car–one set of beams, as I saw it–drove into the intersection, stopped suddenly, reversed, and inscribed an arc in the gloom as it made a U-turn and went back the way it had come. Was this, Oops, I forgot something? Or something else?

The next clip, captured by the camera over the far intersection on the opposite side of the street, picked up Ophelia approaching out of the dark. I lost her whenever cars passed by. And then the thing I was looking for appeared: a set of headlights slowly approached behind her. The front of the car came into range enough for me to see that it was black or maybe dark green or blue, before it parked at the curb, lights out. When Ophelia crossed at the intersection, the headlights snapped on again and the car slowly pulled away from the curb. I captured the last frame and saved it.

I went onto the Net and pulled up photos of full-size late-model cars. The front ends of most of them were no more different than cookies baked from the same batch of dough. A little longer here, rounded or angular there, but altogether, similar cookies. The Audi was among them.

In case he was asleep, I texted Dom upstairs in his room. He saw the text and came right to the head of the stairs.

"Maggie?"

"How many Audis do you think there are in Vaucresson?" I asked.

"Hundreds." He laughed and started down the stairs. "That's what you wanted to ask me?"

"No. May I borrow your scooter?"

"Where are you going?"

"Just a little drive," I said. "Do you know where the Fouchets live?"

"*Ouais.* We took Ophelia home after riding workout a couple of times. Why?"

I motioned for him to come into my office and pointed to the image frozen on my computer screen. "Can you tell what model car that is?"

"You want to know if it's an Audi?"

"I want to know what it is."

Dom squatted down for a closer look. "It's a fairly new model whatever it is. Could be a Lexus or a Mercedes or Audi. Maybe a Peugeot 508; they all want to look like Teslas right now. The way the streetlight reflects on the hood I can't really see the profile of the headlights well enough to tell."

I closed the computer and tucked it into my bag; I might need the captured image for comparison. "Dom, may I borrow your scooter?"

"À *chez* Fouchet? No. I'll drive, you ride on the back."

The Fouchets lived in a pretentious pile of fresh stucco and faux stone on the far side of boulevard de la République, a main street through town. I hadn't intended to go calling, but I was ready with an excuse if anyone saw us cruising the place and had questions. All I wanted was another look at Yvan Fouchet's Audi. Typical of homes in the region, the garage was around back. I couldn't see a car in the driveway, but the downstairs lights were on and through the large front windows I saw someone moving around inside. It was after nine, late to knock on a stranger's door, but I asked Dom to pull into the drive anyway. Intrusive? I'm afraid so.

The front door opened before Dom or I could ring the bell. The woman standing under the light looked as if she were dressed to go out for the evening: skirt, heels, pearls, polished hair and makeup. She also held a highball glass with about three fingers of amber liquid in it.

"Dom Bernard, is that you?" the woman of the house said, stepping outside when she recognized him. "Look how tall you are."

"Madame Fouchet, I want you to meet Maggie MacGowen, Papa's fiancée."

"Oh, yes?" she said, as if suddenly noticing I was there. She offered me her hand. When I took it, saying the usual sorts of things, lovely to meet you, sorry for the circumstance, she was studying me with such a laser focus that she didn't seem to hear me. Her scrutiny made me want to reach up and fluff my helmet-flattened hair. Looking at me still, she asked, "How is Jean-Paul? We haven't seen him for ages. Not since Marian's funeral, I think."

"Jean-Paul is well," I said, mystified. If my daughter were missing and a stranger came to my door at night, wouldn't the first, or maybe second question be, Have you news about my girl? But then, there was that drink in her hand and who knows what she might have swallowed earlier, in either liquid or pill form. Was she inordinately self-contained, or simply numb? I plunged forward. "Madame Fouchet, I'm sure your husband told you that we retrieved a bit of security camera footage that shows some of your daughter's movements Friday. Monsieur Fouchet came by last night to see it."

"Did he?" she said, a frown pulling her perfectly arched eyebrows into a furrow. "He didn't mention it. But then, I've hardly seen him since–"

Finally, a flicker of something like emotion.

"I thought you might like to have a look at what we found," I said.

"Of course," she said, moving aside a step to usher us in. "Forgive me for keeping you standing outside. I apologize, I'm not at my best."

"No apology needed." On my way past her, I caught a whiff of scotch. From her skin, not the glass.

Dom, bless his heart, stopped and gave her a hug. She seemed to cling for a moment before pulling in a breath and breaking away. She patted his cheek. "I can't get over how grown up you are, *mon chèr*." Taking his arm, she led us into her very formally furnished salon. "Are you still riding?"

"No time for anything but books," he said.

"You sound like my Ophelia. No time for horses anymore. Just school and music, school and music. Too bad. She looked so pretty up on her big stallion."

We declined her offer of drinks. While she refreshed her own at a bar cart at the far end of the long room, I opened my laptop on an imitation Louis Quinze table and pulled up the footage from the train station.

"I saw you on the *Jimmy* show, you know," she said, recorking the scotch bottle and crossing the room toward us. "I record it every night in case he has someone interesting on. Who told me you would be a guest? Oh, I don't remember. Now, what is it you have to show me?"

She leaned forward to peer at the computer screen. I touched PLAY and Ophelia appeared beside Nabi.

"Oh!" she exclaimed, leaning closer. "Where is this?"

"The train station car park Friday night." I pointed to the time stamp in the top corner.

"They were supposed to be going for pizza after rehearsal. What was she doing at the train station? More to the point, what was she doing with that boy? We forbade her."

"Looks like he's carrying her cello," I said.

She watched Nabi hand the cello to her daughter, the chaste good-bye exchange, and their separate exits. "The woman from the police told me the boy has nothing to do with whatever Ophelia is up to. Now I can believe her." She turned to me. "Is there more?"

"Not very much." I showed her the next sequence, freezing the last frame after Ophelia, alone on the street, walked on into the dark beyond the camera's range. I said, "Your husband didn't mention seeing this?"

She shook her head as answer.

"Is he home?"

"Probably not. I'm sure he's out patrolling the streets the way he does, looking for Ophelia."

"The way he does?"

She lowered her chin and looked me in the eye. "This isn't the first time my daughter hasn't come home, you know. One time she went into the *haras* to sleep and whatever she saw there frightened her enough that she scuttled back home to the nest. Since then, when she disappears Yvan gets into his car and goes looking for her in case she gets frightened. I think she knows he will. I wonder sometimes if it's a game they play. Hide and seek; he never finds her, and she comes home when she's cooled off."

"You're expecting her to come home, then?"

"I have no idea anymore." She sipped her scotch. "This time is different from the others. She wasn't angry when she left. We gave her permission to stay out late because we'd been getting along quite well lately. Or, at least, I thought we were. So why did she go? Not that it matters now. She's never been gone this long before."

All I could think to say was, "I'm sorry for what you are going through."

She nodded and drained her glass.

Dom cleared his throat; it was time for us to go.

I closed the computer and tucked it into my bag. "Again, I'm sorry for interrupting your evening, Madame Fouchet. But so many people have already seen the video from Friday, and there's been so much talk that I wanted to make sure you saw it for yourself."

"Yes, so much talk. Too much talk."

"Then we'll wish you all the best and say good night."

"Oh, so soon? But wouldn't you like to stay for a drink? Dom, you're old enough now."

He smiled, shook his head. "I'm driving. If I crash my scooter with Maggie on board Papa will never forgive me."

"No, you're right. Some things are beyond forgiveness, aren't they?"

Madame Fouchet stood in the open door watching us walk to Dom's scooter. I wondered if she would call us back, but she closed the door as we fastened our helmets. Dom's face in deep shadows under the streetlights was unreadable.

"That conversation was somewhat disturbing," I said. "You okay?"

"Sure," he said, taking his seat and steadying the bike for me to climb on behind. "Why not?"

"She seemed, I don't know, flirty with you. Is that normal for her?"

He chuckled. "I don't know her all that well—I'm a kid, she's a parent—so I don't know what's normal for her. I'm surprised she remembered my name. I think she had a lot to drink, yes?"

"Definitely." I chastised myself for being judgmental. The woman had to be going through hell. I doubted we had enough in common to ever be good friends, but this was no time to be critical. If she drank to cope, so what?

We were two houses away when a dark Audi passed us. I shifted around enough to see if it would turn into the Fouchets' driveway. When it did, I straightened back and tapped Dom's shoulder. "So?"

He shrugged. "Possibly, yes."

] *Six*

B ROKEN RIBS HURT like hell," I said. "And there's nothing you can do except wait until they heal. Poor Nabi."

Jean-Paul opened the side gate and led me out onto the foot path. I took some deep breaths as we waited for other early-morning runners to pass before we fell into line, setting off at an easy jog until we warmed up–the morning was surprisingly chilly in the hour after dawn–keeping to the left to let faster runners and bikers pass on the right.

"There is more concern about the bruised kidney," Jean-Paul said, holding back to stay beside me; he was a far better runner. I was asleep when they all got back from the hospital last night and he was filling me in on Nabi's examination. "The beating poor Nabi got was absolutely brutal. I hope those kids are taken into custody."

"Taking bets on that?"

"Odds are they get counseling, sensitivity sessions, assignment to community work, maybe. They'll be off the hook before the summer holiday. Before Nabi's injuries heal, anyway."

"No permanent damage, though?"

"Not to the body," he said. "But damage to the heart and soul, who can say?"

In February, outside a refugee camp in Greece, Jean-Paul was badly injured by a bomb. After that, sometimes he cried out in his sleep. Last night, he cried out again.

"How are you today?" I asked.

He took some time before answering. "All things considered, I'm all right. And you?"

"What you said."

We picked up the pace and ran in silence, both of us lost to our own thoughts as we turned off the path that ran behind the house, away from the crowd of bikers and more earnest morning runners, and into the open trails of the *haras*. We were far from alone, however. There were other runners and clusters of chatty walkers all over the park. Twice I spotted homeless men emerge from the dense copse that surrounded the vast central meadow; Ophelia told Nabi that scary people come out at night. I was still surprised that there could be homeless people in a socialist system. It was explained to me that while refugees admitted to France for humane reasons, like Nabi and Diba, were immediately eligible for benefits like health care and housing assistance, documented immigrants, like me, had a waiting period before social benefits kicked in; I was paying for international health insurance. Undocumented immigrants were eligible for *rien*, zip, because they were no more welcome in France than they were in the United States. Was that who these men were, undocumented aliens?

We heard a chorus of shouts ahead on the right where one of the clusters of women walkers seemed to be having an argument with a bearded man. Two of the women, both gray-haired, began to tussle with him, trying to keep him in place when it was clear that he wanted to go. Jean-Paul and several other men turned on their jets and sprinted across the lawn toward them, me in their wake. When I arrived, the long-beard was on the ground with one panting male runner sitting on his legs and two others pinning his arms. Off to the side, a woman, wide-eyed and flushed, held a beautiful cello by its neck.

Jean-Paul was just finishing a phone call when I came up beside him, gasping for breath but managing to hold my mobile with the camera's video function aimed at the action.

The woman with custody of the cello looked down at the captive and demanded, "What have you done with Ophelia Fouchet?"

"Who?" he said, looking puzzled. "What?"

"The missing girl," the woman repeated. "This is her cello. What did you do with the girl?"

"I don't know about a girl." He had an accent I couldn't place, but he understood French well enough. "I found that thing in the woods and I'm taking it to sell at the Saturday *brocante* in Garches. I can get good money for it, so give it back."

The bearded man began to struggle in earnest when the first wails of police sirens pierced the morning quiet. Glaring at his captors, desperate to get free, he pleaded, "Keep the damn thing. It's yours. Just let me go. You have no right."

A little blue-and-white Renault, full lights and sirens, rolled over the low curb of a parking lot near the kiddie playground and bounced across the grass toward us. Two other cars followed.

"*Merde, merde, merde,* let me go!" he seethed.

But the captors held fast until two very young officers of the law took the poor guy into custody, snapping handcuffs around his skinny wrists and wrestling him to lie on his stomach. Out of the second of the backup cars emerged our Detective Fleur Delisle and her partner, Detective Lajoie. When she spotted us in the crowd, me with my phone camera taping, she rolled her eyes and shook her head, but she smiled. She walked straight to Jean-Paul to hear the story, but he sent her to the woman with the cello.

Statements were taken, and the cello was tagged as evidence and placed in the backseat of one of the blue-and-whites by an officer wearing Latex gloves. And through it all, Delisle and Lajoie grilled the bearded man who insisted, over and over, that he had found the cello in the undergrowth when he was looking for a place to spend the night. He kept it because he thought he could sell it at the flea market.

The big question was, in which patch of woods did he find the cello?

Officers thanked the walkers and runners, took their names, and sent them on their way. But Delisle asked Jean-Paul and me to stay; she had something to say. She also asked me to turn off the video.

We walked a few yards away from the clutch of police guarding the still-unidentified bearded man and stood where Delisle could keep an eye on her colleagues.

"I had a call late last night," she said. "Someone from the investigative branch of the national vehicle registration office had a report for me on a request for help identifying vehicles captured by a CCTV camera. Funny thing is, I don't remember sending any footage to them for identification. The really odd thing is that when I have asked for help from that office in the past, the report has taken weeks, if not months, to get back to me. And here we are, not even twenty-four hours after Madame MacGowen had her very helpful video engineer collect a bit of footage that I am given a confirmed identification on four of the vehicles and a sincere apology from the investigator for his inability to identify the others. An immediate report *and* an apology? Unheard of. How do you think that came about?"

Jean-Paul shrugged. I said, "It helps to know people."

"*Merde*," she said, and laughed. After doing her best to shift to stern-cop mode, she said, "We're going to walk that guy back to the place he says he found the cello. I would say, don't follow us, but I know that would be wasted effort. One of you would probably call in a chopper to film the whole thing. So, come along if you must. Just try to stay out of the way."

"Since we're invited to the party, Jean-Paul," I said, taking his arm, "we should attend."

"*Bien sûr*," he said. "But why, Detective?"

"Our chances of finding something among the bushes is fairly slim. But if we do, short of the child's remains, I might need some help getting quick reports out of what can be the vast forests of the bureaucracy I work in so that we can go forward with an investigation. Now that Ophelia's beloved cello has turned up, everything is different."

"One more thing," I said. "Did you have a chance to look at the note I sent you last night?"

"About a car that seemed to have some interest in Mademoiselle Fouchet? *Oui.* I sent an identification request to my new friend at vehicle investigation. Let's see how quickly he answers this time."

Then she waved us toward the parade of police who, under the direction of Detective Lajoie, escorted the bearded prisoner across the meadow toward the woods on the far side. With a little bow, she said, "Shall we?"

Every ten yards or so, the bearded man, who said his name was Voycich, would point to a spot and one of the uniforms would venture into the copse and, finding nothing, emerge brushing leaves and twigs from his or her hair and clothes. With each false alarm, Lajoie grew more cranky and sweaty.

"I had a little wine," Voycich said when Lajoie accused him of leading them on *un ballet d'absurdités*, meaning, Jean-Paul informed me, a wild-goose chase. "And it was dark. There's lots of trees around here, you know. Besides, it was a little while ago."

I ventured to ask. "When?"

"When? Good question," he said. "I didn't mark the day on my calendar."

"Try to remember," Delisle said.

"I don't know. A few days? Four, five, six?"

The day began to warm. As the sun moved higher over the open meadow it felt more like summer than late spring. Delisle, shielding her eyes as she looked down the long line of dense woods, muttered to her partner, "Let's run the asshole in; this exercise is useless. If the girl has been here for six days, we'd smell her."

Lajoie wrinkled his nose. "Yep. Time to go."

"No, wait!" Voycich nodded to a crosshatch of broken twigs at the edge of the lawn a few yards along. "That's the place. I remember now. See, I left some stuff in there so I made a marker so I could find it again."

"A miracle," Lajoie smirked as he gestured for a uniform to go in for a look. "The heat has loosened a memory."

A few moments later, the officer in the thicket called out, "Detective, you better see this."

Lajoie turned to Delisle. "Who do you suppose he's talking to? Detective you or detective me?"

She chuckled. "As you outrank me, old man, I'm guessing it's me."

He laughed, a low guttural *Hah*! Delisle threw him a narrow-eyed glare before she parted some branches and edged her way into the brush. We could hear her thrashing about, then some muffled conversation with the officer who was already in there before they both worked their way out into the sunlight again. Delisle, wearing Latex gloves, held a backpack by its straps.

"That's my stuff," Voycich said.

Delisle pulled out a binder full of sheet music. Catching his eye, she said, "Your stuff?"

"Now it is, sure," he said, defiant. "I found it. It's mine."

"Why'd you leave the cello case behind?" she asked him. "Those things cost a lot of money."

That bit of news seemed to surprise him, but he recovered to say, "It's red. You think people wouldn't notice me walking around with a big red case?"

She laughed. "You think people won't notice a bum walking around with a cello, red or not? Take him in," she said to the uniforms hanging onto Voycich by the elbows. "Get him processed, and for God's sake get him a shower. But secure his clothes for the lab, *oui*?"

"What do you want on the charge sheet, Detective?"

"Let's start with theft of property valued at more than a thousand euros, vagrancy, no documents of legal residency, and shitting in a public space."

Lajoie was on his phone, calling for a crime scene team, watching the pair of uniforms fast-walking Voycich to a car. Again, Delisle, with a bob of her head, moved Jean-Paul and me a few yards away. After a glance at her partner, she said, "I have a favor to ask the TV girl."

"I can't imagine," I said, expecting her to tell us to stay the hell away. Instead she asked me to make a short film for her.

"I told you last night that the *directeur* is having all the secondary school kids assemble in the gym this afternoon to talk about bullying. She asked me to speak to them, voice of authority or something. Scare tactic. I tried to shift it onto Lajoie, but my *commandant* made it an order. Me talking to kids is a bad idea because I know how it will go down. The first little asshole who throws shade at me, I'll go off on him. It'll get ugly." She shook her head. "This generation with their faces in their phones all the time, I think if I can show them a video, maybe it'll be okay."

"What's on this video?"

"First I want them to see what they did to Nabi. And then I want them to feel bad about it."

"That second part," I said. "Any idea how to accomplish that?"

"Short of hauling them all in and letting them know what it's like to sit in a jail cell, or beating the crap out of them, no."

I checked my phone for the time: 7:50. "This assembly is at two?"

She nodded. "Two this afternoon."

"A five-minute video? Ten?"

"Twenty minutes?"

"There isn't time to pull together twenty minutes."

"But you'll give me something?"

"I'll do my best. But no promises that it will be pretty."

"*Très cool.* I'll drive you home now so you can get right on it."

We left Detective Lajoie telling war stories to two uniformed officers while they stood watch over the patch of woods until the forensic science team showed up. The drive home took all of five minutes.

Jean-Paul and I walked into a house full of string music.

"Debussy," Jean-Paul said as he went in search of the source. We found Ari and Nabi in my office busily assembling furniture. Already, they had the work table finished and had set my new computer on top. Ari was putting together the stool my father made when I was a kid wanting to help in his woodshop, and Nabi was at work on the open storage shelves that would go against the side wall. Nabi, with his ruined face, turned when he heard us and gave us a smile and a cheerful wave.

The music streamed from a laptop set up on one end of the work table with auxiliary speakers attached. Jean-Paul asked Nabi, "What is the piece?"

"String Quartet in G minor, Opus Ten," the boy said. "My father loved Debussy, that's why I chose that piece to play for the holiday concert."

I looked at the computer monitor, four young musicians in formal concert dress, on a stage. There was a dark-haired young woman mostly hidden behind a cello, and Nabi in first chair. A mental lightbulb popped on; suddenly I had a soundtrack for Delisle's video. I said, "Good, your holiday concert is on You Tube."

He frowned. "No. The holiday concert is on the teacher's web-page, but it isn't on You Tube."

I looked at the video's address at the top of the screen and pointed. "Then this isn't the holiday concert?"

"That?" He put down his Allen wrench and came across the room looking very somber. "No. That is my father when he was a student at the conservatory in Edinburgh, where he studied violin. One of his classmates posted that old video as a tribute when he heard Papa died. I like to hear him play."

"It's beautiful," I said. "Can you download your holiday concert?" When he hesitated, I added, "On my desktop?"

With a shrug, after I unlocked my computer's access, he did. I restarted his father's performance and paused it. The piece began again, but this time it was Nabi sitting at first chair and Ophelia who was half-hidden behind the cello. There were some differences in tempo and phrasing, but here was the son, playing his father's favorite composer.

"Nabi," I said. "Will you please go put on a clean shirt with a collar, preferably not white, and comb your hair? Where's your grandmother?"

"Cleaning Ari's house."

Ari gave an embarrassed little smile and shrug. I guessed he didn't have much choice in the matter.

"I may need her later. But for now, Nabi, scoot. Meet you back here in ten minutes. Make it fifteen," I said. "Jean-Paul, I'm claiming first shower."

I was back downstairs, showered, dressed in jeans and a T-shirt, wet hair pulled into a ponytail, and putting a charged battery pack into a video camera when Nabi came in from the terrace looking freshly scrubbed and quite stylish, if one could see past the discolorations and lumps on his poor face. I took Dad's stool and a tripod into the salon and searched for a spot that had the right light and background to shoot a conversation with the kid. It took several tries before I found it. With Nabi in position on my dad's stool, camera screwed onto the tripod, I shot a few test frames, added a lamp on the floor behind him to give his image more separation from the wood-paneled wall behind him, and adjusted the camera angle. The room was tall and swallowed sound, so I hooked him up to a small digital voice recorder. The setup was primitive. The sound and the images would not be perfectly synchronized, but it would have to do. There wasn't time to get Guido over with more sophisticated equipment. Besides that, I had my partner busy getting equipment ready to film the assembly at the school; Detective Delisle said she would settle arrangements with the *directeur*.

"This won't take long, Nabi," I said when all was ready. "I'm going to ask you a few questions. Answer them as you wish but aim for brevity and incorporate the question into your answer. Don't worry about messing up because I'll edit out the goofs. Okay?"

"Okay," he said with a shrug. "But what are we doing?"

"Oh, sorry." I looked around from behind the camera. "We're making a little video to show at your school's assembly this afternoon."

He paled, seemed panicked. "Why?"

"Because Detective Delisle is afraid of what she'll say to your classmates so she's letting you do the talking."

"But what do I say?"

"Just answer my questions and try to relax. Don't think about your audience; teenagers, like lions, can smell fear, so stay calm."

He laughed. There was a nervous edge to it, but he laughed.

We started. First question: Tell us about your music and about your father's. From there, a few questions about his family and their tragic passage from Afghanistan, then school, his friendship with Ophelia, the last time he saw Ophelia, and his goals. A few times, I fed him lines to repeat, simplifications of answers he had given. With one small break for water, we finished filming in about thirty minutes. After that, Nabi was released with a warning not to wrinkle the shirt in case we needed to reshoot something. I sent Ari to the rue Jacob apartment to fetch Guido and his equipment

and deliver them to the school. Jean-Paul's assignment was to find
out what media projection equipment was available to us at the
school gym where the students would assemble. With everyone
off to handle their delegated tasks I holed up in my office, alone,
with the door closed. When Jean-Paul had an answer, he braved
opening the door enough to tell me that if we brought the video
on a USB memory stick or could download it from the cloud, the
school would be able to project it onto a giant screen. That made
my life a little easier.

Using the bits and pieces I had, I was able to cobble together what I thought was an adequate little video. At noon, I texted
Delisle with suggestions for follow-up remarks after the video
played. Ari was back after delivering Guido and equipment to the
school gym. I asked him, Jean-Paul, Nabi, and Diba to take a look
at the rough. There was still a little time, a very little time, to make
changes if anything bothered them. Each person had a suggestion
or two. Some were impossible, some were doable, some helped
make the video better. At one-thirty, when Jean-Paul and I headed
to the school, I had a USB memory stick in my pocket, backed up
on the cloud, for a video piece that I hoped would help Delisle get
her message across to Nabi's classmates.

Guido was all set up in the gym when we arrived, with one
camera aimed at the speaker's podium, and the second behind the
podium and off to the side, facing the empty bleachers. He would
man the podium camera and turn the other one over to me.

At two o'clock, the music of Nabi's father, Aarash Ahmad,
blasted over speakers in the *lycée*'s gymnasium, competing with
the racket students made as they thundered into seats on the
metal bleachers. The tribute video of the father, captured playing in a string quartet nearly twenty years earlier filled the pair of
giant screens that dropped from the ceiling. The caption running
under the image, not perfectly centered, I admit, read EDINBURGH
ROYAL CONSERVATORY OF THE ARTS. I had allotted twelve minutes
of concert time for the students to settle into their seats before the
gym lights dimmed and a headshot of Aarash Ahmad that I found
online appeared superimposed over the quartet on stage, his name

captioned, and the date twenty years earlier. Nabi, in voiceover, said, "The greatest gift my father gave me was his love for music. He began teaching me violin when I was three."

The father's image faded into a recent headshot of Nabi taken for his conservatory applications, the father's name fading as the son's emerged. The quartet in the background now, and the music, came from the video of the school's holiday concert that Nabi downloaded for me from the orchestra teacher's homepage. The resemblance of the son to the father, both of them sitting in first chair, was striking. And so was their music. When the students recognized their classmates on the screen, and saw Nabi, there was a low murmuring throughout the huge room. The Debussy faded, Nabi said. "I made a solemn promise to my father that I would never abandon my violin study."

The music remained in the background, the concert stage faded and Nabi, sitting on a stool that morning in Jean-Paul's salon, daylight showing off his massive shiner in all its colorful glory, filled the screen. There was an audible gasp. The camera angle shifted slightly, and Nabi talked about his family being targeted by the Taliban because his father had studied in Europe and because he was a teacher, and that was why they fled. He did not describe the nightmare crossing of the Mediterranean, except to say that their boat went down and all of his family, mother, father, two sisters, and a brother, were lost. Now there were only Nabi, his grandmother, and memories.

We went back to the topic of music, because it was through the orchestra that Nabi met Ophelia, his protector. I could be heard asking, "Did you need a protector at school?" He laughed softly and framed his face with his palms, and said, "You see what happened when she was not here one day.

"Ophelia is so strong. She doesn't want to be like everyone else," he said as the scene switched to the CCTV tape from the train station Friday night. Nabi and Ophelia walked into frame. "She is my only friend here. I miss her. I am worried about her."

Cut to Ophelia walking alone down the street behind the train station with her cello. Suddenly, the muted grays of the CCTV night shot were replaced with the bright, if a bit jerky, video I shot that morning of the bearded man who found the cello being pinned down on a meadow in the *haras*; the cello was in the frame. Nabi said, "Where can Ophelia be?"

The image faded to black, music crescendoed over the low murmur that filled the room when the last clip appeared, their whispered conversations drowning out the last plaintive strains of the piece. The room became bright again to reveal Detective Delisle standing at the podium looking freshly starched and thoroughly formidable as she gave the student body a hard-eyed looking over.

"I am Detective Delisle of the municipal police," she said, voice echoing around the cavernous space, eyes constantly scanning the kids as if she were looking for criminals among them; she reminded me of the nuns at my high school. "We need to talk about harassment."

While she gave the students the legal definition of what constitutes harassment, with my video camera I panned their faces, filming their reactions. Though all of their electronic devices were banned during the assembly, some of the kids kept themselves so busy with God knows what that they might as well have been passengers on a bus and not present in that huge room at all. Some listened with great interest, some with skeptical or perhaps hostile frowns, a few wiped away tears. Some just seemed to have zoned out. An interesting mix.

Delisle asked for questions. The first, no surprise, was about what they had seen in that last bit of video: "Did you find Ophelia in the *haras*?"

"Whore," a single voice from somewhere in the crowd. Delisle homed in on the section the word came from, pointing a finger at a clutch of boys, one of them now blushing furiously. I waited to see what would happen. She warned us that she would go off on a kid if he "threw shade" at her.

Face like stone, that finger pointing directly at a red-faced boy, she said, "You. Come."

"Me?" He pointed at himself, quaking more than a little, feigning innocence.

"You have something to say," she said, open palm out, flicking her fingers for him to come. "Let's hear it."

"Down there?"

All she did was flick her fingers once more and the kid, though reluctant, came forward, but he stopped several yards to the side of the podium. With the crook of one finger, she impelled him to the podium next to her.

Looking at him, she said, "Up there surrounded by all your friends you made a comment about a classmate. It was easy to make when you had your buddies to shield you. But here you are, out where everyone can see you. Will you repeat what you said so we can all hear?"

"Uh, no."

"Why not?"

"Uh, it was rude?"

I was twenty feet behind them, and off to the side. When the boy looked at Delisle he was full face to me, and she was in profile. I had seen never anyone blush as furiously without passing right out. I waited for him to fall over.

Looking him in the eye, she said, "Tell us what a bully is."

"Uh."

She waited for more before repeating, "Uh?"

"Uh, it's someone who picks on someone else. Someone weaker."

"*Tsk, tsk, tsk.*" She shook her head and made eye contact again with the kids in the bleachers. "Someone weaker. An easy target then? Someone who can't defend himself, or herself?"

"I guess."

"Like a person who isn't in the room when you say something rude about her?"

"No. I was just–"

She waited. Finally, he said, "I was just being a smart ass. I'm sorry."

"Don't apologize to me. Apologize to your classmate. And pray she hasn't come to harm before you get the chance. Now, go take your seat and sin no more."

The room was as silent as a classroom ten minutes after the last bell of the day. Delisle looked at the kids and let them squirm for a moment before speaking again. With a gesture over her shoulder toward the blank screen behind her, she said, "You saw what was done to your classmate, Ahmad Nabi. Did you know it took three football players and one girl to inflict that damage? Broke some bones, made him piss blood. Four kids, against one. To make certain that none of you still have the idea that that sort of torture is okay, we need to have a serious discussion about bullying. Your new *directeur*, Madame Jensen, tells me that she intends to make the elimination of campus harassment one of her primary missions. I promise that if any of you give her problems, she has my number on speed dial. Now, I'll turn the podium over to Madame Jensen."

Delisle came over and stood beside me, arms folded over her chest. With a nod at the camera, in a low voice, she asked, "Can they hear me now?"

"No. The only microphone is on the podium."

"Thanks for doing that video for me. It isn't what I expected, but it was okay."

"Hardly my best work, but it isn't as if I had a lot of time to make it pretty."

She laughed, a soft chuckle deep in her chest. "I owe you. That's twice, now."

"Don't think I won't call in the debt," I said.

"I'm sure you will."

I noticed her watching Guido. After a while, she leaned in and asked, "Your guy over there with the camera, he doesn't wear a ring."

"He isn't married."

"Seeing someone?"

"Not that I'm aware. He's only been in Paris since Friday, so he hasn't had much time."

"He isn't–" She bobbed her head from side to side, one shoulder up, asking a question.

"Not gay."

She sneaked a look at him, smiled in appreciation, or perhaps anticipation, caught me catching this assessment, and shrugged before turning her attention back to whatever the *directeur* was saying.

Jensen's remarks were brief. She expanded on Delisle's remarks and announced that the school was committed to addressing and eradicating harassment in any form. There was a new sheriff in town, in other words, and some things were going to be different under her administration. During their first period in the morning there would be workshops on the subject led by experts from the Ministry of Education. Absentees would be heavily punished. A pamphlet was distributed and homework on the subject was assigned. Before she dismissed the fidgety mob in the bleachers, she reminded them that a hotline had been set up for tips about Ophelia Fouchet. After that, she released them back out into the daylight.

While I broke down my camera setup, Delisle found some excuse to go over and chat up Guido. When the *directeur* asked her for a word and the two of them walked out, I draped a coil of extension cords over a shoulder, grabbed up the camera and tripod, and took it all over to Guido.

"How'd it go?" I asked him.

"Depends on which thing you're asking about," he said, taking the camera from me and fitting it into its case. "If you mean your little video, for a quick hack job it was pretty good, but hardly ready for prime time."

"From you, I'll take pretty good for a hack job as compliment enough," I said, shucking the cords onto his pile. "I want to get a look at the footage we shot today to see if any of it is usable for our piece on bullying, assuming we decide to do one. If we can get the *directeur* to buy in, I want to film the efforts of this campus to stop harassment and use it as counterpoint to the ugly shit we're going to have to wade through."

"Think she'll go along?"

"We'll see," I said. "Let's go back to, How'd it go?"

"How did what go?"

"Detective Delisle has her eye on you."

He smiled almost shyly. "I think we have a date. Her English is a whole lot better than my French, but it's still not so good. We're meeting for drinks later."

"Tread gently, my friend," I said, handing him the tripod. "She packs heat."

He laughed.

I looked around for Jean-Paul. During the assembly I'd lost track of him. He was next to Guido when the video started, but I didn't remember seeing him after the lights came back up afterward. I texted him and asked where he'd gotten to. The answer was Monsieur Gold's classroom, along with directions so I could find my way to Ophelia's calculus teacher's domain. I told him I'd be there after I helped Guido get all the gear to the car. I left it to Guido to stow the equipment—he can be very fussy about what goes where—and went into the building.

Nabi told us that sometimes Ophelia would say she needed help with calculus as an excuse to go speak with her teacher. Until I met her teacher, Joel Gold, I assumed she had a crush on him. I was wrong. Monsieur Gold was small, old, and the little hair he had was wiry gray tufts over his ears. Thick glasses made him look owlish. He had a big voice as teachers so often do, and must, but when he spoke to Jean-Paul and me he lowered the volume and pulled three chairs into an intimate circle.

"Ah, Ophelia," he said, shaking his head. "I am so very concerned that something has happened to her."

"Did she confide in you?" I asked.

"Bits here and there," he said, straightening his bow tie. "Enough that I knew she was troubled and sometimes needed a neutral place to wait until the— What shall I call it? The afternoon rush, I suppose. At any rate, until the other students were gone and the coast was clear so that she could get home without being bothered."

"Did she tell you who bothered her?"

"Not in so many words. When I teased her about suddenly appearing all in black like a vampiress she said that she couldn't bear looking like a princess anymore because she felt dark inside. I suggested that we go speak with a counselor, and she laughed me off. She told me not to worry, she said she only hoped to scare away some big jerk."

"Do you know who the jerk was?"

"I can think of three or four who seemed to hover around her. But one specifically? No."

I said, "Did Louis, Maxime, or Octave hover?"

He hesitated before he said, "These are all children, madame. They may have the bodies of adults, but in here—" He tapped his head. "They are *naïfs*. Babies. On Tuesday they may explode over one thing, and on Wednesday another. I have learned over the years that what they say in the heat of a momentary drama needs to be tempered over time before we can truly understand their issues. If the police were to ask me these questions, I might be more inclined to speculate. But to tell you, a lay person, what I only suspect but don't know would be tantamount to gossip, don't you agree?"

"Of course," I said, silently damning his scruples. "Are you aware that Ophelia's friend, Ahmad Nabi, was badly beaten yesterday?"

"Sadly, yes," he said, shaking his head. "And I know by whom. *Directeur* Jensen called a staff meeting this morning to discuss what happened and to tell us which students will not return for the remainder of the school term. We are all very upset, of course, but far more so for Nabi than the others."

"Do you know Nabi?"

"Yes. And I understand that Monsieur Bernard does as well. Am I correct?"

"Not until a couple of days ago. This came up in the meeting?" Jean-Paul asked.

"No, no," Gold said. "From time to time I have spoken with Doctor Massarani about Nabi's assignments; the boy is in my introductory algebra class. Once, I dropped off some of the boy's schoolwork at your home so that Doctor Massarani could review it with Nabi; I am aware who you are by reputation, Monsieur. The doctor and I had such a nice conversation that I stayed for the tutoring session when Nabi arrived. Doctor Massarani has helped the boy immeasurably. Though the boy is bright, very bright, and he has an affinity for numbers, he was in need of serious remediation when he arrived. By end of term, he should be caught up to grade level. Not a surprise, really. Musicians are frequently also gifted in math. Something about the way the brain is wired."

"Do you play an instrument, Monsieur?" Jean-Paul asked the mathematician.

"I do." Gold's face brightened. "Saxophone. Hot jazz. Sometimes after school I jam with the music teacher, the *directeur*–the former *directeur*, that is–and the soccer coach. From time to time Nabi and some other kids in orchestra join in. Nabi loves jazz, and lordy can that kid play! We riffed on *Rhapsody in Blue* last week. Nabi took that old standard to places Gershwin could never have imagined, though he would have recognized his framework. Made my hair, what little I have anyway, stand on end. Nabi, that quiet little kid, has a soul on fire."

He played air sax as he remembered, bobbing in rhythm to music that lived on in his head long after the notes of the jam session had dissipated into the ether. I could see why kids would be drawn to this unassuming-looking little man. With a long sigh, he was back within the walls of his classroom.

"Did Ophelia ever join in?" I asked.

"*Bien sûr*. Of course, yes. The cello makes a fair stand-in for the bass when the bass player has a tennis meet." Suddenly, the joy of remembering that improv session was gone. He gazed out the window behind me, as if hoping to see something–someone?–that wasn't there. "Ophelia, Ophelia, where have you gone?"

"That is the question," I said. "Did you know that her cello was found this morning?"

"Yes. Monsieur Bernard told me when we were waiting for you. I was worried for her before, but now I am frightened. Please, if you learn anything, I would like to be told."

Jean-Paul put a hand on Gold's shoulder, looked him in the eye, and said, "*Bien sûr, Monsieur.*"

We got up to leave, but I quickly sat back down. "Monsieur Gold, what happened to the former *directeur*?"

"At the risk of sharing gossip," he said, "it's my understanding that the ministry received a letter accusing him of carrying on an inappropriate relationship, so he was reassigned to a desk at headquarters until the issue is resolved."

"Any truth to the accusation?" I asked.

He raised his palms. "*Qui sait?* Accusations are easy to make and sometimes difficult to disprove. Same answer for your next question, and probably the next; I simply don't know."

"I don't like coincidences," I said. "I find it curious that both he and Ophelia disappeared on the same day."

He chuckled. "I doubt Samuel Lambert has disappeared from anywhere other than this campus. If he is not at a desk in the ministry, you will likely find him at home tending his roses; he has a passion for gardening even greater than his love for jazz."

"Thank you for your time, Monsieur Gold," Jean-Paul said, extending his hand. I followed his lead and said good-bye. By then, school had already been out for an hour, so though I had hoped to speak with the music teacher, he was gone for the day.

We found Guido waiting in the faculty parking lot. Leaning against the car beside him was our fair detective, Fleur Delisle. She straightened when she saw us.

"I want to thank you," she said, extending her hand to me. "I could not have gotten the point across to the students nearly so well as a few pictures did. The kids, I think, paid attention. At least some did."

"They seemed to," I said. "They certainly sat right up when the lights came on again and they saw you glaring at them."

"I wasn't glaring at them," she said with a frown.

"Guido got it all on video if you want to see for yourself."

She shot him an appreciative glance. "Maybe I'll do just that. Should I bring a bottle of wine?"

I translated what she said for Guido. He grinned, his face coloring a bit. He said, "Tell her she doesn't need to bring anything. I know where to find the key to an entire wine cellar."

"Just keep your hands off my Bordeaux," Jean-Paul said with a laugh.

Delisle understood enough of that to laugh with him.

It was decided that Delisle would drive Guido and the film equipment back to Paris—the least she could do, she said, to thank us—but first, Jean-Paul and I wanted to speak with him about, maybe, making independent films again. We had all missed lunch and the apple and chunk of cheese I'd had in lieu of breakfast were a faint memory. It was after two and before six, so restaurants in town were no longer serving lunch and not yet serving dinner. The options were to go home and make something or to get a *croque-monsieur*, a sort of open-faced grilled cheese sandwich, at the local *café tabac*. The latter appealed to Guido, so we headed to an agreed-upon café in two cars, with Delisle and Guido in the lead. We waved them to go ahead because Jean-Paul wanted to call home to check on things. Ari assured him that all was quiet. Diba, looking for ways to be useful, had finished cleaning the guest house and had moved on to the main house. Ari, apparently also concerned about being a burden, told Jean-Paul that it was enough that we had taken in Diba and Nabi, but he could not expect us to also feed them until other housing was arranged, a problem Ari was working on. So, in the meantime, Diba would be preparing their meals in Ari's little kitchen; she had already gone grocery shopping. Jean-Paul assured him that we did not feel burdened, but when he put his phone away and reported to me, he seemed relieved that our houseguests did not intend to become long-term residents.

We pulled out of the school lot and headed toward the café. I said, "Do you think Delisle is moving on Guido awfully fast?"

"Shamelessly so." I checked to see if he was kidding. He was. Maybe. "Guido is a big boy, Maggie, and this isn't his first pony ride."

"That's the problem. I've seen him fall into and out of affairs too many times over the years not to be wary. I don't know that I have the energy for another go around."

"Are you worried that if things go badly with our detective he'll set off an international scandal?"

"No," I said. "Just a local one. But isn't that enough?"

We caught up to Delisle and Guido at the first traffic signal. Just as the light turned, Delisle put her foot on the gas of that little blue car and with gumballs flashing and her claxon siren piercing the air she shot across the intersection. I was looking for a ball of fire and black smoke when a text from Guide beeped: "She says follow."

I relayed the message to Jean-Paul as I texted back, "What's up?"

"Dunno. Only word I understood was cadaver. What's 'aytan'?"

Cadaver is one of those words that sounds the same in both French and English, but "aytan" rang no bells. I spelled that word for Jean-Paul as we made a sharp turn onto boulevard de la République. He said, "Pronounce it for me." When I did, he said, "*Étang*. It means pond. Looks like we're headed for a pond in the *haras*."

My stomach knotted. I said, "Cadaver and pond, not a good combination, is it?"

He covered my hand with his. "Not good at all."

] Seven

TRAFFIC MOVED OUT OF OUR WAY as we sped down boulevard de la République following the flashing lights of Delisle's car. Two more blue-and-whites, lights and sirens, joined the queue as we crossed an intersection against the signal. Onlookers surged out of houses and shops sitting snug against the road to watch the parade go by. Behind the narrow strip of buildings there was yet another expanse of dense green woods. A cross street, no more than a narrow gap in the greenery, opened on the right. Delisle saw the turn late but took it, tires squealing. Jean-Paul followed and so did our tail. We passed through a tunnel of tall iron fences and hedges that ran along side yards, into the woods, and suddenly out onto a broad, flat meadow. To the right, well-groomed soccer pitches. To the left two ponds, one larger, one smaller, and both rank with green algae. At first, that's what I smelled, the particular stench of stagnant water on a warm day. And then I opened the car door and knew what we would find.

There were two blue-and-whites already parked on the grass near the smaller pond, trunks open as uniformed officers pulled out stakes and tarps to erect a barrier, police protocol to screen a crime scene from prying eyes. And there were plenty of prying eyes. One of the cars in our train stopped near the edge of the meadow to keep the rapidly growing number of onlookers from venturing near.

Delisle's car had barely stopped before she was out and fast-walking across the grass toward the pond. Guido was out just as quickly, but instead of following her he went around to her trunk and began pulling out video cameras and extra battery packs. We pulled in close beside them, with the last police car coming in on our left flank.

"What happened?" I asked Guido as I closed the car door behind me.

"Here." He handed me a little JVC-4K, a high-definition video camera that, with the mic and recorder attached weighed maybe three pounds. This one was new, but I'd used its older brothers often enough. As he screwed down the recorder on his own camera, he glanced up at Jean-Paul. "At some point we have to load the rest of this gear into your car. Fleur doubts she'll be able to take me home later."

"I'll take care of it. You two go ahead." Jean-Paul popped his trunk. "Sorry about your plans, my friend."

And it was too bad, though I had a feeling that Guido and the fair detective would figure things out.

Guido bumped my shoulder. "Let's go."

We crossed the grass but as we approached the tarp screen a uniformed officer looked up from stringing caution tape and yelled for us to stop. Delisle heard him and stepped out from behind; she had already pulled on Latex gloves and stepped into a white crime-scene jumpsuit; she looked like a kid's Halloween version of a spaceman, complete with white booties.

"They're with me," she said to the officer and waved us over. She thrust plastic-wrapped jumpsuits into our hands and as we pulled them on over our clothes she gave us instructions, a similar list of Don'ts that had been delivered to us over the years by investigators at any number of crime scenes. Generally, we were to stay out from underfoot and touch nothing. I wasn't at all sure why she allowed us, or maybe wanted us to be there with cameras, but I was hardly going to ask questions. Instead, as a courtesy I texted Diane

Duval at the studio to let her know, in brief, where we were and why; Zed had told me the day before that in future Diane should be my first contact, a chain-of-command issue. I left it to her to decide whether to alert the news division that there was a report of a cadaver in a pond.

In truth, stopping to send a text was a stall before following Delisle behind the screen. If, indeed, there was a body, I was afraid that it might be our missing girl and I didn't want to see her as I imagined she would look after six days in the water. I was still out-side when a bright blue van pulled up. Out came three men and a collection of large duffels and diving gear. I turned on the cam-era and filmed their progress across the lawn then fell in behind them as they joined their comrades behind the screen. Jean-Paul, I noticed, stayed well back, watching from the side, away from cameras.

Behind the screen, out of the wind, the stench of stagnant water was joined by even stronger notes of something heavy and sweet and horrible and all too familiar; something or somebody was very dead.

While Guido walked around the side of the pond looking for a good shot of the dark and bloated hump rising through the bright green blanket of algae covering the pond, I kept my camera trained on the activity of the divers. Geared up, with me close behind, two of the divers padded in rubber boots to the edge of the water and waded in. I stood on the muddy shore and filmed as they used their hands to push aside green scum, cutting a path that quickly closed behind them. With the camera as a sort of shield between me and what they were doing, I watched them reach the black-clothed mass. Before they could float the body to shore, one of the divers took out a knife, grabbed something under the water, and sliced it, freeing what was now obviously a corpse from a snag or tether so they could retrieve it.

"When they bring it in, be sure to shoot the face." I hadn't noticed Delisle walk up beside me. As she spread a heavy green plastic body bag on the ground she said, "It's important to catch a floater's features right away before the tissues begin to drain and desiccate and deteriorate. On a warm day like this it doesn't take long for the process to begin."

"Okay," I said, but already I was fighting the urge to retch. Thank God we hadn't stopped to eat. Normally I'm okay, but not when a kid might be involved. I raised my forearm to my nose and took a deep breath through the fabric of my sleeve to steady myself. Didn't help. The stench of putrefying flesh preceded the progress of the cadaver toward shore. For a distraction, I asked Delisle, "Who found it?"

"Neighborhood dog." She raised her arm and did the same thing I had, hoping for a clean breath. "*Merde.* Worse than dead fish, yes?"

"Definitely."

"Sorry to ask you to film this but our science crew can't get here for maybe another hour, and that is too long to wait; we'll lose daylight before they arrive."

Guido was about ten yards to my left, standing on the bank beside the third diver and a cart of scuba tanks, taping the retrieval of the cadaver from the side. Camera on his shoulder, Guido began to move along the waterline toward me, following the progress of the men in the water until he walked into my frame. Immediately, he faded back, lowered his camera and came around to where Delisle and I stood. He pulled a little plastic jar of mentholated balm out of his pocket and handed it to me. I passed him my camera, still trained on the cadaver, so I could slather the stuff over my upper lip, a trick I learned the first time I visited a morgue.

"Where did that come from?" I asked, passing the little jar to Delisle.

"The diver over there gave it to me," he said, handing me the second camera, the heavier one. "He has a whole box of them. Basic body-retrieval equipment."

Delisle rubbed the strong-smelling goo under her nose and passed it back to me. I said, "Keep it. You may need it again one day."

Moving a corpse through water doesn't take a lot of strength.

Lifting water-logged dead weight and manhandling it onto shore through foot-sucking mud, however, does. Both divers were panting by the time they had their sodden bundle laid out on the rubber mat at our feet.

I tapped Guido's shoulder to get his attention. "Delisle wants a close-up on the face."

"Looks like fish already got at it," Delisle said. "People dump their aquariums in the pond, so who knows what's out there. Looks like the work of crabs to me. Crabs'll make quick work of flesh."

She stepped forward for a closer look as Guido thrust the running camera back into my hand, doubled over and heaved up his last meal. Hoping I wouldn't follow suit, I took the camera and trained the lens on the face, or what was left of it.

"Throat was cut," Delisle said, putting a gloved finger against a flap of the long, bloodless gash. "Sharp blade, one clean cut."

The poor soul laid out on a bag atop the mud at my feet looked like any of the men I had seen that morning emerging from the woods after sleeping rough the night before. He was fairly tall, definitely underfed and unkempt. Somewhere, he must have a family that would grieve for him. My only feeling, other than revulsion at the sight and smell of him, was relief that this bloated cadaver was not a certain five-foot-two-inch, hundred-and-two- or four-pound fifteen-year-old Goth-attired girl.

] [

THE SATELLITE NEWS VAN from our home network pulled in beside the police cars strung along the lawn. When she saw it, Delisle gave me an accusatory side-eye. I had told her earlier that I called my producer and told her what was happening, but the detective had shrugged it off. Of course, she was busy at the time waiting for a cadaver to be brought to shore. And now here they were.

"*Merde*," she said. "I'm detective in charge, so it's up to me to talk to them. I hate talking to them. Any tips, TV girl?"

"Always pretend you know what you're doing," I said, looking her over. "And ditch the crime scene chic."

Delisle's white jumpsuit was black with pond mud from booties to knees. She discarded the Latex gloves, pulled off the booties, stepped out of the jumpsuit, and reached up to finger-comb stray hair into the bun at the back of her head. While she tucked in her shirt and put on her blazer, I grabbed a towel from the pile of diving gear and handed it to her to wipe away the shiny smear of menthol balm around her nose. When there was nothing more she could fuss over she held up her palms and shrugged.

"You'll do," I said, handing her a clipboard someone had left on a pile of jackets. "Just remember to look directly at the red light atop the camera when it's running. Plant your feet, keep your shoulders back, chin up, don't fidget, and if you need time to think, look down at the clipboard as if it tells you something other than the dive team's work rotation schedule."

She chuckled. "Anything else, my guru?"

"Yes. It doesn't matter what you're asked," I said. "Just give the answers you want to give, and don't volunteer anything."

"Like politicians, yes?"

"Exactly." I glanced over the crowd drawn by the news van. "Who will tell his family?"

"I will," she said. "If we can find a family when the morgue identifies him, if they can identify him. I like that conversation even less than talking to the press. But, here I go. Wish me luck."

"*Merde*," I said, the French equivalent of "break a leg."

The news crew, a cameraman, a soundman, and the generically attractive on-camera female talent in full television makeup, was still getting set up when Delisle, looking as crisp as she could under the circumstance, headed off across the grass to face them.

Jean-Paul was standing over by the cars, chatting with one of the uniformed policemen when Guido appeared from behind the screen, a camera dangling from each hand.

"Any reason to hang around?" he asked.

"No." I took one of the cameras from him and tried to keep up as he strode across the grass. His color had returned, but I asked, "You okay?"

"Embarrassed, but yeah. That wasn't our first floater, Mags. They don't get prettier, do they?"

"No," I said, stomach suddenly roiling just thinking about it. "I'll be happy if it's our last. How long do you think he was in the water?"

He shrugged. "More than a couple of days, less than a month. If *corde* means rope and my French tutor wasn't lying when he said *pierre* means stone, I think someone intended for him to stay on the bottom."

"Shallow water, warm days, wouldn't take long for decomposition gasses to pop a fully-clothed, skinny guy to the surface," I said. "Less than a week, anyway. Did you notice, his throat was cut?"

"Yeah. That's when I lost it. Something was living up inside there."

"Fishies having a dinner party," I said, taking a deep breath and trying to think of anything other than the image of creatures crawling out through the white, bloodless edges of the open gash across the man's neck before the divers zipped him into the bag, ready for the morgue's meat wagon to take away.

Guido said, "I saw your reaction, Mags. Did you recognize him?"

"No. I only know who he wasn't," I said.

Guido and I were about halfway to the cars when the news hen spotted Jean-Paul and made a beeline toward him. She greeted him like an old friend, offering her cheeks for *les bises*. I didn't want to interrupt their chat, but Guido and I might need to work with her or her crew at some time, so I forged ahead, intent on introducing the two of us. We were maybe ten feet away when she tapped her ear and excused herself. I knew the gesture: through an earpiece, the cameraman had summoned her. Jean-Paul walked with her until their trajectory intersected ours. She looked up suddenly, saw me, did a double take, then held out a hand, "You're—" But got no further.

"Chloe, have you met Maggie MacGowen?" Jean-Paul said. "Maggie, this is Chloe Caron, a colleague of yours."

"Hello, Chloe," I said, taking the offered hand. "This is Guido Patrini, my work partner."

"Maggie," she said, giving Guido a token nod. "Delighted to meet you. I recognize you from the *Jimmy* show. We all watched you, of course, our new girl. We wondered if Jimmy would say something that was so absolutely offensive that you'd run right back to America."

"I can't imagine what that something could be, but no, he behaved himself."

"Next time," she said, wagging a finger. "He might be better prepared."

"If there is a next time, I'll be better prepared, as well," I said. "It is lovely to meet you, Chloe, but I think the detective is waiting and the light is fading."

"Of course," she said. "Give me a call. I'm in the studio directory. We'll sneak away for a coffee, yes?"

"Yes," I said.

Pointing at Jean-Paul, she said, "And bring him."

Guido watched her go. When she was out of earshot, he addressed her back: "Nice meeting you, too."

"Don't worry, son," I said, patting his arm. "You still have your magic. Delisle didn't seem to mind that you nearly barfed on her shoes."

"If the face of that guy didn't faze her, why would a little recycled breakfast?"

Jean-Paul bobbed his head, considering the question. "Speaking of food, before we adjourn to the local, let's take a little walk on the wild side."

"Metaphoric walk, or an actual walk?" I asked.

"A short walk."

Guido glanced at the sky. "It's getting dark soon."

"Won't take long," Jean-Paul said. "Bring your camera."

We started across the meadow, past the soccer fields and into the woods beyond. There was no path, so we ducked branches and pushed our way through the undergrowth until, after maybe twenty yards, we came out onto a familiar meadow. I looked around to

catch my bearings. The *haras* was a huge, meandering, open park-
land. Across the way were the tennis courts, the kiddie playground,
and the curved walkway that led to the foot path that ran behind
Jean-Paul's house. To our right, remnants of police tape snagged
on a branch after police left the scene that morning waved in the
light evening breeze. Following Delisle, we had driven around a
long neck of the park to get to the pond, but we were never far as
the crow flies from where we began that morning.

I caught Guido's attention and pointed toward the tape. "That's
where Ophelia's backpack and cello case were found."

His response was to turn on a camera and zoom in on the flag
of tape. "Light's gone. I'll come back tomorrow."

Jean-Paul gripped my elbow. "You see?"

"My imagination is in overdrive," I said. "I can come up with
half a dozen scenarios about what happened in this strip of woods
sometime after nine-fifty Friday night. I don't like any of them."

"No," he said. "There isn't much to like about any of this."

"His throat was cut," I said. "Where's Nabi's knife?"

"Wrapped in a kitchen towel in the safe in my office floor. I
opened it, Maggie. That knife has never been used. The blade still
has protective plastic on it."

"I just wondered," I said. Nabi told us that Ophelia gave him
the knife, and that she carried one like it. Could she have used
her knife to slit a tall man's throat, weight him with stones, and
drag him into a pond? Not likely. Not bloody likely, unless she
wasn't alone.

We made our way back through the strip of woods to the cars.
On the other side, as we picked twigs and leaves from each other,
Jean-Paul suggested we go find that meal we were headed for when
Delisle was called to the scene at the pond. Guido declined the
invitation. He and Delisle had made plans for later after all, so he
wanted to get back to rue Jacob to get ready, whatever that might
entail. We said good-bye to our detective and the three of us headed out in Jean-Paul's car. We dropped Guido at the train station,
promising to get the camera gear to rue Jacob in the morning
before our scheduled meeting with Diane Duval at the studio.

"Dinner at the bistro?" Jean-Paul said to me as we drove out of the lot.

"Later, if you don't mind," I said, rubbing a rash that suddenly popped out on the back of my hand. What had I brushed against in the woods? "There's someone I want to talk to. Know anyone at the Ministry of Education?"

"Do you feel like sharing why you want to speak with this person?"

"Because I don't trust coincidence."

] Eight

WE FOUND SAMUEL LAMBERT, the secondary school's furloughed *directeur*, in front of his tidy little cottage in Villepreux, an outer Paris suburb, washing garden tools under a hose. Joel Gold, the math teacher, told us the man had a passion for gardening. The sun was long gone but there was enough light from the street that, standing on the sidewalk and peering over the gate in his iron rail fence, we could see the meticulously maintained flower beds and graveled walkways that filled his long front yard. I breathed in the heady perfume of his roses, a lovely antidote to the sticky stench of death that seemed to have settled deep in my lungs.

"Monsieur Lambert?" I said to get his attention.

He turned off his hose and looked over to see who was there. "*Oui?*"

"May we speak with you?"

Lambert hesitated, studying us, but in the end he walked closer. He was tall and thin, with the sun-browned skin and rangy build of a longtime outdoorsman. He was also surprisingly young, mid-thirties maybe. I always thought of school principals as wizened old relics, but he certainly was not. Indeed, he gave off a sort of wiry energy.

"What can I do for you?"

"May we speak to you about Ophelia Fouchet?"

"Ophelia?" He drew back, wary, garden fork gripped in his hand. "What have you heard?"

"About where she might be?" I said. "Nothing. It's been six days now."

"*Merde.*" He frowned as he thought that over. "I hoped, I strongly hoped, she was back. But what brings you to my door?"

I said, "Monsieur Lambert, were you close to Ophelia?"

"Close to her?" His expression hardened. "My relationship with Mademoiselle Fouchet concerns you how? You are family, police investigator, education ministry official?"

"None of the above," I said. "My name is Maggie MacGowen and this is Jean-Paul Bernard. I'm a filmmaker. I'm exploring the idea of doing a piece about bullying. Actually, about harassment generally. One of your charges, Ahmad Nabi, was badly beaten yesterday because Ophelia was not around to protect him. Monsieur Gold told us that sometimes Nabi and Ophelia joined your faculty jam sessions. I thought that perhaps the kids confided in you."

"If they had, and I then spoke to you about it, that would be a breach of their confidence, would it not?"

"Yes. Unless they told you about something that might put them in peril or might rescue them from peril. Or help locate the missing girl."

"Locate the missing girl, yes," he said, bristling, I thought. He set down the garden fork and walked right up to the gate. "I know absolutely nothing, not one thing, about where young Ophelia might have gone this time, but if I did I would move heaven and earth to persuade her to come back. However, if you want to talk about bullying, I will be only too happy to have that discussion. There's bullying of the sort that got Ahmad Nabi a thumping. And there's bullying of the sort that can ruin a man's career–hell, ruin his life–with nothing more than an accusation on an anonymous note. And what can he do to redeem himself? Nothing. Everything he says in his defense only digs him in deeper in the public eye."

"That's what happened to you?" I asked.

"Happened? Is happening still," he said with heat. "I am all for this Out the Pig movement. It's way past time that we paid attention to girls and women when they say they have been abused or harassed by some idiot so unsure of his manhood that he needs to keep women down or believes that females only exist for males to toy with. But we have reached a point where, as a society, we are so eager to punish abusive bastards that we don't bother to examine the veracity or motives of the accuser. In our zeal we have opened a new Reign of Terror. At the first word of accusation, it's off with their heads! Or off with their dicks, as it were. And how do we, the innocent victims, defend ourselves during this public bloodbath?"

"Monsieur," Jean-Paul said in a quiet voice.

"I have been ruined," Lambert fumed, volume rising. "And I don't even know by whom."

"Monsieur," Jean-Paul said in the same quiet voice. "Have you eaten dinner yet?"

"What?" Fully flummoxed by the question, Lambert leaned toward Jean-Paul as if he hadn't quite heard and might find the words hovering in the air. "Eaten? Did you say eaten?"

"Yes. Have you eaten dinner yet?"

"I– No. Why?"

"There's a very good little bistro just down the road that serves a more than decent *pot au feu* on Thursdays. We missed lunch and we've had a very upsetting afternoon. I wonder if you'll join us for a meal."

"Now?"

"*Bien sûr*, yes, now. I'm starving, and I know that Maggie is interested to hear what you have to say. Am I right, Maggie?"

"*Bien sûr*," I said. "Yes to both starvation and conversation."

"Well." He looked at his hands, saw they were sufficiently clean, tucked in his button-down shirt, and said, "*Allons-y*, let's go. If I'm thinking of the same bistro, they serve a very nice house Burgundy with the Thursday special. It's close, we can walk."

And we did. The bistro was a very old and very traditional neighborhood eatery. Customers walked in and chose their own seats at one of the two long tables that ran the length of the room, sitting down next to friends and strangers alike. Maybe not the best environment for a private conversation, but certainly a good place to pull in a variety of opinions on any subject you might bring up. There were two choices on the menu board outside the door, *pot au feu*–beef stew–or poached white fish. On the table there were stacks of squat glasses, carafes of red and white wine and tap water for diners to pour as desired. We sat, small plates of cold, thinly sliced pickled fish and pickled root vegetables, along with a basket of fresh bread and sweet butter, were placed in front of us, and we all chose the beef stew. What could be more French than this?

I gave Jean-Paul's hand a squeeze and smiled. I said, "Lovely."

"*C'est ça*," he said, returning the squeeze; that it is.

I was floundering for a way to begin this conversation, a bit concerned about setting off Lambert's temper and starting a general brouhaha in the crowded restaurant over the issue of harassment, thereby not ferreting out of him the specific information I wanted. But he played the opening gambit first.

"So, Madame MacGowen, you make films?"

"Please call me Maggie, and yes I do." I gave him a short summary of how my work had landed me in France. He was intelligent, engaging, and he was certainly savoring his food and wine.

The proprietress, a woman maybe in her sixties, white apron over her flowered dress, carrying a stew tureen and a stack of thick crockery bowls on a tray worked her way between the long tables, greeting customers, exchanging little jokes and comments until she came to a stop beside Sam Lambert. She unloaded her tray and began ladling thick stew into bowls, talking the entire time.

"Monsieur Lambert, here you are," she said, looking at him as she placed a steaming bowl in front of me. "And you have brought my old friend Monsieur Bernard. How are you, Monsieur?" she asked, taking up a second bowl. "It has been too long. How is that handsome boy of yours?"

"Dom is fine," Jean-Paul said, accepting a heaping bowl from her. "I'll tell him you asked after him. We left him at home to fend for himself tonight."

"Next time, you'll bring him. And make it soon." Then she looked at me and waited to be introduced. All niceties taken care of, stew served, with a parting "*Bon appétit!*" she went back toward the kitchen, collecting empty plates and bowls along the way.

The *pot au feu* was earthy and rich and maybe the best thing I had ever tasted. Certainly the very best thing all day. After we had agreed that our meals were exceptional, Sam, as he asked to be called, said to me, "I believe that we did not come here to discuss *pot au feu*, yes?"

"Yes," I said. "Sam, will you tell us about Friday?"

"Ah, Friday." He replenished his glass. "Horrible Friday. What can I say? It started as any Friday would. Nothing at all unusual. We've gone to a five-day school week, so we release the students earlier in the day than in years past. It was a lovely day and I was looking forward to having a few hours of daylight to visit the garden shops and prepare the garden for tomatoes I wanted to plant Saturday morning. And then, with a single telephone call, my entire professional life came to a standstill. I couldn't believe what I was being told. There was this horrible accusation. An anonymous but sufficiently credible-sounding accusation. While it is being looked into by the Ministry of Education, I was put on leave, to begin immediately. No one would answer my questions. I had no way to defend myself. No one to confront."

"What did you do?"

"What could I do?" His voice was very low, his face flushed. Then he shrugged, looked up at me with a wry little smile, and said, "I went home and planted tomatoes."

"You just went home and stayed there?"

"No. I felt terrible. Ashamed. But for what? I had done nothing," he said. "I wanted to hide myself. But I thought, I'm not guilty, so why would I behave like a guilty man? Most Fridays I play in a pick-up combo after the dinner service at a café in Vaucresson. So, I gathered up my clarinet and my music and went."

"Which café?" Jean-Paul asked.

"Bertholds," he said.

"I know it well. What time did you arrive?"

"What time? You sound like the police, Jean-Paul."

"I don't mean to," he said with an apologetic little nod. "Maggie has been working on a timeline of Ophelia Fouchet's movements Friday night. She was seen in the general area around Bertholds at about nine-fifty Friday night, so I wondered if she might have gone inside, or whether you had seen her at all. Joel Gold told us that sometimes she jams with teachers and other pupils. It would be natural for her to go to the café to listen, or even to play. She had her cello with her."

"I arrived as usual around nine o'clock, maybe a little after. We always have a drink or two while we decide on the evening's playlist. Anyone can join in, but if I had spotted Ophelia Fouchet Friday night I would have run like hell out of there."

"Why run?" I asked.

"Because it is Ophelia I am accused of having an inappropriate relationship with."

"Ah," I said, surprised that I was not surprised. "When we showed up at your gate asking questions it's a wonder you didn't throw your garden fork at us."

He laughed. "I resisted the urge because I needed to know what you wanted."

"The police have probably already asked you most of the same questions we have," I said.

"No, they have not. The ministry assured me that because the accusation against me is anonymous they will keep their inquiries discreet and in-house for the time being. Anyway, as far as they are concerned, I have been accused of an ethical breach, not a legal offense."

"I assumed the accusation was for sex with an underage girl."

"Maggie," Jean-Paul said. "The age of consent is fifteen. Unless the accusation was that Ophelia was coerced or forced, there is no crime."

"Correct," Sam said. "I was furloughed because the relationship I am accused of is a violation of ministry policy for faculty and administrators."

"But, surely, after she went missing, someone had questions for you."

"So far," he said, refilling my glass and raising his to me, "only you."

"*Merde*," I said, loving this universal swear word and wish for good luck more all the time as I clinked my glass to his. By then I was silently applying a string of *merdes* to the itchy rash on the back of my hand acquired during our romp in the woods that afternoon. Except that the rash now looked more like a cluster of blisters.

"Have you hurt yourself?" Sam said, reaching across the table for my hand.

"I must have run into some poison ivy," I said as he lowered his head for a closer look at the blistered skin.

"Poison ivy was eradicated from France years ago," he said. "There are nettles, of course. But is it possible you brushed against rue?"

"I wouldn't know," I said. "Rue is an herb, right? What does rue look like?"

He shrugged. "It's an evergreen. Pretty yellow flowers. Quite common, butterflies love it, but some people have a severe skin reaction. It can be worse than this. Were you out in the sunshine?"

"It was almost dusk when we went into the woods."

"You're lucky. Exposure to the sun makes rash from rue erupt. Horrible stuff."

I turned to Jean-Paul. "I should have kept the white jumpsuit on."

He took my hand, studied the rash on the back, then turned it over and kissed the palm. "We'll have Ari take a look at it."

The proprietress put a tray of cheese in front of us and asked if we wanted the *gâteau au chocolat* or the apricot tart for the finish. I would have declined, except that dessert was included and I had seen the chocolate cake when it was set in front of other diners. A narrow, dense, rich, nearly black chocolate wedge. I didn't care that I had already eaten enough. I said, *"Le gâteau, s'il vous plaît, Madame."* And my companions ordered the same.

When she walked away again I looked across at Sam. "If you can stand it, I have one last question."

"I'm afraid, but all right."

"What make of car do you drive?"

"I don't drive a car."

"I have a last question as well," Jean-Paul said.

"Oui?"

"If the ministry should find against you, what would the punishment be?"

"Assuming consent, I could be demoted, counseled–scolded, that is–and relocated," he said. "Relocated no matter the determination. And for the rest of my working life I will have a dark cloud hanging over me."

"Dommage." I said, and gave his hand a little pat, because the situation truly was a bloody pity.

Coffee arrived with the chocolate cake. Sam looked at it and sighed. "You have both been so kind, letting me vent and then feeding me instead of– Well, instead of doing several things I can think of. If you will keep a confidence, I would like to run something past you because you seem to be familiar with the situation. A suspicion only, backed by no facts at all."

"Please do." Jean-Paul set his first forkful of the rich cake back on his plate. "I don't know that we can help you, other than to listen."

"It's this," Sam said, gesturing for us to lean closer. "You asked whether Ophelia confided in me. And the answer is no, not directly. But there was a query about her. When I think back, it seems that the apparent equilibrium of Ophelia's life began to collapse some months ago, shortly after we distributed a pamphlet to students, 'Non au Harcèlement,' put out by the Ministry of Education. The pamphlet defines what constitutes harassment and lists references for further reading. At the back there is contact information for anyone who feels harassed or bullied. It was maybe a week later that someone from the office of the *juge des enfants*– Do you know who they are, Maggie?"

"I'm guessing that it's child protective services of some sort."

"Something like that, yes," he said. "So, this official came to the school and asked me questions about Ophelia. Were there signs of physical abuse on her? Did she seem to be in immediate peril? Had I observed a change in her mental health? I could only answer that she appeared to be healthy, there were no outward signs of physical abuse, and that she was keeping up with her school assignments. Indeed, she is an excellent student. None of which indicates that she is not a victim of abuse in some form. A week after that visit, Ophelia ran away for the first time. When I next saw her, she had dyed her hair and was dressed in garb my grandmother would have described as *vêtements de deuil*."

I turned to Jean-Paul. "What is that?"

He thought for a moment before he said, "Widow's weeds I think you say."

"Dressed all in black, as in mourning." I opened my bag and pulled out the printout David Berg had given me at lunch the day before. Aloud, I read the definition of domestic abuse: "'Harassment of one's spouse, partner, or co-habitant by repeated acts that degrade the other's quality of life and cause a change to the other's physical or mental state of health.'"

Sam extended his hand and I gave him the printout. After reading the highlighted passages and looking to see who was responsible for issuing it, he said, "That's exactly what I was asked. Do you know something?"

"I know very little," I said. "But I've heard that life *chez* Fouchet is not always peaceful. Tell me, if Ophelia went to the authorities claiming that her parents abused her, what would happen?"

"Not enough," he said. "It is a great scandal, you know, that we don't protect our children legally until there is gross mistreatment. Ophelia could walk into the office of the *juge des enfants* by herself and file a complaint; she has that right. But the system takes a clinical approach to family problems, not a legal one as I think is more often the case in America. In France, everyone concerned would be brought in for a conversation. Not testimony, you understand, just a conversation in judge's chambers. The judge would hear the child's complaint, listen to the parents, and then there would be a *justice negocié* and everyone would go home."

I looked at Jean-Paul for an explanation. He said, "A negotiated agreement to get along in the future and perhaps to go for counseling."

"That's it?" I said.

"Yes," Sam answered. "Unless it could be shown that the child was in physical or psychological danger."

"By running away and changing her appearance, was Ophelia trying to show that her mental state had been changed?"

Sam raised his hands. "When you find her, ask her."

] *Nine*

WHEN WE FINALLY GOT HOME, the house was dark except for a light in the kitchen. Apparently, everyone was already tucked up for the night. I was tired, but too wound up after a crazy day to go bed.

"I think I'll have a swim," I said as we walked through to the salon. "Will you join me?"

"Yes." Jean-Paul said, and crossed the room to flip on the pool and terrace lights. Right away his phone dinged with an incoming text from Ari. He read it to me: Ari thought he might have found a new living arrangement for Diba and Nabi until the end of the current school term, but if it worked out they would need to stay with us through the weekend unless that was a problem. It wasn't, of course. As we walked upstairs to change, Jean-Paul said, "As Ari seems to be awake still, out of respect for his traditional sensibilities, will you mind terribly wearing a swimsuit?"

I laughed because with so many people in the house it hadn't occurred to me to swim *au naturel*. My American prudery? I said, "Sure, not a problem, this time."

We put on suits and collected towels and went back downstairs. The pool was solar heated to about seventy degrees. At first the water felt cold, but before the end of the first lap I didn't notice. Through college, I was a competitive swimmer, not gold-medal caliber but fairly competent. Early on, to filter out crowd noise and other distractions, I learned to put myself into a sort of oblivious or meditative zone by concentrating on nothing except the movement of my body through the water. That's where I was when Jean-Paul gave my foot a tug. I was startled, a little disoriented for a moment before I figured out that he was trying to get my attention. I swam beside him to the side of the pool and that's when I heard the ruckus somewhere on the foot path beyond our garden wall.

As I hauled myself out of the water I heard our neighbor, Holly Porter, and at least two men, arguing. She yelled, "Stop it right now," in English. From the tone of it, the response had to be a French obscenity, followed by a third voice demanding in heavily accented French, "Put that down! Step away!"

I grabbed a towel and tied it into a sarong around my waist as I followed Jean-Paul to the gate. He yanked it open and with it came a hulking youth who, caught off guard and off balance, fell flat on his face onto the stone pavement of the terrace. The kid must have been leaning against the gate, maybe trying to cover his handiwork on its backside. I grudgingly appreciated his skill as a cartoonist while deploring the obscene image he had created of a bearded man wearing only Arab headgear committing a bestial act on a still incompletely drawn squealing pig. When Jean-Paul pulled the kid to his feet, a wide-tipped felt marker and a flashlight rolled from his hands.

Holly and the man with her, who I assumed was her husband, Kevin, stood in the open gateway, eyes wide, mouths agape when they saw blood spurt from the boy's nose and stream down his face and onto his shirt.

"Dear God," Holly said. Then she shook herself and aimed her flashlight at the drawing on the gate, outrage taking over. "Do you see what he was doing? We were out for a walk and we caught this kid defacing your property with that nasty picture. Kevin was just calling the police when— Oh hell, Maggie, this is just so awful."

Hearing the commotion, both Ari and Nabi came out of the guest house. I took Holly by the arm and brought her into the yard, the husband right behind her, and closed the gate before Nabi and Ari could see the graffiti on the back.

"Louis?" Nabi said, venturing around the end of the pool toward us. "What are you doing here?"

The bloody boy, Louis the tormentor, apparently in his humiliation at being caught began to cry, a catch of breath at first, followed by choking sobs. I untied my wet towel and pressed it to his bleeding nose. I said, "You better sit down, Monsieur Roussel. We'll call your father."

"No, please, don't," he begged.

"You know this kid?" Holly asked.

Nabi answered: "We go to the same school."

Holly got her first look at Nabi's battered face, and then she looked at Louis, whose nose might be broken. She asked Nabi, "Did he do that to you, son?"

Shyly, Nabi nodded.

Louis turned to him. "It wasn't just me, you know."

Jean-Paul laughed, one short bark. "You aren't helping yourself, Louis. Sit down and let Doctor Massarani look at that nose."

Ari hesitated before he agreed to help the little miscreant. He leaned over the kid, pinched the bridge of his nose and gently wiggled it, then gave it a sharp snap to realign the displaced cartilage. He had Louis put his head back so he could get a look into the nostrils, though with all the blood I doubted he could see much. When he was finished, he stepped back and announced, "Yes, broken. By morning you should have two black eyes. Not as bad-looking as the ones you gave Nabi but really ugly just the same. With a broken nose, as with Nabi's broken ribs, there isn't much that can be done. Your parents might want to take you to the clinic in the morning, but there's no emergency. Just try not to fall on your face again until it has healed."

Ari started to say something more, but stopped, took a deep breath and dropped his head. After a moment, he put a hand on Louis's shoulder. "Forgive me, young man, I should never have spoken to you in that way, but my anger at you got the best of me. Please, Louis, help me understand why you continue to harass Nabi. You've been removed from school on a discipline advisory and, I hope, punished by your parents as well. Yet you persist. Why?"

Nabi pulled up a chair and, elbows on knees, chin on fists, watched Louis search for an answer. Having none to offer, Louis said, "Don't look at me, Nabi," and started to cry again.

I turned to Ari. "Icepack?"

He nodded. "Please."

When I came back outside with a plastic bag of crushed ice wrapped in an old towel, the Potters, who had introduced themselves to Jean-Paul and Ari, were taking their leave.

"Our munchkin is in bed, in theory at least," Holly said. "The *au pair* we loved went back home last week so Kevin and I can only sneak out together for quick evening walks until we find someone else. We need to get back before the kiddo misses us. Call if you need us to testify or anything."

"I doubt things will get that far," Jean-Paul said. "But thank you."

She took a step toward Nabi. "Are you the violinist we hear?"

Nabi, chagrined, blushed under his bruises. "I'm sorry if I disturb you."

"Disturb us? Oh, heavens no. When my daughter hears you play we go outside to listen. She has just begun piano lessons, but I think she likes violin better. Please, keep playing."

"All right," he said with a shy nod. "I will."

When the Porters were gone, Jean-Paul handed his phone to Louis and told him to punch in his father's number.

"You can't tell my parents," Louis said, sounding panicky. The hand holding the icepack shook, and not from cold. "My mother is in the hospital again and my father is with her. Please leave them alone."

"No, Louis," Jean-Paul said. "What you have done is far too serious. Your father needs to get you help before you dig yourself in so deep no one will be able to get you out again. Now, your choice, give me your father's number, or I go to the hospital and get him."

Louis gave in, put the ice down on a table and tapped his father's number into Jean-Paul's phone. While Jean-Paul did his best to explain the situation to Guy Roussel, I went upstairs and got dressed. On my way back outside, I detoured to the garage and found a plastic tarp and some painter's tape to cover the graffiti on the gate. No one needed to see that obscenity, certainly not Nabi.

Or Ari. While we waited for Roussel *père* to arrive, with Louis being tended by Ari, Jean-Paul got dressed and I shrouded the image on the gate, after taking photos of it.

By the time I finished, Ari had managed to engage both Louis and Nabi in a quiet conversation about school and their mutual difficulties with a chemistry class.

"I'm lost," Louis said. "I know I'll never pass the science portion when we take the *baccalauréat* exams. My father will kill me if I don't qualify for university. And now, until the end of the term I'm on home instruction and it's even worse. What am I supposed to do, teach myself what I don't know?"

"If I didn't get help from Doctor Massarani," Nabi said, "I would be in big trouble."

"You're doing better than me," Louis said.

"Nabi will be home from school recovering from his beating for the rest of the week," Ari said. "Why don't you join us for a chemistry session tomorrow morning? Ten o'clock."

Nabi nailed his bleeding tormentor with a stare as if daring him to accept. After a pause to consider, Louis said, "Thank you, sir, yes, thank you. If it's okay with Nabi."

"Whatever," Nabi said, but I thought I saw a small glint of victory in his attempt at nonchalance.

While I eavesdropped on this interesting exchange, I picked up Louis's discarded icepack and laid it on my itchy hand. Ari noticed.

"Are you injured, Maggie?" he asked.

"No. I ran across something in the woods today." I showed him my puffy rash. "I was told it may be a reaction to rue."

"Calamine lotion might help. Just keep it out of the sun or it might blister more."

Nabi said, "Rue," not much more than a sigh as he looked at my hand.

"Rue?" I repeated.

"It's just— Random thought. In *Hamlet* when Ophelia goes crazy she says something about rue. I don't remember exactly how the speech goes but it's something like 'you wear your rue with a difference.'" He said the line in English. "Friday night when I was walking with Ophelia to the train I teased her about it, because she wears those black clothes and her name is Ophelia, and she had lied to her parents about what she was doing. My French isn't so great and maybe it just didn't translate. She said rue is a noxious weed and you shouldn't touch it. One time when she tried to hide overnight in the *haras*, she got a bad rash from rue. I tried to explain to her then that rue can also mean regret, but she didn't get it. She said I wasn't making sense. I told her to look it up."

"Shakespeare?" I said. "You quote Shakespeare, Nabi?"

I'd embarrassed him. "No," he said. "Yes, well, I think about it sometimes, because of my father. When my father was a student in Scotland he went to all the Shakespeare plays he could because he thought if he was there he should study the culture so he'd know what people were talking about. To be, and not to be, and all that. When we decided to leave Afghanistan he hoped that, somehow, we would end up in Britain and if we did then knowing Shakespeare would be useful. We read the plays together and he explained them. He said that Shakespeare is like opera, you have to know what the story is about before you go see it so that you can appreciate the presentation, the way it sounds and the way it looks, because it's hopeless trying to understand what anyone is saying."

"Your father was an amazing man," I said.

Nabi smiled, and nodded. "Because I know *Hamlet* I met Ophelia. Because of her name. I never knew anyone named Ophelia before. I asked her why her parents named her that."

"It's a pretty name."

"I guess, but Ophelia is so sad she kills herself. So I wondered why they chose her name for a baby."

Louis, who seemed confused by the entire conversation, suddenly sat up. "Ophelia killed herself?"

"In the play," Nabi said. "Not in real life. Not our Ophelia, just the character in the play."

Nabi was still trying to explain things to Louis when the doorbell rang. On my way to let in Monsieur Roussel, I overheard Louis ask Nabi what it was like to lose his mother. Nabi told him, "It's very lonely."

] Ten

I THINK WE MIGHT FIND MORE peace and quiet together in a tent in a snake-infested jungle than we seem to have at home," Jean-Paul said Friday morning as we drove through the gates that hid the courtyard of number seven rue Jacob from the prying eyes of passersby on the street outside. "Maybe it's time for us to just sneak away."

"Not today, though," I said. "After lunch, Guido and I will screen the final cut of the Normandy piece for Diane Duval. If she signs off on it, we'll decide on the rest of our fall projects. Diane has been great this week about giving me space to settle in, but from here on, my work schedule will get more intense. Doesn't mean you and I can't sneak away for a long weekend soon. *Sans* snakes, preferably."

"I'll look into it. Maybe the Edinburgh Shakespeare Festival, whenever that is."

I laughed. "Why not? What's on your schedule today?"

"The usual, some meetings to talk with people about this and that," he said as he parked next to a tiny red Smart Car in front of the blue door that led to Isabelle's second-floor apartment. "Mostly a lot of that, not enough agreement on this."

"This and that, huh? I think one day I'll walk around behind you all day with a camera and try to figure out what exactly you do."

"The camera would probably self-destruct out of boredom."

"After what you told me about holding your finger in the dike, I sincerely hope that's true."

We unloaded gear left in the trunk the day before after filming at the school and the pond and hauled it all upstairs. I had an apartment key, and Guido expected us, but I knocked; it was his pad now and who knew what we might walk in on. Detective Delisle answered the door.

"*Bonjour*, good morning," she said, gathering us in. Her hair was down loose and she wore skinny jeans, a linen shirt, and no shoes, looking very comfortable, indeed. There were roses in her cheeks. "Guido is setting up in the basement for a last peek before the studio screening. He said to send you down. Would you like coffee?"

"Please," I said with a smile, ignoring the elbow Jean-Paul shot into my back; she seemed very proprietary. He came downstairs with me only to help carry gear and to say hello to Guido. He visited the wine cellar and chose half a dozen bottles to take home, and then he left to do whatever it is he does. Guido and I settled in for a look at the last go-around of film edits and transitions that we had discussed earlier before handing our final cut over to Diane. I was more than happy with the piece as it was now, which mattered not one bit if Diane was unsatisfied with something.

Guido clinked his coffee mug against mine and said, "*Merde*," for good luck.

"Same to you, partner. Ready to go?"

"Not yet," he said. "I want to show you something I smashed together based on our conversation about a harassment film."

Guido had made a five-minute piece, a teaser, using bits from the film I made for Delisle, clips from the school assembly, and some footage he had shot during his explorations around Paris: a swastika spray-painted on the main Paris synagogue, the burned-out remains of a kosher market, a white-haired matron confronting a young woman about her hijab, women in a street demonstration against sexual harassment carrying signs with their motto, BALANCE TON PORC—Out the Pig. The soundtrack was Nabi playing a serene passage from Debussy, Op. 10, a stark contrast to the ugly images.

"Wow," I said. "You put this together this morning? What was Detective Delisle doing while you were sequestered down here?"

"Fleur went out for an early run. Then she came back and kibitzed; she is quite interested in filmmaking after yesterday. Actually, I've been tinkering with this little teaser for a while, ever since you brought up the issue. All I did this morning was splice in some of yesterday's footage. What do think?"

"As a teaser for a film about harassment, it's powerful."

"*Harcèlement*, you mean," he said, doing his best to growl the R at the back of his throat. "There's some mean shit going on over here, Maggie. Just like everywhere else."

"What do you think about expanding our project to look at the issue of harassment across the eurozone? It will mean some travel."

"Time might be a problem, but yeah," he said without hesitation. "Definitely."

On foot, Guido and I followed Delisle's little red Smart Car across the cobblestone courtyard and out the gates onto rue Jacob. She turned one way, we the other.

"So?" I said after waving her on her way.

"We're good," he said. "Fleur doesn't waste any time waiting for invitations, but so far that's okay. The language thing is awkward, but she doesn't waste a lot of time talking, either."

"Watch six, my friend," I said as a caution to watch his back. "And don't give her a key to the wine cellar."

At the Odéon Métro stop we descended into the underground transport maze that took us across Paris to Issy-les-Molineaux, where we came up into daylight again. The walk across the bridge to reach the studio was to be the last of the sun I saw until just after five o'clock that afternoon when I crossed the river again to catch the train home.

Diane Duval and I sat across from each other at a table in an open sort of hub area among the various production offices under her command. I leaned forward, elbows on the polished surface, in business mode. But she was the image of unhurried casual elegance, sitting sideways on a chair pushed a few feet away from the table, an elegant arm poured over the chair back, one slender leg draped over the other.

"You have been busy the last few days, Maggie," she said, a sardonic smile lifting one corner of her mouth. "You sent footage from a car bomb on Wednesday and alerted us to a murder scene on Thursday. What should we expect from you today?"

I laughed. "Nothing newsworthy, I hope."

"With all that has been going on, have you had time to consider what project you want to do next?" Diane asked.

"I have. As the new kid on the block I'm open to your suggestions," I said. I heard the undertones; she was miffed with me for some reason. "But unless you have something else in mind, I'd like to follow the Normandy sequence with the saga of the convent library that was discovered during the renovation of my mother's building. I confess that I'm concerned about the tight production schedule and we have a head start on this one."

"A convent library in Paris?" Her tone was rife with skepticism. "I thought we agreed to go after more hard-hitting topics. Where's the hard-hitting part of a story about a convent library?"

"The part that involves Russian oligarchs, international money laundering, mercenaries for hire, the attempt on my partner's life, the murder of a young Swedish nurse in Greece, and a decades-long argument between the local diocese, the Louvre, and the pope over very old and extremely valuable texts."

She wasn't sold, yet. "How personal are you going to get with it?"

"That's a variable. The story began before I entered the picture and it was, it is, far larger than me alone."

"I remember the news coverage," she said. "By your partner, do you mean Guido, or Jean-Paul Bernard?"

"Jean-Paul."

"He is notoriously camera shy. Will he co-operate?"

"I'll ask, but whether he will or not is his to decide."

"It is your project, of course, and I am confident that you will give us something wonderful." She made a note, just a few quick taps, on the laptop within her reach. "And, as you said, you have a head start. But I hope that you will decide to focus on the extreme efforts of various players to claim the library and in doing that you will keep yourself in the background as much as the story will allow. All right, then, have you a plan for the film after?"

"After that, bullying," I said, wondering what her issue was, because I knew, after she essentially pushed me offscreen on the library project, that something was up. "I want to go beyond workplace harassment and look at *le harcèlement scolaire*–schoolyard bullying–because the issue has been quite neglected by the media. Incidents of Islamophobia and anti-Semitism, harassment of immigrants generally in European schools has become more blatant, more violent, and more pervasive. The abusers, the bullies, often feel confident that they are justified; they are rarely punished. It's frightening."

"You said European schools. You want to take the topic beyond France?"

"I do, if you'll give me crew and travel support."

"Of course, yes. Good. Get with Bruno to work out the logistical details when you're ready to schedule shooting." When she tapped another quick note into her computer I wondered if she was checking off another talking point on a list. When she finished, she leaned forward as if to confide something. "Maggie, you should know that we had some blowback after your appearance on Jimmy Jardine's show. The issue, of course, is one that came up during the taping: Why have we hired an outsider to examine French society for a French audience? You gave Jimmy a very good answer, but the reaction of the public is an emotional one, void of logic. Your work will sit better with French viewers if they are reassured that the problem of harassment is a global one and that you are not picking on your new host country."

"I'm not surprised that I am an issue for some people," I said.

"Blowback blows itself out. The audience will warm to you, Maggie. Give them time."

"I hope you're right."

She closed the laptop and sat back again. "Harassment in the school is a perfect topic for you to tackle. But I'm surprised. I thought you would do something with the missing girl you've been so interested in."

"The girl is where my interest began," I said, leaning back as I realized how nervous I had been about this meeting. "By protecting a Muslim refugee from schoolmates she may have set herself up as a target. Her disappearance may also be her response to abuse at home, or her perception of abuse. If she's found alive, she'll have an important story to tell. And if she isn't, well, her story still needs to be told."

I told her about Nabi and all he'd been put through, and she liked the idea of using him as the human-interest hook that we wrapped the story around.

"But be careful, Maggie. You have already seen how dangerous the haters are."

I spent the rest of the afternoon pulling up articles about the issue of harassment across the eurozone. The biggest challenge for me before we began to film would be winnowing the mass of material to fit our allotted air time. I was lost in reportage about the recent disappearance of Jews from Germany when Diane tapped me on the shoulder and said, "Don't forget to have a life. Go home."

While I waited for the five-twenty, I texted Jean-Paul and told him I was out on the loose. Instead of texting back, he called; he was already at home.

"Tell me there were huzzahs all around when you screened your film," he said.

"Not even one huzzah," I said. "But Diane is happy enough with us that she greenlighted our proposition to look at the harassment issue across the eurozone."

"When do you begin working on it?"

"Right away," I said. "In about six weeks people will start disappearing for the summer holiday. Most of our time until then will be eaten up by research and logistics, but with luck we'll squeeze in a couple of good shoots by mid-June and pick it up again in September. Having a full crew will help."

"An all-union crew, I suppose."

"Most likely," I said. "There is one position, though, that is up to me to hire. Diane asked who I want for hair and makeup. I don't know anyone except the woman who takes care of Jimmy Jardine. Do you want the gig?"

"*Bien sûr*," he said, trying not to laugh. "I'll go out right now and get some of those magazines—you know the sort, Tips for This Season's Hot Looks—and start studying."

"A fine idea," I said. And maybe it wasn't a bad idea at all.

He had two pieces of news, one very good, he said, and one he hoped wasn't bad news. The first was that Ari was notified that he had passed all the required exams and interviews, his Cambridge medical school transcripts had been certified, and he was now licensed to practice medicine in France. On Saturday, Jean-Paul was taking him to shop for a new suit for job interviews. The second bit of news was that the living arrangements Ari had been working on for Nabi and Diba had fallen through.

"Maggie, how do you feel about Nabi and Diba staying on a while longer?"

"I have no problem with that," I said. "Nabi needs us right now, if us includes Ari. I wish that Diba didn't feel she has to keep herself invisible. She is quite delightful to be around. I think we should celebrate Ari's good news with a little party. Shall we ask Diba to plan the food?"

He chuckled. "I remember saying to you one time that you are the peanut butter to my jelly. Maggie, *je t'adore*. Yes, let's ask Diba to plan the menu."

"I love you, too." I remembered that when he told me I was his peanut butter I was wiping juice that squirted from a fresh tomato off his chin with my shirttail. He meant that we were comfortable together. If anyone wanted to be my jelly, I was happy it was Jean-Paul. "My train is here. See you soon."

I merged into the tide of evening commuters as they sorted themselves into various train cars and then into seats when they got inside. As I looked for a place to sit, the clutch of people directly in front of me found seats leaving me directly behind a very large man. He heaved a familiar-sounding sigh and dropped into the first open aisle seat.

I asked, "The window taken, Monsieur Roussel?"

"You?" he said, managing a sheepish little smile. He moved his bulk over and conceded the aisle to me. "You want to sit next to me?"

"Why not?" I said. "You're the only person I know on the train."

"Why not, eh?" He took a deep breath, and when he looked over at me, he said, "Should I list all the reasons why not?"

I shook my head. "How was Louis this morning?"

A shrug while he assembled an answer. "Better than he deserves. I had him checked out at the clinic first thing this morning. The doctor said there was nothing more to be done for the nose, but he arranged for us to start counseling. Together."

"I hope that works out," I said.

"That makes two of us. I wish I could find some way to engage Louis."

"He is quite a talented artist," I said. "We didn't show you the gate he decorated last night. Though the subject matter was repugnant, the drawing was very skillful."

"The boy is always scribbling," he said, dismissing the compliment. "Wasting time when he should be studying. And about the gate: I will pay for any repairs. Please just tell me what it will take to make that right."

"Ask Jean-Paul. I don't know that he's as concerned about the cost as he is making the graffiti go away. It is offensive."

"What did my son draw?"

I pulled out my phone and showed him a shot I had taken before I covered the gate.

"*Imbécile,*" Roussel muttered as if to himself. He turned his attention to the passing scenery and I thought that meant our conversation was over, maybe unwelcome; the man had a lot to contend with. But, with his face still averted from me, he said, "You know, Madame, your Muslim friend, Doctor Massarani, is the most Christian man I have ever encountered."

"My Muslim friend is a good Christian? Would you explain that please?"

"He didn't just turn the other cheek, he opened his arms and welcomed Louis in." Roussel, brow furrowed when he looked at me again, seemed to be puzzling through yet another of the great mysteries of humankind that had walked up and hit him unawares. "After everything Louis has done to hurt Ahmad Nabi, Doctor Massarani offered to help him with his schoolwork. I dropped him off at your house this morning at ten, as arranged. There was tension, yes, but also courtesy. When I went back at noon to pick up Louis, I found the two boys in the swimming pool, laughing and playing some sort of ball game. A woman was putting out lunch on the terrace and your doctor asked if Louis could stay to eat. I didn't know what to say."

"What did you say?" I asked.

"Nothing. Louis said it all for me. He said that after lunch they were going to have a second chemistry lesson." He raised his palms and shoulders, the go-figure gesture. "My Louis volunteered to sit down with his books. How is that possible?"

"Monsieur Roussel," I said.

"Please call me Guy. After all we've been through, *oui?*"

"Guy," I repeated. "Doctor Massarani is a well-trained pediatrician. He has dedicated his life's work to caring for children. The tragic reality is, his own little ones, and his wife, were killed during a bombing raid before he could get them out of Aleppo."

"I didn't know," he said, face full of sincere sadness. "I didn't know."

"Clearly he sees something in Louis that he can help. Or maybe it's Nabi he's helping. If you want my advice, which is worth everything you paid for it, I think you should let him."

The sound he made was somewhere between a laugh and a sob. "If only he could help me, too, eh? Where do I sign up?"

"I think you already have," I said. "Tell me, how is your wife?"

"You said once that at some point your husband refused further cancer treatment, and that he was at peace at the end. Do you remember?"

"I do."

"Adèle has reached that point. She wants to go home."

I put my hand over his on the armrest between us, he gave it a squeeze, and we traveled the rest of the way in silence.

Jean-Paul was waiting for me on the platform at the Vaucresson station. I asked Guy Roussel if we could drop him, but he said he had a car, so after exchanging friendly *bises* we said our good-byes. Jean-Paul watched this with a very confused look on his face as he walked toward us. He and Guy exchanged a quick handshake, and Guy continued on his way.

After witnessing that chaste exchange of cheek kisses, Jean-Paul said, "I have no words."

"Poor man is going through hell," I said, moving in for a more interesting round of *les bises*. "The whole family is. Has Louis gone home yet?"

"No. The boys are playing video games on the terrace until Louis's father comes for him. So, Madame, have you invited the Roussels to dinner tonight?"

"I have not. But someone should. If my mom were here she would have all her friends organized into a dinner tree so that someone was taking a hot meal to that family every night."

"Is that what people do in California?"

"Some people do. Which reminds me, I haven't spoken with Mom all week. I'd better call her." Even though she had not given birth to me, the woman who raised me was every bit my mom. "What are we doing for dinner?"

"Taking cheese and bread and a bottle of wine up to our room and hiding?"

"Lovely idea," I said. But of course, we did not. Instead, we met Dom at the neighborhood restaurant owned by his friend Nathalie's parents.

It was Friday night and the small restaurant was crowded with locals, some of them fresh off the train and still carrying briefcases. I received many wide-eyed glances because here, sitting next to Jean-Paul Bernard, was the woman many of them had been curious about and about whom no small number had gossiped even though they knew nothing about me except that I had moved into the home vacated by the lovely, late Marian Bernard. I had to smile at the number of them who subtly checked out my chest, expecting to see the Hollywood boob job Monsieur Gomes went on and on about. More than one gawker was clearly disappointed at the rather ordinary-sized bumps pushing out the front of my cotton shirt.

The conversation at our table, between breaks for introductions to yet more people who stopped by to greet the *Messieurs*

Bernard, and snoop, was about where we were going to go for our
summer holiday. As was French custom, we would take off for the
entire month of August. I proposed that we spend at least a week
in Southern California with Mom. I wanted to see her, check on
the tenants in my house, and take care of various loose ends. Dom
could visit with his Los Angeles school friends, and we would still
have time for exploring. After that, we would come back to France
and straight into the middle of a tug-of-war between Jean-Paul's
mother, who had a beach house in Villierville west of Le Havre,
and my grandmother who would be in residence at the family
farm in the Camembert region on the Cotentin Peninsula. Dom, of
course, would also be expected to join his maternal grandparents
for at least a week wherever they were during August. My daughter,
Casey, had to be included in the mix. She would arrive after finals
in mid-June and stay until early October when she would go home
to begin her senior year. My grandmother wanted her to work with
the family's cheesemaker and I wanted her with me, wherever that
might be. Casey wanted to stay in Paris, in Isabelle's apartment,
unless we took off for somewhere interesting.

"My God," I said. "The summer holiday sounds like a month-
long version of the battle over who goes where for Christmas dinner.
What if we rent a house on some faraway island and tell folks that
if they can get themselves to us, they're welcome. In the meantime,
we're lying on a beach with margaritas balanced on our bellies."

They chuckled their oddly similar chuckles. Jean-Paul took my
hand and kissed it. "*Bonne idée.* Who do you tell first? Your mom,
mine? Your grandmother? Dom's grandparents? Casey?"

The answer to that was the arrival of our entrées. That is, the
island idea, nice as it was, went no further.

Fabienne Simon came in with her husband and children. They
stopped to say hello on the way to their table. Fabienne also greeted
the woman seated directly behind me. I heard the sibilant edges of
a brief whispered exchange between them. I made out, "Yes, she's
the one." So did Dom, who covered his mouth with his napkin to
keep from spewing his mouthful of pickled *haricots.* His father,
trying not to laugh, flicked his son's hand as a warning. I looked

from one to the other, both of them holding back giggles, and gave them a queenly wave because, apparently, I am the one. Dom had to leave the table but Jean-Paul, like a good trained diplomat, with a last snort and a deep breath, regained composure. And the meal continued.

That Friday marked the beginning of the second week without Ophelia. As we ate, I kept expecting to hear her name among the bits of conversation that rose above the general welter of voices and dishes and chairs scraping on the floor. But it did not, until her parents walked in the front door.

The room fell silent for a moment, every conversation, every fork and knife stilled. And then, a bit at a time, the susurrus of voices began to build again as the Fouchets crossed the room and were seated. A few people greeted them, quietly, as you would greet members of the family at a funeral. Claire Fouchet looked coldly, stiffly composed, and Yvan, though he wore a crisp white dress shirt and a beautifully tailored, perfectly pressed suit, was a wreck. His hands shook as he stared unseeing at the menu card placed in them.

Jean-Paul tapped my arm to get my attention and I realized that I had been staring, transfixed. I looked down at my plate, embarrassed to be caught. He said, "Like passing a collision in the road, it is difficult not to look, yes?"

"Yes. Exactly like that."

Dom had paled. "Papa, do something."

"What do you suggest, my dear son?"

"I don't know. No one is talking to them." He leaned toward his father. "It isn't normal."

"No, it isn't. Nothing for the Fouchets is normal right now, Dom. Do you want me to go speak with them?"

Dom raised his palms, at a loss.

"All right." Jean-Paul pushed his chair back and rose. And then he held out his hand to me. "Shall we, *ma chérie*?"

I pasted on a smile, folded my napkin next to my plate, and took the offered hand as I got up from my chair, in no hurry. "Is there a plan?"

"Only to say hello."

Monsieur Fouchet still held the menu card in a death grip when Madame Fouchet ordered for them both. The waiter was just leaving their table when we walked up.

"Claire, Yvan, it is nice to see you out again." Jean-Paul gave his cheeks to her, his hand to the husband. Though I had met them both earlier he said, "I want to introduce my fiancée, Maggie MacGowen."

As she offered me her hand, and he did his, each for a brief and formal press, I smiled at her and said, "I was just telling Jean-Paul how much I admire your peonies."

"My peonies?"

"Yes," I said with a little nod I hoped looked sincere. Jean-Paul slid a chair behind me and I sat. He went to the opposite side of the table and did the same. "Peonies simply don't thrive in the dry climate of Southern California where I lived before coming here. I see them all over this part of France. They are so beautiful that I hope to plant them in the garden for next spring. Any advice is welcome."

"Peonies are the more beautiful because they last such a short time, don't you agree?" As soon as I mentioned peonies, the change in Claire Fouchet was sudden, unexpected certainly. She relaxed, her hard lines softened. So far there was no mention that we had met before. Maybe her husband didn't know that Dom and I had gone calling, so I did not bring it up. She reached across the table and covered her spouse's shaking hand with her own steady one as if to hide his tremor, I thought, and not as a gesture of affection. Or, was she drawing our attention to his distressed state? "Some years peonies flourish, and some years they hide. I can coax them and bribe them, but they do what they decide to do. A mind of their own, just like people, *oui*?"

"Temperamental like all creatures of nature, I suppose," I said.

She turned to Jean-Paul. "Thank you, my friend. Kind of you to come over. The way people keep their distance one would think we had something contagious. At first, everyone was around trying to help, but now–" She shrugged her elegant shoulders. "True friends still call, but I suspect that our situation has become tiresome even to them. Certainly it's tiresome to us, yes Yvan?"

"Tiresome? I suppose. I have begun to wonder if we are ghosts," he said. "Are we dead and don't know it? We think we are still here, everything looks the same, but no one sees us. And if they do, they seem frightened."

"I can't imagine what you are going through," I said.

Their waiter came with a bottle of wine and we fell into the sort of sudden silence that happens when people are caught sharing a dirty joke. Watching the server pull the cork, Claire changed the subject.

"Maggie, do you ride?"

"For fun," I said. "I have a pair of rescued horses that enjoy eating wildflowers along the trails of the Santa Monica Mountains and will tolerate me in a saddle to get at them. I have no formal training. Do you ride?"

"Not in competition anymore, but yes. You must join us on club rides. We trailer the beasts and go somewhere we can set off across the countryside for a day or two. It's lovely. Jean-Paul, I don't see you at the stables anymore."

"No time," he said. "My houseguest, Ari Massarani, keeps my ponies in good shape."

"We see him at the equestrian center," Yvan said. "He has a wonderful seat, well-schooled."

"He's an Arab," Claire said. "All Arabs ride."

Their first course appeared so we excused ourselves to rejoin Dom.

On our way back to our own table, in a low voice I said, "Do you think all Arabs ride?"

"No more than all Americans wear fanny packs." He bumped my shoulder with his. "Peonies? Where did you pull that from?"

My turn to shrug. "I know all sorts of things. For instance, I happen to know that she is past president of the Hauts-de-Seine Peony Society, and that you have a birthmark shaped like Paraguay on your butt."

He craned his head around as if he could sneak a look back there. "I do?"

"I'll show you later."

"I'll take that as a promise."

When we rejoined Dom, he said, "Your food was getting cold, so Nathalie's mother took your plates to the kitchen."

"Think we'll see them again?" Jean-Paul asked as he settled back into his chair, clearly unconcerned. "I was just getting acquainted with that nice piece of salmon."

"Maggie, my father always says that it helps to know people. He's not the only one in the family who has connections." Dom looked across the dining room and gave someone a signal with a flick of his chin. Right away, freshly prepared meals were set in front of us. After thanking the waiter, Dom raised his glass. "Thank you, Papa, for sacrificing your salmon to comfort the Fouchets. And, Maggie, I hope you understand what you're in for with this man."

"You egged him on," I said. "It's you I'm keeping a watchful eye on."

Dom's friend Nathalie, who I suspect was responsible for ordering fresh entrées to be prepared for us, served the cheese and coffee when we finished. Dom told us there was a movie showing at the Cinéma Normandie, the multiplex down the boulevard, that they both wanted to see. After we finished the meal, Nathalie handed her apron to her mother, the young people bid us good night, and went happily on their way.

"The evening is ours," Jean-Paul said as we watched them go. "Would you like to take a walk?"

"Where to?"

"It's Friday." He glanced at his watch. "Approaching the hour that two other young people happened to be out loose in town one week ago. Shall we begin at the train station car park?"

I took his arm. "I like the way you think, sir. *Allons-y*. Lead on."

It was a dry, clear, warm spring evening with only a sliver of moon. Perfect for a stroll with a lover. We drove to the train station and started to walk from there, following Ophelia's footsteps the week before. Through the dark alley, and out onto a main street, past shops, to the last place the CCTV captured her before she merged with the night. We were mid-block. Immediately around us there were more professional offices than shops, and nothing was open. A dentist next door to Fabienne Simon's family law practice, an insurance agency, a frame shop, and so on. At the next intersection we could see Bertholds, the bistro where Sam Lambert and his friends jammed on Fridays, only a few doors down on the cross street. It was nine-twenty when we walked inside.

Sam spotted us right away and waved us over to join him at the bar. Joel Gold was also there, without his bow tie.

"So, friends," Sam said. "You've come to hear some hot geriatric jazz, have you?"

"We thought we might," Jean-Paul said. "We were out for a walk and stopped in to say hello."

We ordered drinks and joined Sam and Joel and their bandmates at a long table in back. The last of the diners in the restaurant seemed to be finishing up. Several couples drifted into the bar after eating. Other guests began to arrive, regulars, it seemed, by the way they were greeted. In all, counting musicians, there were about thirty people filling chairs and leaning on the bar. The conversations hovered around music, jazz specifically, and I was lost. I love jazz, but as a listener, not a musician. Those worlds overlap, but they are far from the same place. It didn't really matter, though, because everyone was having fun, and so were we. After a couple of beers, Sam went off to the toilets and Joel Gold slid over into the seat next to me.

"Sam is happy you're here. But tell me the truth, did you come to hear some pretty good jazz, or are you out looking for a ghost?"

"A ghost?" I said. That's what Yvan Fouchet had said about himself, a ghost haunting a world that was no longer familiar.

"Odds are," Gold said; he'd had more than one drink, too. "It's been a week."

"I still want to know what happened to her," I said.

"Fair enough." He stood and whistled to get everyone's attention. "Friends, Vaucressonais, countrymen, lend me your ears. One week ago tonight, at about this very time, a teenage girl named Ophelia Fouchet disappeared. Sam tells me that at around nine-fifty Friday night she was seen in this very neighborhood. So, I'm asking you, on your way over here last week did any of you notice a young girl carrying a damn good cello in a hard-shell red case?"

There was a murmur of conversation and then a woman stood up. "We saw her, Joel. I mean, hard to miss a kid lugging a cello that's nearly as big as she is."

Jean-Paul rose to face the woman. "Where did you see her, Madame?"

"Near here, at the corner, right Bennie?" she asked the man beside her. "The girl was just standing there looking up and down the street like she was waiting for someone. It's not something you see every night, is it? A girl out alone at night with a cello."

"Have you seen posters about a missing girl?" I asked.

"*Bien sûr.* Everyone has. But the girl they are looking for is a little blond girl, and the girl I saw was very dark. Algerian maybe? Or a gypsy, all dressed in black."

"It's the same girl," I said. "Did you speak with her?"

"No. We drove on by. Funny though, because someone called and asked Bennie the same thing. Who called, Bennie?"

"*Une poulet.*"

I turned to Jean-Paul for a translation. He asked Bennie, "A woman cop? Detective Delisle?"

"That's right." Bennie lifted his glass and drained it. "Don't know how she knew where we were Friday. Gave us a jolt; Big Brother, *oui?*"

Jean-Paul and I exchanged knowing looks. Vehicle registration identified the cars picked up by the CCTV and gave the report to Delisle. Our friend Bennie and his partner were a dead end as far as new information, though for a moment I'd had hope.

"Hey, Joel," a man at the far end of the room called out. "What time are we talking about?"

"Any time," Jean-Paul answered. "Did you see her?"

"*Ouais.* Like Sylvie said, you don't see many kids out at night lugging a cello. But it was later, and not right around here. After the boys riffed on 'Blue Train' I had to go home."

A voice near my elbow: "Sam, you're no John Coltrane, but that was sweet."

Sam was back, leaning against the wall near the end of the bar, listening.

Jean-Paul exchanged nods with him before addressing the man who spoke up. "Where did you see the girl?"

"Let me think." He tapped the table, eyes in a squint. "You know that drive-through coffee bar on boulevard de la République? I take the shortcut through the *haras* some mornings and stop by for a coffee. She was near there. I wondered about it because the coffee bar was closed and nothing else is nearby. Where was she going with a cello at that time of night?"

"What time was it?" I asked.

"Sam, what time did you finish trying to be Coltrane?"

Sam shrugged. It was Bennie who answered. "Ten-thirty, maybe ten-forty-five. 'Blue Train' was at the end of the first set before the break."

"So, add ten or fifteen to whenever that was, and that's when I saw her."

Sam, still leaning against the wall, asked, "Anyone else?"

When there was no answer he pushed himself upright and said, "Then let's have some music. That's why we're here, isn't it?"

We listened through the first set, enjoying the people around us as much as the music. The combo was an eclectic collection of musicians and instruments, something like a weekend pick-up game at a community park with all levels of skill and equipment. What the players all had in common was sheer joy in what they were doing for an openly appreciative audience. They started with an old standard, "Take the 'A' Train," and segued somehow into "L'air de Toréador" from Bizet's *Carmen*. While Joel Gold on clarinet was very good, it was Sam Lambert's saxophone that rocked the piece. He truly gave himself over to the music. By the time the last of the toreadors marched out of the bullring, he was exhausted. But happy.

After the applause, whistles, and back-slapping were done with, and fresh drinks ordered, we said our good-byes to Joel and Sam and walked back out into the night.

"Zowie," I said. "The math teacher and the principal. *Quelle surprise.*"

"As you say, people are full of surprises." Jean-Paul took my arm as we retraced our steps back to the train station.

"I found it odd at the restaurant earlier," I said, "the way that Claire Fouchet shifted gears so quickly. The first time I spoke with her, she was a stick. But tonight in the restaurant as soon as I mentioned her flowers she was entirely different. It was as if a mask fell off, and boom, there was relaxed Claire underneath. You know what else was odd? She never mentioned the visit I paid to her Tuesday night. Did she not recognize me?"

"I can't say. Yvan had met you, or at least seen you before, and he said nothing either."

"With Yvan, I just happened to be there when he wanted to talk to you. He was in such a sorry state when he waylaid us in the driveway Tuesday that I doubt he even knew I was there."

"That might be true," he said. "We can't expect the Fouchets to be normal when their lives have become so very abnormal. And, by the way, before we left the bistro, I saw you go speak with the man who thought he saw Ophelia near the *haras.*"

"He gave me his contact information and I texted it to Delisle."

"You don't think she's so distracted by one Guido Patrini that she won't follow up?"

"I happen to know that tonight he is out with his downstairs neighbor and she is on call in Vaucresson. She already texted back."

"What did she say?"

"She sent a thumbs-up emoji."

He laughed. "The new international language, emojis."

At the train station, we were panhandled by a young and filthy man. From the look and smell of him he hadn't bathed or eaten regularly for a very long time. Odd the way young homeless men all seem to look alike after a while. The young women seemed to take more pains with hygiene and weren't as easily recognizable as people living in the rough as the men were. Out of pride, or as a way to remain invisible, I wondered?

Jean-Paul asked the panhandler his name and when he had last eaten. The answers were Yegor and yesterday. Jean-Paul asked if he wanted a meal and a bed for the night and when Yegor said yes, I steeled myself, expecting one more joining our growing household. Instead, Jean-Paul made a phone call. When he put the phone back into his pocket, he told Yegor, "A man named René is on his way to give you a lift to a shelter. It's a decent enough place, trust me. He will be here in five or ten minutes, driving a pale green van. He already has two other passengers."

"Is he a cop? Immigration?"

"No, he's a monk. I'll leave it to you to decide whether you will get into René's van, or not. And now, I wish you luck, and good night."

With that, we continued to the car and drove home.

"Like Paraguay?" Jean-Paul asked as we waited for the garage door to open.

"Like Paraguay," I said. "I'll show you when we get upstairs."

"Hmm," he said, smiling to himself.

"Thank you for not bringing Yegor home," I said as we walked through the kitchen."

"Our house isn't big enough for all the Yegors out there, *ma chérie*. And there aren't enough beds or hot meals in all of France, or anywhere else I know, to take care of half of them. I'm surprised you didn't ask him whether he had seen Ophelia."

"I thought about it," I said. "But I have a feeling he wouldn't talk to me about it, or the police for that matter. If he saw something, maybe when his tummy is full again he'll talk to your friend Friar René if you plant the right questions in René's ear."

"*Une bonne idée, chérie. Une très bonne idée.*"

] Eleven

S ATURDAY MORNING, AFTER WE returned from a foray
through the village farmers' market, Jean-Paul took Ari to
buy a new suit to wear during his upcoming job interviews.
Ari had argued that he could probably find something adequate
at a *brocante*–a swap meet–or at a second-hand shop in the *ban-
lieues*, the less-than-prosperous outer suburbs north of Paris. But
Jean-Paul vetoed the idea. It was going to be difficult enough for
Ari as a foreigner to get a position in a medical practice or hospital anywhere except some rural French village where there was a
terrible doctor shortage unless he could impress the interviewers
with a combination of impressive résumé, French language skills,
and impeccable French tailoring. Ari had taken care of the first
two requirements, and now it was time for the third, a good suit,
non? So off they went.

Nabi, excused from work that weekend because his boss,
Marco, was afraid his battered face would scare off sausage customers, left early to make up the violin lesson he had missed on
Wednesday after he was beaten and displaced by his grandmother's employer. Diba, in an interesting development, was next door
baby-sitting for the Porters so they could attend a company day
cruise up the Seine to Giverny for lunch; they wouldn't be home
until dinner. Dom had gone somewhere for the day with Nathalie
and various other friends.

By ten o'clock they had all scattered and I was blessedly alone with the quiet house all to myself, except for the painter who showed up just as Dom was leaving. On Friday the painter had covered the graffiti on the backside of the garden gate with a coat of primer paint. He left it to dry overnight, and now he was back to apply a top coat. He was a nice enough older man, happy to be left to his work without wanting a lot of chitchat. With headphones on, he set right to work lightly sanding the primer in preparation for the finish coat.

There was still some unpacking I could do, but I felt unusually tired. Or maybe I was simply on overload; being a foreigner was hard work. I thought about taking a run, a swim, or even saddling one of Jean-Paul's ponies and trying not to disgrace the Bernard family name as I bounced along the equestrian trails in the *haras*. Instead, I pulled a chaise into a far shady corner of the back garden and curled up with my laptop. I spent some time just woolgathering while watching a mother bird fly back and forth to her nest in the tree over my head, something different and squirmy dangling from her beak every time she returned. Mothering the young can be exhausting. I knew that from experience, and marveled at the bird's stamina.

Eventually, I mustered the energy to turn on my computer with the intention of doing some basic research on the issue of school-yard harassment beyond France. In the film we planned to make, I wanted to use Nabi's situation as a personal hook that would lead to a broader inquiry. I didn't get very far because in the process of saving an article about a trial in Germany, my hand began to itch and that made me think about rue. I looked up rue so I would know what to look for so I could avoid it. When it wasn't in bloom, rue looked like a lot of things. Brushing against it could cause a nasty rash and blisters, especially if the rash was exposed to the sun. The plant attracts butterflies, flavors grappa, and was used historically as an abortifacient. A link to that last nugget of information led to the possible meanings of rue in Ophelia's speech in *Hamlet*.

I made a note to self: stay out of the woods, and then out of

curiosity because of Nabi's comments to Ophelia about rue in
Hamlet, I downloaded the play. I had never read *Hamlet* or seen
it performed, though, like just about everyone, I can quote some
bits that have become part of the idiom: "Get thee to a nunnery";
"Alas, poor Yorick, I knew him" (said while holding a skull, or, in
the case of a certain pompous college friend, every time she held
a head of lettuce); or "Something is rotten in the state of Denmark."

I managed to stay awake through act 1, scene 3, where Ophelia's brother, Laertes, warns her about Hamlet's impulsiveness
and unclear intentions and cautions her not to "...lose your heart
or your chaste treasure open to his unmaster'd importunity." By
then, I knew why the nuns at my convent high school had never
assigned *Hamlet* to their assemblage of supposed virgins: too much
talk about sex. Before the end of act 1, I did exactly what I would
have done if that difficult play had been assigned by the nuns; I
found the cheater version.

Hamlet is a strange and lurid tale, with the ghost of cruel Prince
Hamlet's father floating about the castle scaring everyone. And
poor Ophelia, caught between a controlling, scheming father and
rapacious Hamlet who has apparently deflowered her and maybe
impregnated her, insulted her for giving in to him, and abandoned
her. So she throws herself into a brook and sings until she drowns.
That last part was worrisome.

I closed the computer, leaned back, and tried to sort the bits
I knew about the flesh-and-blood Ophelia into a cohesive story.
Lulled by the soft *chuh-chuh-chuh* of the painter's sandpaper in the
background, the mother bird back-and-forth, back-and-forth overhead, I fell asleep.

"Madame?" A soft voice broke through the fog. "So sorry to
disturb you, Madame, but I have finished."

I opened my eyes enough to see the painter perched at the very
edge of the stone-paved terrace, giving me a tentative little wave.
I took a deep breath, opened my eyes all the way, and got to my
feet. Trying not to weave back and forth, I said, "You're finished?"

"*Ouais.*" He took a step back, bowed slightly as he swept an
arm toward the gate. He had it propped open until the paint dried.

Across the opening he strung tape and WET PAINT signs to keep people away. "Please come and see."

I followed him over to admire his handiwork, the stone pavement hot under my bare feet. "Wonderful job, Monsieur. Thank you so much."

"You are satisfied, Madame?"

"Yes, perfectly satisfied, Monsieur. A work of true craftsmanship. We can't thank you enough for coming out on Saturday."

He smiled and gave me a very gallant full bow from the waist. "Always a pleasure to be of service to Monsieur Bernard, Madame."

The painter gathered his neatly folded drop cloth and his bucket of tools and presented me with the nearly empty paint can just in case we needed to do touch-ups. I saw him out the front door. I had only just set the paint can on the garage shelf with other nearly empty paint cans when the doorbell rang. I padded out in still-bare feet, expecting the painter to be there saying he had forgotten something.

"*Bonjour*, Madame–" It was Claire Fouchet, with her arms full of bright peonies loosely wrapped in newspaper. "MacGee?"

"*Bonjour*, Madame," I said. "What beautiful flowers. Please come in. And please, call me Maggie."

"*Merci*, Maggie. And I am Claire." She unloaded the flowers into my arms. "Forgive the intrusion, but you said last night that you are interested in planting peonies. I took a chance that you were home so that I could get a look at your garden and see where the plants will do best. I hope I haven't interrupted something."

"Not at all. Let me put these wonderful flowers in the kitchen and we'll go have a look."

When I came back she was already outside, studying the yard beyond the paved terrace.

"So, Claire, what do you think?"

"Peonies want four or five hours of full sun, so I think that over there by the side of the guest house would be your best choice. It will help if you have that linden tree trimmed back to allow more morning sun. Whether you plant peonies or not, all three of your lindens could benefit from a good pruning next winter."

"I'll mention it to Jean-Paul."

"That's right, he's been away," she said. "Marian loved this garden. She and Jean-Paul gave the most wonderful parties out here. Of course, you'll want to make it your own. Marian always said she didn't have the courage for peonies. Maybe that will be your signature planting here, Maggie."

My phone buzzed with an incoming text and, while Claire went on with instructions for planting peonies, I pulled it out of my pocket only far enough to see what it was. I didn't recognize the number, but the signature made my heart race. "Let's talk. Where? When? Signed Déchaînée." Déchaînée was the moniker on the letter to the editor commenting on Roni Pascal's April article. The woman who said she called the wife. I fairly itched to get back to her, but while the wife of the man in question was standing beside me that would hardly be wise. Instead, I tried to find my way back into Claire's peony tutorial.

"I didn't realize peonies were so temperamental."

"Not once they get established. Getting them to establish, however, requires diligence and patience." Without shifting her focus from the yard, she shifted the topic. "You seem to have taken quite an interest in my daughter."

"I have, yes. You know that her friend Ahmad Nabi is staying here with us for the time being. Her disappearance has been very hard on him."

"I had heard that, yes." She turned her head just enough to look at me. "Why is he staying here?"

"For several reasons, but primarily because he and his grandmother have nowhere else to go right now. They are lovely people, and we are enjoying them."

"I never understood what my daughter saw in him."

"I hope you'll have the chance to ask her very soon."

Finally, her eyes filled. I don't know that I had ever before met a person whose emotions were kept so firmly under control. She must have had a lot of practice.

"Is the boy here now?" she asked.

"No. He's at a violin lesson."

"I've never met him. I saw him play in a school concert, but we weren't introduced. My fault. Do you think he would speak to me?"

"I'll ask him if you wish."

She relaxed just a little. "Please, if you would, Maggie. Tell him it would be just me. Ophelia's father is too upset for rational conversation; you saw him last night. The doctor has given him a sedative, hoping he'll sleep before he collapses. The poor man doesn't know what to do when he can't snap his fingers and get what he wants. Right now, he wants his Ophelia."

"I don't know how you manage to put one foot in front of the other."

"Hah!" With a sad little laugh she said, "I just sleepwalk through the day."

"Maggie?"

I turned and found Diba out on the foot path looking into the yard over the wet paint tape. She had a little girl by the hand.

"Sorry to interrupt," she said, smiling, seeming quite happy, and speaking to me in English, of course. "But, if you don't mind, may I bring Madison over for a swim?"

"Of course," I said. "Are you lifeguarding for her?"

"Oh yes. Nabi will be home soon and he'll swim with Madison, too. He's more fun than I am, but I can manage fine until he arrives; I am a good swimmer. We'll just go get Madison's things and be right over."

"Paint on the gate is still wet, Diba, so please come through the front."

"Thank you. Say bye for now, Madison."

"*À bientôt*, Madame," Madison chirped, and skipped off toward her house next door.

Claire had watched the exchange with puzzlement.

"Diba is Nabi's grandmother," I said. "Would you like to meet her?"

"Oh my! What would I say?"

"What do you want to say?"

"Give me time to think about it."

"Nabi will be home soon. I'll ask him if he wants to meet with you. Does Jean-Paul have your number?"

"I'll write it down." After she did, I thanked her for the flowers again, and she shot out the front door in a great rush. Was she afraid for some reason that she would run into Diba? Or perhaps Nabi? I hadn't mentioned that if she wanted a conversation with Diba she would have to speak either English or Pashto, unless she had a translator handy.

In the short time gap before Claire Fouchet's fast exit and Diba's arrival, I returned Déchaînée's text: "This afternoon? Tomorrow? Somewhere in Paris? Name the time and place." The answer came right back. "Today, 3:00, Van Gogh's ear, d'Orsay." I told her it was a date just as the happy swimmers walked through the front door.

While Diba changed into her swimsuit upstairs, I busied Madison putting cookies on a plate and counting plastic pool cups for fizzy lemonade. We had the snacks and a large vase of peonies set out on a table by the pool when Diba came down again wrapped modestly in a big terry robe. She and Madison were in the pool practicing swimming underwater when Nabi came home. After asking him about his lesson, I asked him if he was willing to speak with Ophelia's mother. He said he wouldn't mind, but only if Ari was there, too. And maybe, he added, Louis.

I was still thinking over that last one when he said, "Would it be okay if Louis came over to swim now? He's pretty bored stuck at home all the time."

"Ask your grandmother," I said. "I was just leaving. If she says it's okay, tell Louis to use the front door, please. The paint on the gate is still wet."

No one mentioned the reason we had to paint the gate in the first place. I wondered if Louis would have something to say.

It was noon, and I was hungry. I also wanted out of the house and away from the backyard noise, as happy as it was. I texted Jean-Paul to see how the suit project was going. He said they had the suit and they were now at the tailor. Did I want to join them for lunch? Of course, I did. I went upstairs, combed my hair and put

on more presentable weekend clothes, and shoes, told Diba I was
leaving, and drove to the train station.

We were to meet at a halal Lebanese restaurant, Noura Marceau,
on the Right Bank, directly across the Seine from the Eiffel Tower.
Before going inside the restaurant, eternally the tourist, I stopped
to gawk at the view. Ever since I was a little girl, I dreamed of one
day living in Paris, and somehow, now I was. At least, I was living
Paris-adjacent. The realization that I was there, with my charming
prince, still seemed like a dream.

Jean-Paul was already seated at a table, drinking tea. Before he
looked up and saw me, I caught him covering a little belch behind
his hand; my prince was the more charming for it. Ari arrived right
behind me, loaded with shopping bags: shoes, dress shirts, ties. The
suit would be ready for a fitting on Tuesday. I didn't know whether
Jean-Paul subsidized this spree or not, but Ari announced before
we ordered that lunch was his treat. I asked for chicken shawarma,
a favorite, and when the waiter went away, told Ari and Jean-Paul
about Claire's visit.

"What does she want from Nabi?" Ari asked, clearly suspicious
about her motives.

I shrugged. "I'm guessing that she wants Nabi to tell her everything he knows about Ophelia. The only surprise for me is that she
didn't race over to grill him last week as soon as she heard he was
back in town. She must have questions."

"Her reaction has been odd from the beginning," Jean-Paul
said. "I remember her being the sort of mother that Americans call
a helicopter parent, always hovering over their kids. But other than
passing out posters with an outdated photo, what has Claire done
to help locate her daughter?"

"Stayed at home near the telephone?" Ari said.

"I'm sure she has a mobile phone," Jean-Paul said. "And I am
very sure that her daughter knows the number."

"Yvan, on the other hand, seems to be out looking for her all
the time." I broke off a piece of pita and used it to scoop some
hummus from the bowl set in front of us. "Claire told me the doctor
gave him a sedative. When we saw him last night at the restaurant

he couldn't stop shaking. Why did she dress him up and take him out?"

Jean-Paul lifted one speculative shoulder. "After a week, it may be time for them to accept a new reality."

"You mean that Ophelia isn't coming home?" I asked.

"Something like that."

I took a deep breath. "Time for a different topic. Ari, we need to have a party to celebrate your re-entry into your chosen profession. Who shall we invite?"

Ari blushed. "Let's keep it just family."

"Does family include Diba and Nabi?"

"By now, yes, I suppose it does."

"Good, because I'll need Diba's help with food," I said. "But are there friends or people you work with at the community center you want to include?"

He dropped his head and chuckled. When he looked up again, he said, "The community center? Where would we put them all?"

Jean-Paul looked from him to me. "What if we give a party at the cultural center? A caterer, music. A real party. What do you think, both of you?"

"It's up to Ari," I said.

He shook his head. "If word got out there was food, I guarantee that a thousand people would show up. And maybe more. What if, instead, we make it a surprise during my regular Wednesday shift? We bring in some juice and some sweets, and I let them know that I will be leaving soon."

"Good-bye and congratulations all at once," Jean-Paul said. "Very nice."

Ari suddenly grew serious. "I will miss my students and associates, of course. But most of all, Jean-Paul, I will miss you. You have been mother hen and Father Christmas to me for the last two years. It is only because of your friendship and your kindness that I am ready to move on with my life."

"You give me too much credit," Jean-Paul said, coloring a bit. "I think the best thing I did for you was stay out of your way. Most of the time, I was in America falling in love with Maggie and you were here mowing the lawn. If you found that helpful, then wonderful."

Ari laughed. I kissed Jean-Paul's cheek. And we ate our lunch.

"Plans for the rest of the day?" Jean-Paul asked while we lingered over tiny cups of Lebanese coffee, something like espresso shots with just a hint of cardamom. One cup was enough caffeine to keep me awake until Tuesday. Ari had seconds.

"I have a mystery date," I told them. "What does *Déchaînée* mean?"

Jean-Paul did that little French shrug that I had decided was the equivalent of the American "Uh" when someone wanted just a moment to think. "Literally, it means unchained, in the sense that you've unchained the beast. Think 'enraged.'"

"Well, then, I'm off to the Musée d'Orsay to meet Enraged at three o'clock."

Ari glanced at his watch. "It's Saturday. You'll never make it past the ticket queue by three."

"*Merde*," I muttered, pulling out my phone to text the woman I was to meet in front of Van Gogh's severed ear.

"No problem," Jean-Paul said. "I'm a member. We can skip the queue and go in the members' entrance."

I looked at Ari and raised my palms, the gesture that meant, I hoped, No problem here. He laughed, because of course Jean-Paul would have a solution. I said, "We?"

"I haven't been to the d'Orsay for a while, so if it's all right with you, while you're meeting your mystery person, I'll just wander. Where are you meeting?"

"Van Gogh."

"Then I'll be communing with Daumier. Text me when your meeting is over."

The museum, as Ari warned, was crowded. Van Gogh's self-portrait with bandaged ear was a popular attraction. People jockeyed for position to see the little painting–"Not even as big as the *Mona Lisa*, is it, Alf?"–that somehow seemed to vibrate in its frame. I milled around the edges, searching for a stranger who seemed to be doing the same.

"Maggie?"

I turned, feeling unusually wary. There was a crowd, after all. Maybe the coffee left me edgy. Or the expectation of the next random bomb. The woman who said my name was attractive because of the intelligence on her face. That, and like so many French women, there was a simple elegance about her clothes and the way she moved. I had never seen her before, but she looked like the cadres of professional women I commuted with. I said, "How did you know me?"

"I looked you up before I decided to talk to you. You're a film-maker." She hooked her arm through mine; anyone seeing us would think we were old friends the way she bent her head close to mine. "Let's go upstairs where it's quieter."

"Thank you for meeting me," I said as we headed into a side stairwell.

"You told Roni Pascal that Ophelia Fouchet is missing. That's the only reason I'm here."

"Do you know Ophelia?"

She hesitated. "We've met."

"Through her father?"

She nodded. "I'm impressed you made the connection."

A clump of wrestling, tickling tweeners who were generally oblivious to anything except each other progressed in a generally downward trajectory toward us. We had to separate and press ourselves against the wall to let them pass. When the kids were gone except for a trail of voices reverberating in the enclosed stairwell, she walked up two steps to rejoin me.

Voice kept low, she said, "The only notice I found about Ophelia was a runaway teen post on an Interpol sex trafficking site. Is she a runaway?"

"I don't know," I said. "She has run before, but never gone far and never for this long. It's been over a week now and there has been no sign of her. Some of her things were found in the woods in the *haras* in Vaucresson. No more than a hundred and twenty yards from where they were found, a vagrant who'd had his throat slashed was pulled out of a pond; he went into the water roughly the same time she went away."

"A dead man?" she said, seeming not to believe me.

"Very dead."

"And Ophelia is involved in some way?"

"I don't know. I don't know who he was, and I am only beginning to get some idea about who she is. More importantly, I don't know where she is or why she is gone."

"I downloaded some of your films to get an idea who you are, Maggie. Are you doing a film on runaways?"

"Not specifically. Generally, I'm interested in *harcèlement scolaire*–schoolyard harassment. The deeper I look, the further I'm led."

"And somehow your inquiry into schoolyard bullies led you to me?" She smiled. "I promise, I never beat up a kid in my life, though I was sorely tempted to have strong words with that pack of pre-teens in the stairwell just now."

"Hormones run amok," I said, walking with her to the huge wall of windows that ran the width of the gallery at the top of the stairway. The centerpiece was a massive, floor-to-ceiling see-through clock. Paris was spread out below us as far as the eye could see; dazzling. We stood in front of the windows like any tourists and gawked. I asked her, "Do you have a name other than Déchaînée?"

"Lara," she said. "For now, just Lara."

"Lara," I repeated. "I confess that coming to you for information about Ophelia Fouchet is a long shot, but worth a try. Ophelia's disappearance is part of a larger story, and I think that harassment is at the core. Something happened about a year ago that turned her apparently orderly life on its ear. My snooping around led, circuitously, to you through the series Roni Pascal's magazine published last year about workplace harassment, but Roni probably told you that."

"Yes, well, I can see how revealing some unsavory truth about a man would upset a family's equilibrium," she said. "The last thing I wanted to do was hurt Ophelia and Claire. My name is nowhere in the article, nor was his; I was adamant about that. But anyone who was at all familiar with my story would know exactly who Roni was writing about."

"How did Roni find you?"

"We have been good friends for years. A big part of her motivation for writing the series on workplace harassment was watching the hell I went through with Yvan unfold. She begged me for almost a year to let her use what happened to me because it was a good example of how manipulative and vindictive the harasser can be, and how little power his victim has."

"You were victimized by Yvan Fouchet?"

She raised her palms: yes, of course, isn't it too obvious? "Was I naïve, too ambitious, just stupid to fall into a relationship with a man of his stature at work? Of course. When I was hired by the firm, fresh from university with a first-rate engineering degree, he was a mentor, a guide, a protector. I rose through the company– on merit–and we became closer, traveled to meetings together, worked on projects together. He was, at first, paternal. But over time the relationship progressed as they often do until we shared a bed. I thought we were in love, even though he made it clear that because of Ophelia he could never divorce Claire; I know, I am a fool. After a while, of course, the secrets and lying, and him, wore thin, or maybe finally I saw our relationship for what it was, a cheap affair. I told him I wanted to break it off. He refused, and that's when the harassment began. If I quit him or tried to expose him, he promised that I would be fired, and he would make sure I was blackballed so that I would never work in our industry again. After that, you can forget any thought that this was a consensual relationship. Sex on demand, whatever, whenever. I was trapped unless I wanted to abandon my career, the life I had built. My pride. You have to understand that when you're in the middle of such a situation you have precious little pride left. Save myself? What self?"

"There must be a handbook somewhere these guys use."

"I know that mine is an ordinary story. And I was an ordinary idiot."

"When Roni's article came out, you were fired?"

"Oh, no, I was fired months before that. What happened was, I got a very large industry-wide award. Name and picture in all the professional journals, interviews, a big raise in salary, a new office, a new title. I decided that I was now powerful enough to break away from him. I sent out résumés, I set up interviews. Word got back to him. People called him for references even though I did not list him because that industry is, after all, a small world of its own. And he kept his promise. I was fired. One day I walked in the front door and Security walked me right back out. No explanation—none needed, of course—only the required severance, no references. I demanded an explanation, I got none. That's when I first went public.

"Because I was given no cause, I challenged the company. It seemed more likely to me that they would back down before Yvan would. But I was wrong. When the only business news reporter I could interest in my situation went to the company, the answer he got was that employee issues are confidential and there would be no comment. I persisted, not about the sex or the harassment, that was too shameful, but about the way I was fired. I wanted to force the company to explain why I was terminated. Yvan parried my thrust by planting horrible rumors about me throughout the industry; he is a powerful man in our little corner of enterprise. No one would hire me after that. I was poison. Now I sell scarves at Galeries Lafayette and sleep on my sister's couch."

"That's when Roni came to you."

She nodded. "She was angry. As a journalist she thought she could do something important by bringing situations like mine into the light of day. What happened to me happens to people, men and women, all the time. I made Roni promise that if Yvan sued, because I knew he would, the magazine would pick up my legal fees."

"And he did sue," I said.

"He sued the magazine, but not me. He didn't want my name to appear anywhere near his after that article came out. I knew his family, I knew many of his friends because he trotted me out even when Claire was around. I think it turned him on to have the wife and the mistress in the same room. The grounds for the suit was invasion of privacy because it is such an easy suit to bring and it is so quickly resolved. The magazine's offense, according to Yvan, was interfering with his business life, not snooping into his sex life. Roni never mentioned his name in the article, but he argued that there were references that would logically lead people in his industry to assume it was about him and therefor the magazine breached his privacy. The judge agreed."

"And awarded him one euro."

"And an apology. Don't forget the apology. That second part felt like daggers to me."

"So, you called his wife as a last resort," I said.

"Said who?" she snapped.

"A woman who signed herself Déchaînée in a letter to the editor."

She relaxed, laughed softly. "I forgot. Of course. That's how I signed myself whenever I contacted Roni on her work server. That's how I thought of myself during the entire mess."

"The tiger unchained, looking for fresh meat?" I said. "What did Claire have to say?"

"She knew. I think she always knew. We met, and I told her everything only because she insisted."

"In the letter, you said the wife, meaning Claire of course, acted when no one else would. Your last word was *schadenfreude*. What did she do that gave you the cold pleasure of seeing Yvan's comeuppance?"

She narrowed her eyes and studied me as I asked that question. She said, "Does anything escape you, Maggie?"

"Not if I do my homework."

Nodding at that, she said, "Claire went to a *notaire* and filed for divorce on the grounds of fault. Yvan's fault, of course, because of our affair. I promised that I would give testimony in support; what do I have left to lose? If she won, and she would, she would retain primary custody of Ophelia and he would pay significant damages. What gave me satisfaction was knowing that Yvan would have no control over the course of things."

"But Claire hasn't gone through with a divorce," I said. "They're still together. Do you think he forced her to back down?"

Palms and shoulders rose, meaning the answer was a mystery, but she said, "Don't underestimate Claire. She's tougher than you might think. She's had to be."

"What she did certainly explains the open war *chez* Fouchet over the last year. Poor Ophelia is collateral damage."

"I feel sorry for her. She has a good heart, and like her mother, she always found little ways to challenge Yvan."

"Out of the goodness of her heart, last fall she took a Muslim refugee boy under her wing and protected him from school bullies. She also let her parents think he was her boyfriend."

"Good for her. A Muslim boyfriend would not sit well with Yvan." Her gaze shifted back to the panoramic view of the Right Bank. "Yvan is brilliant in his field, and he can come off as charming. But he is a despicable human being."

"He isn't doing very well at the moment."

"I'm sure he isn't. He likes to be in control." She turned to me. "Odd, isn't it, the way we feel better after sharing secrets we thought needed to stay hidden? I still feel guilty about letting Yvan Fouchet into a position to manipulate me the way he did, but I am not ashamed anymore. It's he who should feel guilt and shame. Do you think he does?"

"If he feels guilty about anything, I would think it's that he drove his daughter away."

"I am very, very sorry about Ophelia, wherever she is, whatever has happened. She deserves better."

Jean-Paul wandered out of the stairwell, his eyes, like everyone else, on the view. He knew Lara was skittish about meeting me, so when he noticed we were there, he turned around to head back down.

"Jean-Paul?" Lara called out, a happy look on her face as she started off toward him. He hesitated, but, being who he was he put on a smile, changed direction, and came our way.

"Suzanne," he said as they exchanged *les bises.* "What a nice surprise."

"I didn't know you were back from America. I am so glad I've run into you."

As they went through the usual long-time-no-see questions and answers—I'm fine, you're fine—Jean-Paul was drawing her over to me. He took my arm and, facing her, said, "I didn't know you'd met my Maggie."

"Suzanne?" I said.

She dropped her head to show chagrin, and with a shamefaced hint of a smile when she looked up again, she said, "I thought Lara was an appropriate name to use, the beloved mistress Doctor Zhivago dumped in favor of his less-loved wife. Except I have a strong feeling that my Doctor Zhivago did not love either of us as much as he loved having us both under his thumb."

She took a breath and smiled at Jean-Paul. "I'm sorry, that must sound very mysterious to you. Disregard it, dear Jean-Paul. We were having a bit of girl talk, weren't we Maggie? Affairs always end badly for someone, don't they?"

"And perhaps the recovery takes time," he said.

She took a breath. "You two know each other? What a small world. Except, Jean-Paul seems to know everyone. Do you still ride?" she asked him.

"Not recently," he said. "And you?"

"No." A sad sort of chuckle. "Horses require a great deal of time and money. I miss the club rides very much, but not the feed bills."

"I understand that very well," he said with a gracious nod.

"I didn't realize it was so late," she said with a glance up at the giant clock. She put a hand on my arm and leaned in, offering her cheeks to me first, and then to Jean-Paul. With a last glance at me, she said, "We'll talk again, yes?"

"I look forward to it," I said.

"Let me know what you hear about Ophelia." She gave my arm a squeeze, turned and hurried down the stairs.

Jean-Paul waited for a moment before walking over and peering down the stairwell to make sure she actually was gone. When I joined him, he said, "Suzanne is Déchaînée?"

"That's how she signed herself." We crossed the upper gallery and went down the stairs on the opposite side to lessen the chance of running into her. "You knew her through the equestrian center?"

"Yes. She helped coach the younger riders and came out on some of the group rides in the countryside. As I think about it, she and Ophelia seemed to get along very well."

"For a while," I said, "she also got along very well with Ophelia's father."

"I heard rumors," he said.

"So did Claire. Suzanne told me that when she tried to break it off with Yvan, he had her fired, and then he blackballed her in the industry. She went from upper level executive to selling scarves; she's bitter."

Looking at me sidelong he asked, "How bitter?"

"She called Claire. She also gave an interview to a magazine. He sued the magazine. The public record of the judgment led me through some wormholes to Suzanne. I keep hearing that Yvan needs to be in control of things. If he had done nothing about the article, I wonder how many people who matter in his life would have seen it, much less recognized him as the sleazy workplace abuser; no one was outed by name. I think he couldn't let it rest. The great war *chez* Fouchet, and the alienation of the daughter, began at just about the same time that he won the lawsuit."

"Hoist by his own petard," Jean-Paul said in English. We had stopped in the *Allée centrale des Sculptures* that filled the center of the museum's ground floor to admire a sculpture by Camille Claudel, Rodin's rejected mistress. The piece depicted a young woman on her knees, Camille, desperately trying to pull back an old man, Rodin. The title is *L'Age mûr*, Maturity. Gazing at the agonized face of the woman, Jean-Paul said, "Do you know the word *pétard*?"

"I don't."

"It means fart. But it also means little bomb, the sort that was used to blow open gates and doors. I like the expression because it could mean Yvan farted on his own plan, or he blew it up. Nice, yes?"

"Not as versatile as *merde*, but nice, yes."

"Are you familiar with the tragedy of Camille Claudel?"

"A bit. Rodin left her for another mistress. She died in an asylum during the German Occupation."

He nodded toward the sculpture. "This piece made him so angry he denounced her publicly."

"The moral is?"

"Unzipping the fly can open a Pandora's box," he said.

"It can also open a gateway to heaven. One just has to be careful."

He laughed and wrapped an arm around me and we walked outside. Rue Jacob was only a few blocks away, so I texted Guido to see what he was up to. His answer was, "Date night!" Almost immediately after, Delisle sent a text. The car that seemed to follow Ophelia Friday night was, indeed, an Audi.

] *Twelve*

JEAN-PAUL CRIED OUT IN THE NIGHT, waking me. His nightmares about bombs started in February when he and a colleague were injured in a blast, but by May they had tapered off. Until the car bomb on Wednesday. During every one of the last four nights since then, explosions had invaded his dreams.

Unable to go back to sleep, and not wanting to wake him by turning on a light, I crept downstairs with a book, hoping to fall asleep reading on the couch. But it was hopeless. I kept going back over the little pieces I had gathered, looking for answers, adding questions. When Suzanne told me that Claire filed for divorce, which clearly she hadn't gone through with, I thought I understood why Ophelia went to the *juge des enfants* last fall and filed charges of abuse against one or both of her parents. She was filing for the divorce her mother dropped. When that failed, she changed her appearance because, as she told Joel Gold, her calculus teacher, she felt dark inside and could not bear looking like a princess anymore. That's also when she began running away. To get her parents' attention? To punish them? *Schadenfreude*, Suzanne said in her letter to the magazine. The cold pleasure of seeing the enemy suffer. Was that Ophelia's motive?

I was stretched out on the sofa, unopened book hugged to my chest, watching petals drop from a vase of Claire's wilting peonies as I finally began to doze off, when I was struck by a random thought. I sat right up again.

On Monday afternoon, when Dom showed us the missing children flyer that Claire and her friends were passing out in the village, he said, "If they want to find Ophelia, they need to use a different photo." That wasn't the last time I heard some version of the same thing.

While Yvan Fouchet ran around in a frenzied search for his daughter, Claire did not. Was it possible she knew where Ophelia went and had not told him? Did she find satisfaction of some kind watching him deteriorate? *Schadenfreude*, Suzanne said, a cold satisfaction.

Jean-Paul woke up and found me missing from the bed, so he wandered downstairs to check on me.

"Ça va?" he asked, planting himself at the far end of the sofa and weaving his legs among mine as he stretched out.

"I'm fine. Couldn't get back to sleep."

"Did I wake you again?"

"Do you remember what you were dreaming?"

"No."

"Good."

He took hold of one of my feet and began to massage it. "What are the heavy thoughts at oh-dark-thirty that keep you from going back to sleep?"

"Revenge," I said. "It all begins with revenge."

"All what begins with revenge?"

"Bullying, running away. Everything. Why do Muslim religious extremists say they bomb synagogues and random crowds of people? Revenge for Israel's treatment of Palestine. Why do Christians harass Jewish children in public schools until they are driven out? Because they fear Jews will draw Muslim terrorist attacks to the school, at least that's the excuse for this generation. Some Muslims, rejected out of fear they are terrorists, become angry enough to commit acts of terrorism. And we cycle back to the beginning."

I gave Jean-Paul my other foot to rub. The massage felt good, but it also let me know he was still awake. "A high school girl dumps a set of friends and befriends a new kid. Out of revenge, the old friends mercilessly bully, then beat, the newcomer. Poor Louis Roussel, not only does his crush have no interest in him, his mother is dying and his father is preoccupied. If he hurts Nabi, does his own pain hurt less? *Schadenfreude*, taking pleasure in someone else's pain."

"*Schadenfreude*? No wonder you can't get back to sleep."

"One more," I said.

"One more foot? I only count two."

"One more example of the domino effect of revenge."

He yawned. "I'm listening."

"Yvan Fouchet sexually harassed your friend Suzanne. When she tried to break it off, he had her fired, then blackballed her. After other remedies failed, Suzanne, wanting revenge, called Claire. Vengeful, Claire filed for divorce, blaming Yvan. Thunderous fights ensue, but no divorce happens. The next move is Ophelia's. She goes to children's court and files abuse charges against her parents. Nothing happens. She stops being their princess and starts running away."

"Out of revenge?"

"What would you call it?"

"*Schadenfreude* has a sadistic connotation. So, considering the sequence you laid out, it's apt. In this family game, who gets the next revenge play?"

"Good question. The more I think about it, the more convinced I am that Ophelia is not a runaway this time. And she isn't coming back."

"Be careful," he said, untangling himself and getting to his feet. He reached for my hand and pulled me upright. "If what I think you believe is true, you're treading treacherous waters."

"Where are we going?"

"To bed," he said. "There are other uses for beds than sleep, my dear."

Sunday morning, we went for a run later than usual because we slept in. All things considered, it was an uneventful outing. Except for running into our neighbors, Holly and Kevin Porter, that is. They fell into stride with us and asked if we had any objections to them offering a live-in nanny-housekeeper position to Diba. Their little girl loved her and Nabi both. Their *au pair* had returned home and they were desperate for help. After making sure they meant for Nabi to live with them, as well as Diba, we assured the Porters that we had no objections, but the decision was Diba's to make.

Because it was Sunday, after our run, we showered and dressed, collected Dom, and went to Jean-Paul's sister Karine's house nearby for family brunch. Karine's husband, Émile, was an internist who worked in a large family medical practice. I watched Jean-Paul work Ari into his conversation with Émile as the two of them, beers in hand, manned the backyard grill. Dom and his two cousins went down the street to play basketball at a small park. That left me to be grilled in the kitchen by Jean-Paul's mother and sister about wedding plans. So far, our plan was to sneak away to the town hall as soon as I had been in the country for forty days and announce the deed to everyone after the fact. There would still have to be a party because Jean-Paul's mother and my grandmother would insist. I escaped the conversation by grabbing two bottles of beer and taking them outside.

"Couldn't stand the pressure, huh?" Émile said with a chuckle. "You know they'll get their way in the end, don't you?"

"I don't want to spoil their fun," I said. "How are you doing? Has Jean-Paul persuaded you to hire Ari yet?"

"I've seen the man's résumé and transcripts, Jeep made sure of that. If it were up to me, he could start tomorrow morning. But my colleagues need to agree, and that may not easy."

"Because Ari is a Muslim?"

"No. There are Muslims in our practice now. The issue is, Ari is a foreigner. It helps that he has worked with *Médecins Sans Frontières* and will have mutual acquaintances with some of my colleagues. All I can promise is, I will get him an interview."

It was still early afternoon when we got home. Guido called and asked if we would join him and Detective Delisle—Fleur—in the village for pizza later. We thought that was a fine idea. Jean-Paul asked if I wanted to go with him to the equestrian center for a ride, but I declined because Claire Fouchet had called earlier and invited me to come over that afternoon to see her garden. She seemed disappointed that I couldn't come until late afternoon, something about the shadows late in the day, but any time was fine. Jean-Paul said the horses could wait, if I didn't mind him tagging along. He'd love to see the Fouchets' garden, he said, but the truth was, he didn't want me to go there alone.

Diba and Nabi, chaperoned by the always protective Ari, were on the terrace, deep in conversation with the Porters. The last of the household, Dom, was picked up by his grandfather for nine holes of golf, whether Dom wanted to golf or not. Roland, Marian's father, came inside only long enough to be introduced to me and to take a look at what had become of his late daughter's office. He shook his head, gave the room a shrug, smiled like a martyr, kissed my cheeks, shook Jean-Paul's hand, and left. After a rather long phone conversation with Detective Delisle, I put a large round of Camembert from my grandmother's cheesemaker into a basket, and with Jean-Paul driving, went to keep a date with Claire Fouchet.

The black Audi was parked in the driveway when we arrived. When we spoke earlier, Claire told me that she would be in the garden. Just ring the front bell, she'd said. Yvan would be inside watching tennis and he would show me the way. But if he fell asleep as he sometimes did, and didn't answer the bell, then I should just come right in and walk through; I would see the garden from the foyer. I rang the bell, and no one answered.

"She told me that if no one answered I should just walk right in. I don't feel comfortable walking into someone's house," I said to Jean-Paul after an appropriate wait. "I hardly know Claire."

"Let's go around to the back."

We followed the driveway to the back of the house and peered over the garden gate. Claire was off in a far corner, on her knees, packing fresh earth around the base of a spindly rose bush. There were four other young rose plants already in the bed, and five sixteen-gallon plastic pots from a nursery scattered on the lawn behind her.

"Claire," I called.

"Oh, Maggie! And Jean-Paul, too. How nice." Though I was expected, we seemed to have startled Claire. She rose to her feet and came across the lawn to open the gate. "Sorry, I lost track of time. It always happens when I'm out here. I thought I would just pop in that last rose and be finished before you arrived. Did you ring the bell?"

"No one answered," I said. "Your garden is beautiful."

"Yvan is in the house. Why didn't he bring you through?" She glanced toward a back door, shrugged, and put her hostess smile back on. "Probably fell asleep. Most of my friends would just come right in; I never hear anything when I'm out here. And, thank you, my garden is a great solace to me, especially now. Come and see."

"We are enjoying the peonies you brought us," I said as we, at last, were admitted through the gate. "I wanted to share this Camembert from my family's *fromagerie* with you."

She looked at the wheel of cheese in the basket and gave the label an appreciative nod. "I know this cheese well. Your family produces it?"

"They do. The cheesemaker, his father, and his grandfather before him, have made our estate cheese for nearly a century."

"But you're American."

"My mother was French. I was born in Normandy."

"I had no idea." If she had watched me on Jimmy Jardine's show, as she said she had, and if she were paying attention at all, and at least somewhat sober, she would have heard that factoid get discussed to death. Were I in her shoes, I would not be able to focus on anything except the great big fact that my daughter was missing. I'd be a wreck, like Yvan. I found it a bit jarring that on that bright Sunday afternoon Claire seemed almost perky. Credit the garden? Or acceptance of her family's new status quo? A pill?

Claire carried the cheese in its basket as she walked us on a circuit along her graveled paths. We were in the suburbs, so it wasn't a huge garden and the tour didn't take very long. We visited the peonies and discussed the roses–my father had a passion for roses. She told us she recently dug up an old hawthorn hedge to make room for the new rose bed. Quite an undertaking, we were told with some detail, because the old plants had root balls that went down five or six feet. Took a week to dig them all out, and a load of fresh soil to fill in the hole they left.

We oohed and we aahed before thanking her and telling her we wouldn't take up more of her time.

"Lovely of you to stop by," she said. "We haven't had guests for, well, for a while. Won't you come in for a glass of lemonade or something stronger? Jean-Paul, I'm sure Yvan wants to say hello and have a word or two about horseflesh."

Without hesitation, Jean-Paul said, "Yes, thank you very much. A lemonade sounds perfect. Maggie?"

"Perfect," I said, taking my cue.

She ushered us across a stone-paved patio and through a set of French doors into a sunroom off the kitchen. As soon as we were inside, she leaned though a door connecting to the salon and called out, "Yvan, we have guests."

There was no response, so she called again. After a moment of silent waiting, she shrugged, and with a little smile rife with the forbearance of a martyr, asked, "Where can he be? I hear the television so he can't have gone far. Have a seat, I'll just go see where he's got to."

We stood. When she was gone, I leaned close to Jean-Paul. "I have a bad feeling."

"Do you?"

"Claire sounded so odd on the phone. Is it customary around here for people to walk inside someone's house when no one answers the door?"

"I hope not."

Claire screamed. Just once. I wondered later if we had been waiting for it, or for some form of the second shoe dropping. We rushed toward the sound of her voice, across the salon to a small study off the foyer. Yvan was, indeed, in front of a televised tennis match. But hanging by the neck from a rope wrapped around the massive overhead beam I doubted he was seeing very much.

Jean-Paul reached up and pressed his fingers against one of

Yvan's purple, swollen wrists, feeling for a pulse. His eyes came up to mine and he shook his head. My phone was in my hand. I snapped a picture of the deceased and sent it to Detective Delisle with a note, and then I dialed one-seven, the police emergency code, and handed the phone to Jean-Paul to speak with Dispatch. While he explained where we were and what we saw, I guided Claire back out into the salon and poured her a stiff scotch from a half-full bottle on the drinks cart.

Claire was dry-eyed, quiet. She looked at the glass in her hand for a moment before she decided to take a sip.

"The police should be on their way," I said. "Why don't you sit down until they get here?"

She did, perching on the edge of a straightbacked chair, ankles crossed, a well-posed portrait.

"Poor Yvan," I said, hovering near. I was shaken, certainly, by Yvan's ugly death, but I was also angry with Claire, growing angrier still as I watched her try to conjure up a mask of shock. A few years ago, I saw another man who was hanged. He was unconscious when the rope was placed around his neck, but he died of asphyxia. A horrible thing to see. Bulging eyes, lolling tongue, foam around his nose and mouth. And now I'd seen it twice. Damn her.

"When did Yvan die, Claire?" I asked, failing to sound dispassionate. "I won't ask how; the police will tell us that."

"When?" She looked around the room as if an answer floated there for her to pluck. "When? How would I know that? I was out back; you found me there."

"You were in the garden when we arrived, but I think Yvan was already dead this morning when you called and invited me to come over."

"That's absurd."

"Is it? I noticed when Jean-Paul felt Yvan's wrist for a pulse that his fingers were already stiffening. Rigor mortis takes a few hours to set in."

"Think you know everything, don't you?" she snapped.

"Not nearly enough," I said. "But I know you tried to use me to discover your husband."

I heard voices in the foyer. Keeping an eye on Claire, I stepped out far enough to see Jean-Paul usher in four uniformed officers. I was relieved they were there. Claire paled, and drained her scotch in two hearty quaffs.

"I would have been better off if I hadn't called you, wouldn't I?" She got up and refreshed her glass. "I've never been a good judge of people. If I were, I would never have married Yvan. What a misery he made of my life."

"And Ophelia?"

"Ah, my dear Ophelia." She sank back into her chair.

"And Ophelia?" Detective Delisle walked into the room with Jean-Paul and Detective Lajoie looming in the doorway behind her. She gave me a glance but went straight to Claire. "Before you tell me about your husband, I would like to hear what you were going to say about Ophelia, Madame Fouchet."

"You have reason not to believe me, but I do not know where my daughter is." Claire looked up at me. "I lied when I told you that Yvan would follow her in the car. It was I who did that. Whenever she was out at night, I kept my eye on her, afraid something bad would happen."

"On Friday?" I asked, and she nodded.

We were interrupted before she could say anything more by the arrival of an emergency medical assistance team, the SAMU. Lajoie went out to the foyer to speak with them. Delisle never took her eyes off Claire. Over the muffled conversation drifting in from the study where the emergency responders were dealing with Yvan, Delisle prodded Claire to continue. "You were telling us about Friday night."

"Friday." Claire took a breath. "I knew there was no pizza party; I called one of the other parents and checked. So I waited outside the school until rehearsal was over and then I watched Ophelia and that Arab boy walk to the train station. When he came out onto the street without her, I went looking."

"And you found her?" Delisle asked, notebook in hand.

She nodded.

"And followed her?"

"As far as the *haras*, yes. I lost her there. She was always afraid of the people who come out at night, so I thought she must be meeting someone." A tear coursed down her cheek. "I couldn't follow her onto the meadow in the car, and there was no place nearby to park. There were few other cars at that time of night, so I was able to stop in the road long enough to see her go into the woods carrying her cello. I waited for her to come out again, but when she didn't I thought she might be taking a short cut through the woods to the boulevard. I am familiar enough with the *haras* to know where she would come out, so I drove over to the soccer pitch. And that's where I found her."

"Did you speak with her?" Delisle asked.

Claire threw back her head and took a few deep breaths, clearly on the verge of melting into tears.

"Madame?"

After a long exhale and a sip from her glass, she said, "When I drove up, I saw two people, a man and a woman, near the woods, struggling. When I heard the woman scream, I knew it was my Ophelia. A horrible wretch of a man had her by the arms and wouldn't let her go. I saw the flash of a knife and blood on her. I ran, and with all my strength, I dove into him. The knife fell to the ground, I picked it up, and—"

She struggled to regain composure. Impatient, Delisle prodded, "What did you do?"

Claire nailed her with a watery-eyed glare. "I slit his throat."

"Was Ophelia injured?"

She brushed her hand along the inside of her left arm from the elbow to the palm. "Some cuts. Little cuts except for one near her wrist. It wasn't deep, but it bled a great deal. I tied my scarf around it."

The only reaction Delisle revealed was a tiny lift of her left eyebrow. "Continue."

"We couldn't leave that man lying out in the open for anyone to find. There was a bag of horse tack in the trunk of the car. I told Ophelia to go get a lead rope for me. I tied the rope around the man's middle and dragged him into the pond."

"Why?" I asked. "Why not call the police?"

Claire drew back as if miffed by a stupid question. "And put my daughter, my entire family, through a tawdry scandal? What sort of girl is out in the *haras* late at night consorting with those addicts and perverts? And that *bête* who attacked her? Who would miss him, anyway? Good riddance."

I had to sit down. Delisle's face flamed with anger. I asked her, "Can I get you a drink?"

The detective looked at me and shook her head, more at what Claire had said than the offer of a drink. "One would not be enough," she said before turning her attention back to Claire. "Ophelia helped you do this?"

"She brought me the rope," Claire said. "That was all she did. I told her to go sit in the car and wait."

Delisle crossed her arms and shook her head, not buying the story. "Madame Fouchet, you are a slender woman. You want me to believe that you dragged an adult man across the field, weighted him with rocks, and sank him in the pond? Alone?"

"Tell her, Jean-Paul." Claire looked across the room at him. "You have seen me wrangle a reluctant fourteen-hundred-pound horse into and out of a trailer many times. Tell her that with a strong rope I could get that man into the pond alone."

He held up his palms, maybe yes, maybe no. He said, "Yvan was hanged with good double-braided lead rope. Is that what you used on the man?"

She started to nod but stopped herself. "I didn't notice the rope Yvan used."

"Madame Fouchet," Delisle said, reclaiming control. "Your daughter was in the car, waiting during all of this?"

Claire shook her head. "When I finished, she was gone."

"Did you look for her?"

"I hoped she went home."

"Did you hear from Ophelia at all after that night?"

After a long sigh, Claire said, "Ophelia left a note addressed to me and Yvan in her room. I didn't find it until sometime late on Saturday. It's a poem, I suppose you'd say. At the end of the poem

Ophelia wrote a single word, 'Enough.' And then she signed her name. I showed it to Yvan and asked if he knew what it meant, but he did not. He said it looked like school work because the poem is in English and many of the words are unfamiliar. The passage was all about plants. My daughter and I had been getting along quite peacefully lately, so I thought maybe it was a gift to me because she knows how much pleasure the garden gives me. Later, I searched online and found that it comes from Shakespeare, *Hamlet*, and it's about Ophelia, her namesake, running away from a cruel father and the prince, and that's when I knew my girl ran away and would not come back until she was ready."

I had to suck in some air to keep from popping her in the nose. "Is that what you want?"

"No," she snapped. "I want this all to be over. I want my life back."

Before I could say anything more, Delisle asked her, "Where's the note?"

Claire pulled a folded sheet of lined notebook paper from her pocket, frayed at the edges from much handling. Gently, she opened it and handed it to Delisle. The detective read it, scowled, shrugged, and handed it to me to decipher. My heart sank when I realized what it was; I had read the passage just the day before. *Hamlet*, act 4, scene 7.

Delisle was watching me. She said, "And?"

Before answering her, I asked Claire, "Did you explain what this is to Yvan?"

In a cold, clear voice, she said, "Yvan had a very bad night last night. Full of guilt and self-loathing. This morning I sensed he was near the edge. I brought up the note again, yes. And what I thought it meant."

"Madame MacGowen?" Delisle held out her hand for the worn bit of paper. "Tell me."

"It's a suicide note."

] *Thirteen*

W ATCH YOUR STEP." Detective Delisle led me and Jean-Paul down a small grassy embankment below an overpass where a culvert ran under an equestrian trail in the *haras*. "The cadaver dogs were sent into the *haras* first thing this morning to search for her. They found her before noon. It looks like Ophelia climbed up inside there and finished what she started earlier."

Ophelia's body had been taken away hours earlier, but the sickly-sweet stench of death still hung in the air Monday afternoon. I held my breath and leaned over the edge of the culvert for a quick look inside. The culvert was the usual sort of concrete tube with an accumulation of leaves and grass and random detritus in the bottom. A trickle of muddy runoff water ran down the middle. Not a cozy place to die. There was barely room for Ophelia to sit upright, but the equestrian trail would be familiar to her, and it was out of the way. Exactly what Ophelia sought late on Friday before last.

Next to her body, the search team found an empty vial of Xylazine, a horse tranquilizer, and a used syringe. The Fouchets' veterinarian confirmed that last fall he had written Yvan Fouchet a prescription for the powerful sedative to manage a skittish mare that fought being trailered for travel. The speculation was that

Ophelia, who would know how to inject an animal, had found the vial and syringe kit in the bag of horse tack, where it was kept, when she got the rope from the car for her mother Friday night. She then took the kit to the culvert with her and injected herself. From the position of the body, she curled up, fell into a coma, stopped breathing, and died.

"Ophelia still had her mother's scarf tied around the cuts on her wrist," Detective Delisle said, leading us away from the mouth of the culvert. "The decomposition, as you can imagine, was advanced. But the wounds are visible. The doctor said the pattern is not consistent with defensive wounds. It is far more likely they are hesitation wounds."

"She tried to slit her wrist?" I said.

Delisle nodded. "She seemed to persist in her effort, but it isn't easy to kill oneself that way. I wonder if the poor man we found in the pond came upon her and tried to stop her but she fought him for control of the knife. Her mother assumed he was attacking her, and events transpired as they did. Another misunderstood Good Samaritan."

"Has the man been identified?" Jean-Paul asked.

"Not yet. Maybe never. His pockets were empty, no identification of any kind."

"I wonder," I said. "Do you think Claire Fouchet had the presence of mind to empty his pockets before she put him in the water? If I were you, I'd take a look in her new rose bed."

Delisle laughed, a sad little chuckle. "Nothing that woman might do would surprise me anymore. I know she used her daughter's disappearance as an opportunity to torture her husband literally to the point of death. Whether he was a volunteer or not in the final act, he was her victim. She seems so normal. What sort of human would go to such extremes?"

I said, "Detective, a couple of days ago we watched a man drive a van down a crowded sidewalk before he blew himself up. Can you explain that?"

"You were near *marché* Mouffetard on Wednesday?"

"We were."

"That's a whole other level of crazy." She took a deep breath. "What did the Fouchet woman gain from all this?"

"*Schadenfreude*," Jean-Paul said, slipping his hand around my elbow. "The cold-blooded pleasure of watching someone get his just deserts."

I asked, "Has anyone decided whether Yvan hanged himself, or did he have help?"

"We have to wait for the autopsy. But if Madame Fouchet could drag a man into a pond, she could throw a rope over a beam and pull a man off his feet."

"Tragic," Jean-Paul said.

Ari arrived, driving Jean-Paul's car up a maintenance road toward us; the forensic science team had used the same road when they retrieved Ophelia's remains earlier. Nabi was in the front seat beside Ari, with his head bowed. After Ari parked, they sat in the car for a few minutes and I wasn't sure that Nabi would get out.

One stormy night Nabi thrust his life vest on his mother, took his grandmother's hand and jumped with her into the Mediterranean. The two of them survived, the rest of their family disappeared. No remains. No marker. Just gone. He had insisted that he wanted to see where his friend had been found. He could not let Ophelia go until he saw for himself where she died.

The car doors opened, and Nabi and Ari emerged. Nabi carried a bouquet of spring flowers. With a last word from Ari, and a last nod from Nabi, they walked over to join us.

We folded protectively around the boy. With a little bow, he said, "May I have a moment alone?"

We stepped back and watched him walk over to the end of the culvert. Shyly at first, and then with more curiosity, he looked inside. Then he got down on his knees and laid the flowers inside where his friend had quietly left this life.

While we waited for him, Ari said, "Nabi heard at school today that he was admitted to the Paris conservatory. He'll start in fall."

I shot Jean-Paul an accusatory glance.

"Not me this time," he protested. "I didn't call anyone."

Ari chuckled. "Credit his violin teacher. Jean-Paul is not the only man in France with influence."

Jean-Paul bumped his shoulder against mine. "*Tu vois?*"

I bumped him back. "Yes, I see. This time. And congratulations to Nabi. When he's ready, we'll have a party to celebrate."

We were quiet on the drive home, Jean-Paul and I in front, Ari and Nabi in the rear. Nabi would need time to accept this new loss, but he had more support now to help him than he had when he first arrived. I thought about Nabi quoting a line from *Hamlet* to Ophelia, teasing her about the various meanings of rue. She had left her parents a beautiful and sad passage from the same play, a speech where Hamlet's mother, Gertrude, announces that young Ophelia is dead by her own hand. I thought about our Ophelia lying down on a bed of leaves and grass and cold muddy water to take her life. And I wept for her.

] [

There is a willow grows aslant a brook
That shows his hoar leaves in the glassy stream.
There with fantastic garlands did she come
Of crowflowers, nettles, daisies, and long purples,
That liberal shepherds give a grosser name,
But our cold maids do "dead men's fingers" call them.
There, on the pendant boughs her coronet weeds
Clambering to hang, an envious sliver broke,
When down her weedy trophies and herself
Fell in the weeping brook. Her clothes spread wide,
And mermaid-like a while they bore her up,
Which time she chanted snatches of old lauds
As one incapable of her own distress,
Or like a creature native and indued
Unto that element. But long it could not be
Till that her garments, heavy with their drink,
Pulled the poor wretch from her melodious lay
To muddy death.

–Hamlet, act 4, scene 7

About the Author

Edgar Award–winner Wendy Hornsby is the author of thirteen previous mysteries, eleven of them featuring documentary filmmaker Maggie MacGowen. Professor of History Emerita, Wendy lives in Northern California. She welcomes visitors and e-mail at www.wendyhornsby.com.

More Traditional Mysteries from Perseverance Press
For the New Golden Age

K.K. Beck
WORKPLACE SERIES
Tipping the Valet
ISBN 978-1-56474-563-7

Albert A. Bell, Jr.
PLINY THE YOUNGER SERIES
Death in the Ashes
ISBN 978-1-56474-532-3

The Eyes of Aurora
ISBN 978-1-56474-549-1

Fortune's Fool
ISBN 978-1-56474-587-3

The Gods Help Those
ISBN 978-1-56474-608-5

Hiding from the Past (forthcoming)
ISBN 978-1-56474-610-8

Taffy Cannon
ROXANNE PRESCOTT SERIES
Guns and Roses
Agatha and Macavity awards nominee, Best Novel
ISBN 978-1-880284-34-6

Blood Matters
ISBN 978-1-880284-86-5

Open Season on Lawyers
ISBN 978-1-880284-51-3

Paradise Lost
ISBN 978-1-880284-80-3

Laura Crum
GAIL MCCARTHY SERIES
Moonblind
ISBN 978-1-880284-90-2

Chasing Cans
ISBN 978-1-880284-94-0

Going, Gone
ISBN 978-1-880284-98-8

Barnstorming
ISBN 978-1-56474-508-8

Jeanne M. Dams
HILDA JOHANSSON SERIES
Crimson Snow
ISBN 978-1-880284-79-7

Indigo Christmas
ISBN 978-1-880284-95-7

Murder in Burnt Orange
ISBN 978-1-56474-503-3

Janet Dawson
JERI HOWARD SERIES
Bit Player
Golden Nugget Award nominee
ISBN 978-1-56474-494-4

Cold Trail
ISBN 978-1-56474-555-2

Water Signs
ISBN 978-1-56474-586-6

The Devil Close Behind (forthcoming)
ISBN 978-1-56474-606-1

What You Wish For
ISBN 978-1-56474-518-7

TRAIN SERIES
Death Rides the Zephyr
ISBN 978-1-56474-530-9

Death Deals a Hand
ISBN 978-1-56474-569-9

The Ghost in Roomette Four
ISBN 978-1-56474-598-9

Kathy Lynn Emerson
LADY APPLETON SERIES
Face Down Below the Banqueting House
ISBN 978-1-880284-71-1

Face Down Beside St. Anne's Well
ISBN 978-1-880284-82-7

Face Down O'er the Border
ISBN 978-1-880284-91-9

Margaret Grace
MINIATURE SERIES
Mix-up in Miniature
ISBN 978-1-56474-510-1

Madness in Miniature
ISBN 978-1-56474-543-9

Manhattan in Miniature
ISBN 978-1-56474-562-0

Matrimony in Miniature
ISBN 978-1-56474-575-0

Tony Hays
Shakespeare No More
ISBN 978-1-56474-566-8

Wendy Hornsby
MAGGIE MACGOWEN SERIES
In the Guise of Mercy
ISBN 978-1-56474-482-1

The Paramour's Daughter
ISBN 978-1-56474-496-8

The Hanging
ISBN 978-1-56474-526-2

The Color of Light
ISBN 978-1-56474-542-2

Disturbing the Dark
ISBN 978-1-56474-576-7

Number 7, Rue Jacob
ISBN 978-1-56474-599-6

A Bouquet of Rue
ISBN 978-1-56474-607-8

Janet LaPierre
PORT SILVA SERIES
Baby Mine
ISBN 978-1-880284-32-2

Keepers
Shamus Award nominee, Best Paperback Original
ISBN 978-1-880284-44-5

Death Duties
ISBN 978-1-880284-74-2

Family Business
ISBN 978-1-880284-85-8

Run a Crooked Mile
ISBN 978-1-880284-88-9

Lev Raphael
NICK HOFFMAN SERIES
Tropic of Murder
ISBN 978-1-880284-68-1

Hot Rocks
ISBN 978-1-880284-83-4

State University of Murder
ISBN 978-1-56474-609-2

Lora Roberts
BRIDGET MONTROSE SERIES
Another Fine Mess
ISBN 978-1-880284-54-4

SHERLOCK HOLMES SERIES
The Affair of the Incognito Tenant
ISBN 978-1-880284-67-4

Rebecca Rothenberg
BOTANICAL SERIES
The Tumbleweed Murders
(completed by Taffy Cannon)
ISBN 978-1-880284-43-8

Sheila Simonson
LATOUCHE COUNTY SERIES
Buffalo Bill's Defunct
WILLA Award, Best Softcover Fiction
ISBN 978-1-880284-96-4

An Old Chaos
ISBN 978-1-880284-99-5

Beyond Confusion
ISBN 978-1-56474-519-4

Call Down the Hawk
ISBN 978-1-56474-597-2

Lea Wait
SHADOWS ANTIQUES SERIES
Shadows of a Down East Summer
ISBN 978-1-56474-497-5

Shadows on a Cape Cod Wedding
ISBN 1-978-56474-531-6

Shadows on a Maine Christmas
ISBN 978-1-56474-531-6

Shadows on a Morning in Maine
ISBN 978-1-56474-577-4

Eric Wright
JOE BARLEY SERIES
The Kidnapping of Rosie Dawn
Barry Award, Best Paperback Original. Edgar, Ellis, and Anthony awards nominee
ISBN 978-1-880284-40-7

Nancy Means Wright
MARY WOLLSTONECRAFT SERIES
Midnight Fires
ISBN 978-1-56474-488-3

The Nightmare
ISBN 978-1-56474-509-5

REFERENCE/MYSTERY WRITING

Kathy Lynn Emerson
How To Write Killer Historical Mysteries: The Art and Adventure of Sleuthing Through the Past
Agatha Award, Best Nonfiction. Anthony and Macavity awards nominee
ISBN 978-1-880284-92-6

Carolyn Wheat
How To Write Killer Fiction: The Funhouse of Mystery & the Roller Coaster of Suspense
ISBN 978-1-880284-62-9

**Available from your local bookstore
or from Perseverance Press/John Daniel & Company
(800) 662–8351 or www.danielpublishing.com/perseverance**